DEADLINE TO DECEIT

CW01663147

Deadline to Deceit

CHELLE DAWN

PUBLICATION

First published in the UK in 2026
Copyright © Chelle Dawn, 2025

All rights reserved.
No part of this publication may be reproduced, stored or transmitted in any form by any means, electronic, mechanical, photocopying or otherwise, without the prior written permission of the publisher.

The rights of Chelle Dawn to be identified as Author of this work has been asserted by her in accordance with the Copyright, Designs and Patents Act, 1988.

This is a work of fiction. Names, places, events and incidents are either the products of the Author's imagination or used fictitiously. Any resemblance to actual persons, living or dead, or actual events is purely coincidental.
A CIP catalogue record of this book is available from the British Library.

ISBN: 978-1-9192771-0-3

Also available as an ebook

Part One

~ 1 ~

SARAH

The shriek of the alarm slices through my skull like a drill. I slam my hand down on the clock without opening my eyes.

"Today will be a great day," I whisper into the morning silence. "Today will be a great day."

I stay still for a moment, tucked into the warmth of the duvet, breathing through the slow rise of anxiety that pulses behind my ribs. It's always worse in the mornings, that strange blend of hope and dread that clings to the start of every day.

Three weeks. That's all I have left to finalise the NexTech project before my presentation to the board. Three weeks to prove that I've climbed all the way back. Daniel Reed, our CEO, has been hinting, nothing overt, but enough to make me believe. A board-level position. Redemption in the form of a polished title and a seat at the table where decisions are made. Not bad for someone who was once known as a corporate pariah.

I sit up and swing my legs over the side of the bed, the cold floor anchoring me. My body remembers the fall before my mind can stop it.

Gen22.

The project that shattered my career.

It's been six years, but the memory still lands like a punch to the gut. I was once the rising star of Gen22, handed the reins to a flagship product that was supposed to redefine industry standards. It had everything, innovation, resources, a crack team. And it fell apart. Publicly. Spectacularly. My name was stamped on every headline.

"Gen22 Meltdown: Gen22's Brightest Star Falls Hard."

"Product Catastrophe Triggers Near-Bankruptcy."

No one mentioned the pressure I was under. No one saw the corners being cut behind closed doors. No one cared that I tried to stop it. They just saw the failure.

Back then, I'd raised every red flag I could. The software had major issues, flaws that would become disasters in a live environment. My team and I worked around the clock, scrambling to fix what we could, but the deadlines were immovable. Unreasonable.

One afternoon, after a long strategy meeting, Philip Ogden, Group Operations Manager, cornered me outside the boardroom.

"Sarah," he said smoothly, "you're letting perfection get in the way of delivery."

"There are real risks," I replied. "We're not ready."

"You're being paranoid." His voice was quiet but hard. "We can't afford delays. The revenue from this launch keeps the lights on."

He didn't say it outright, but the threat was clear, stop pushing back or be pushed out.

I asked him to take my concerns to the CEO, Simon Carhill. He promised he would. He didn't. Instead, he told others I was obstructive. Overly cautious. Not a team player.

The product launched. It failed within days. Critical clients dropped us. Contracts were torn up. And I became the scapegoat. I was called inexperienced, unstable under pressure. The board didn't fight to keep me. They let me fall, hard and fast.

After the firing, I barely moved for weeks. My apartment, once my sanctuary, became a prison. I lived off crisps and instant noodles. The only light came from the glare of my laptop as I obsessively read every article written about my downfall.

Eventually, my mother showed up and hauled me home like I was sixteen again. She packed my bags while I stared blankly at the wall.

I returned to my childhood bedroom, which had become a storage space for dusty vinyls, record players in various stages of disrepair, and my mum's overflow wardrobe. The walls still had faded stickers from my teenage years. The closet smelled faintly of lavender and mothballs.

It was humiliating.

But also... necessary.

I spent a lot of time staring out of the small bedroom window, watching the neighbours walk their dogs or take out the bins, living their ordinary, untarnished lives.

Eventually, after days of silent limbo, my mum sat beside me and said, gently but firmly, "You need help. And you need a shower."

I started therapy the following week.

Dr. Harriet Cole was the first person in months who didn't flinch when I said my name. She didn't blink when I told her about Gen22. Instead, she asked, "What do *you* think happened?"

She didn't fix me. But she listened. And she helped me separate the truth from the shame.

After a few months, she nudged me toward getting a job. "Something simple," she said. "Something quiet."

I ended up working at a little independent bookshop on the high street. Just me, a till, a radio and a maze of shelves. No board meetings. No urgent emails. No one expecting anything but change and a smile.

I loved it.

There was something sacred about the hush of a bookshop. Customers would drift in and out, heads bowed over pages, the smell of coffee lingering in the air from the cafe next door. I got to know the regulars, Mr. Calder, who always bought second-hand sci-fi. Amina, who ran the cafe and left me chai lattes in exchange for thriller recommendations. A quiet teenager who used to linger in the poetry aisle and leave with dog-eared Plath collections.

That job gave me space. It gave me breath.

But after a year and a half, I felt the itch return. The desire to build something again. So I started applying. Carefully, selectively. Most doors stayed closed. My name still pulled up search results that made recruiters nervous.

Then came NexTech.

I was upfront in the interview. I told them everything. I figured I had nothing left to lose. Somehow, they hired me. As an assistant project manager, a far cry from where I had been, but a start. And over the last four years, I've climbed my way back.

***

I walk into the kitchen and flick the kettle on. The room is quiet. Sleek. Calm. I bought this flat two years ago, as a reward to myself. The white countertops gleam under the early light, and the oak floors are warm under my feet.

I wrap my hands around a steaming mug and take it to the window. Outside, the city is just beginning to wake up. Buses rumble past, streetlights flicker off and a jogger in a neon vest paces down the pavement.

This is my life now. Balanced. Built piece by piece.

I glance at the time. I've got a meeting at ten with the team leads. We're still ironing out integration bugs for the demo. It's nothing catastrophic, just the usual late-stage chaos. But I can already feel the pressure tightening in my chest.

I'll see Dr. Voss tomorrow. NexTech offers in-house wellness sessions and I've been seeing her once a week since I took the lead on this project. She reminds me to breathe, to track my spirals before they overtake me.

She knows about Philip. About the boardroom betrayal. About the panic that flares up every time I hear words like *deadline* or *launch.*

Last week she said, "You're not broken, Sarah. You were betrayed. There's a difference." It stuck with me.

Sometimes I revisit the memory of my first day at NexTech. I remember standing in the lift, clutching my ID badge, heart pounding. Everyone was polite. Professional. No one whispered behind my back, or if they did, they did it out of earshot. I sat in meetings and kept my head down, speaking only when necessary. I didn't want to draw attention to myself.

But with each project I delivered, I earned a little more trust. A little more responsibility. A little more of myself back.

And now here I am. Heading up one of the company's most important initiatives. Preparing for a pitch that could redefine my future. Daniel trusts me. My team respects me.

And most days, I almost believe I deserve it.

Today will be a great day.

Even if I don't fully believe it yet, I'll say it until I do.

Whatever happens next, I'm ready.

Because I didn't just survive the fall, I rebuilt from it.

And I am not done yet.

~ 2 ~

It was about four weeks into my role at NexTech when the CEO Daniel Reed invited me to lunch. It was part of the company's 'Welcome to NexTech' induction initiative, but I saw it as something more, an opening. A chance to make myself visible at the top.

From the moment he shook my hand, I knew Daniel was exceptional. There was something razor-sharp about him, not just intelligent, but strategic, intentional. His suit was expertly tailored, the kind that whispers wealth rather than shouting it, and his shoes were so polished I could see my reflection in them. I estimated he was in his mid-fifties, his salt-and-pepper hair and faintly receding hairline gave away his age, but his posture, his energy, even the effortless way he owned the space around him, made him seem ageless.

We had lunch at an understated but expensive Italian place, the kind that doesn't need to advertise. Daniel spoke with ease, asking about my background, my goals, and my impressions of the company so far. To his credit, not once did he mention Gen22. He didn't allude to my past or question my capabilities. He treated me like a peer, not a cautionary tale.

He shared some of his own story too. NexTech, he said, was just one of his many business ventures, his "day job," as he put it, with a self-aware smirk. His real passion lay in investments, mentoring startups, and scaling niche tech into big players. But NexTech, he admitted, was special. His legacy, perhaps.

As the conversation shifted from corporate to personal, I found myself admitting things I hadn't meant to. That I was almost forty, single, child-free and entirely content with that. I'd once considered the traditional path, marriage, children, the house with the ivy-covered fence. But somewhere along the line, I realised I valued freedom more. I liked making decisions without needing permission or negotiation. I liked my space, my silence, my independence.

Daniel nodded with quiet understanding. He was divorced, he told me, with two grown sons who lived abroad. His tone held no bitterness, just acceptance. Two people who had each, in different ways, chosen solitude over entanglement.

From that day on, he took a special interest in my progress. Not in a patronising way, but as a mentor who genuinely saw potential. He pushed me forward, assigning me to high-profile projects, took care of my budget approvals, and, more than once, stepped in to unblock red tape when others dragged their feet. He trusted me. And I worked every day to earn that trust.

In four years, I rose from Assistant Project Manager to Group Project Director. I now lead a team of eleven highly capable project managers, each working on different arms of new system development. It's the most challenging role I've held since Gen22, and the most rewarding. My scars from the past haven't disappeared, but they've thickened into armour.

Alongside Daniel, the other pillar in my working life is Emily Chen, my best friend, my confidante, my IT whisperer.

Emily is one of the most brilliant people I've ever met, quiet, precise, and criminally underappreciated. She's the sort who can write code like poetry and spot bugs that entire teams miss. But because she's soft-spoken, introspective and not particularly good at office politics, she's been overlooked time and again for promotions.

Her latest snub was particularly cruel, passed over for the Senior IT Manager role in favour of someone who, frankly, couldn't hold a candle to her, working directly for Mark Bishop, the obnoxious Group IT Director. Arrogant, self-serving, and disturbingly smug. Mark is the sort of man who interrupts mid-sentence, explains things no one asked for, and somehow still manages to command respect because he's tall, handsome, and speaks in confident tones.

Emily won't admit it, but I think she has a bit of a crush on him, which baffles me. Then again, attraction isn't always logical. Despite his grating personality, I can't deny Mark's looks have a certain clean-cut allure that makes people overlook his flaws.

Lately, he's been nosing into my projects with a little too much interest. He shows up in meetings he wasn't invited to, asks questions that sound helpful but feel like veiled challenges and has started looping himself into conversations I know he has no business being in. It rattles me. It's subtle, but it's deliberate.

Emily, as always, is too polite to call him out. That's one of the reasons we work, she softens me, and I steel her.

We met on my very first day. I had just arrived at the office, fresh-faced and deeply aware of my past lingering just beneath the surface. I was ushered down to IT to get set up and there she was, tucked into the far corner of the room, long black hair swishing rhythmically as she bobbed her head to music leaking from oversized headphones. When she finally looked up, she smiled at me, warm, open, unguarded.

She introduced herself and showed me to a desk, her voice calm and unhurried. I was assigned to support a mid-level project, mostly note-taking, tracker updates and meeting coordination. Nothing I hadn't done in my sleep years ago. Emily was the IT lead on the project.

"So," she said, still focused on her screen, "you're definitely slumming it here. What's the real story?"

Blunt. Unexpected. And surprisingly refreshing.

I shrugged, offering only a half-truth: "Just needed a break from senior management."

She didn't push. Just nodded. "Fair."

We became fast friends. Over late-night emails, shared commiseration over bad coffee and whispered conversations during all-hands meetings, I gradually let her in. I told her about Gen22. About Philip Ogden. About the public humiliation, the media frenzy, and the fallout.

She never judged. Just listened. And slowly, we built something solid, a friendship rooted in trust and quiet loyalty.

Four years later, I trust Emily with more than just work. She knows when I'm spiralling before I do. She knows the look I get when something's gone wrong, or when someone's pushed the wrong button. She covers for me when I need time and drags me out for drinks when I'd rather retreat into spreadsheets.

She's still awkward about Mark, though. She claims it's nothing, but I've noticed the way her voice changes when she says his name. I don't push. We all have our blind spots.

As for her love life, or lack thereof, I've stopped teasing her. She's never dated anyone in the time I've known her. I suspect her shyness amplifies around anyone she's remotely interested in. And honestly, she seems content. But unlike me I think she dreams of meeting Mr Right someday. Maybe that's why we understand each other.

Now, as I sit on the edge of my bed, willing my body to move, I think of both of them.

Daniel, the mentor who gave me a second chance when no one else would and Emily, the friend who never treated me like a cautionary tale.

Three weeks to go.

Three weeks to finish this project, deliver the presentation and put the ghost of Gen22 to rest once and for all.

I inhale deeply, stretch out the tightness in my shoulders and swing my legs over the side of the bed.

It's time to rise. Time to lead. Time to make it count.

Because this time, the narrative belongs to me.

~ 3 ~

I grab my phone from the nightstand and open up my calendar. I have a full day of meetings and as usual someone has booked a call in the one gap I had remaining, Lunchtime. Great! I guess I will be eating on the go again. I really need to start booking out lunchtimes as busy, to give myself half a chance at a break. But it shouldn't be too much longer until things calm down. Once the project launch has happened, and with any luck there won't be any hiccups, there is usually a couple of weeks of respite until the next big thing is added to the agenda.

Today I am heading into Head office, instead of working remotely, which I usually do for half the week. I had washed my hair and set out my clothes the night before, which I am thankful for as it allowed me an extra twenty minutes in bed. I quickly shower and put on a little makeup. I wouldn't usually bother if I were working from home, unless on a client call, which usually means a smart top for appearances, paired with pyjama bottoms and slippers, which remain out of view.

On my way out the door I grab a protein bar for later, my cat Mushu looks over at me sleepily from the sofa as I leave. I've decided that in my next life I'm coming back as a cat. What a life it must be to lie around all day, with your only concern being the timing of your next meal.

Arriving at the office at 8:30, my first stop is at the coffee machine, which is located on the first floor. I grab one of the company branded cups and press the buttons for a Mocha. Leaving it dispensing, I grab a paper cone and fill it with jelly beans. I'm sure that these two combined are the reason I've added two inches to my waist line. Not the fact that I have no motivation to go to the Gym.

I make my way to the project room, saying hello to various people as I pass. I sit in my usual spot and take out my laptop. As I open the network folders to access the document I had been working on, my heart falls to the pit of my stomach. Where dozens of documents once were, there is nothing, the folder is completely empty. Suddenly the bright airy room feels too small, a cloud passes in front of the sun, darkening the corners like an omen.

I fumble for my phone in my bag and call the one person I know I can count on to pick up, Emily. In a panic. "Emily, Help!" I say before she can get out a single word.

I explain what has happened. "Ok, calm down" Emily Starts, " We can retrieve the documents from the backup servers that routinely copy all documents each night. Everything should restore to be exactly as it was yesterday" For a moment, it felt like I was back in the Gen22 aftermath, helpless, cornered, about to be blamed. I blink twice, steady my breathing and do my best to shake it off.

I can hear Emily talking to another member of the team, asking them to retrieve all documentation relating to my project and to save it back on the network. Coming back to me Emily says, "Ok, it will take about half an hour for the files to be recovered, but then you will need to check all documents once they have been received." If she were in the room I would Kiss her! "Thank you so much, if you weren't already my favourite person..." I say.

However, I really don't need this today. Fitting this in between all the calls and meetings I have scheduled, will be half of my day gone by the time everything is verified and with only three weeks until the presentation left, the timing couldn't be any worse.

***

By 11:30 I have almost finished verifying everything is as it should be, when I notice there are two Project Financial reports. I open them up side by side. My pulse rockets. My report shows a clean balance sheet. The other? It's bloated. External vendor audits, third-party testing fees. Over £100k added. My name is still on both. But at the bottom of the inflated one, a signature, Board-approved.

My head is spinning. A knock startles me. I slam the laptop shut, pulse racing. One of my Project Managers steps in, calm and clueless, "Hey" he says, "you coming to this meeting? Everyone is there." Reminding me that I am expected in the conference room.

I lock my laptop and walk across the office to a conference room full of the people involved in the project. Emily is sitting at the large table and I take the seat opposite her, still in a daze. What have I just seen? Emily glances over the top of her screen, her voice low. "Are you okay?" I nod slowly, as I realise that every set of eyes are peering over their own laptops, patiently waiting for me to start the meeting.

Every minute of the next hour drags excruciatingly on and I can barely concentrate on what is being said. When the meeting is over, I quickly rush from the room with Emily at my heels. "Sarah, are you ok? You don't seem like yourself." She says with concern in her voice. "Come with me" I whisper, "I need you to see something. It doesn't make any sense". Emily starts to question me, as we continue to walk at pace through the office. "Not here!" I hush, "Wait until we are in the Project Room".

I close the Project Room door behind Emily, "Come and look at this, there was a file transferred this morning for the project financials. It definitely isn't what I submitted" my breathing feels heavy "It's been signed off by the board with almost a hundred grand of additional costs, things like third-party testing fees and external vendor audits" I say shaking my head in disbelief.

I have so many thoughts going through my head right now. This isn't a rounding error, it's a smoking gun. A hundred grand in padded costs doesn't just slip past unnoticed. Someone's either siphoning funds or setting me up. Emily looks at me, her brows lowered in confusion, as I unlock my laptop.

I go to open the document in question, but it is no longer there. I can't explain it, "It was here, an hour ago." I mutter. "Someone must've deleted it." I look at Emily, then quickly back at my screen. I continue to click through the files unsuccessfully, finally turn back to Emily, who is standing staring at me. "Please, just... don't mention this to anyone. I need time to figure it out.".

Emily nods. "Ok, well let me know if there is anything that I can do to help." I am pretty certain that I will be calling her on her offer, but right now, I desperately need to catch up on the work I missed this morning, as well as handle the rest of my calls.

Though i fear my ability to concentrate is far below where I need it to be. What if I'm wrong? What if it's just an honest mistake and I bring down another storm on myself? But what if I'm right, and someone's rewriting my work. Rewriting me?

***

My four until five o'clock call finishes half an hour early, so I take the opportunity to go down to the IT room to speak to Emily. As I walk over to her desk, I notice that she is the only one there, head down and her headphones on. The music is loud enough for me to hear it, so it doesn't surprise me that she jumps as I tap her on her shoulder. When she removes her headphones I ask where everyone is. Emily shrugs her shoulders. "probably gone home already." she says.

The empty office gives me the perfect opportunity to see if we can find anything out about the document. "Who was it that you asked to retrieve the files for me?" I question. "The new Graduate

IT technician, which could explain how he sent the erroneous file." Emily responds.

Maybe his inexperience explains it, I think to myself. But it doesn't explain who removed the file after the fact.

Emily and I are lost in her screen contemplating our next step, when we hear a throat being cleared behind us. I hadn't noticed anyone walking into the room, so I am startled by the sudden presence. Emily quickly clicks through to another spreadsheet, as I turn around to see Mark standing looking over us at her screen. "Oh, Hi Mark. Can I help you?" says Emily, smiling.

Not wanting to stay around, I tell Emily that I will see her later and half smile at Mark before walking out of the room. His gaze hovered a moment too long on Emily's screen, not quite curiosity, not quite disinterest. I couldn't be sure.

Frustrated that I have no clearer idea about the financial report than I did this morning, I pack up my laptop to go home for the day knowing that tonight, at Emily's house, I'm drawing battle lines. Because if someone's messing with my project, they clearly don't know who they're dealing with. I've been here before and I will be damned if I allow myself to get burned again.

~ 4 ~

On my way over to Emily's, I stop at the local food court to grab us both something to eat. I decide on a ready-made lasagne that we can just throw in the oven, giving us more time to discuss the next steps and potential explanations.

As I am pulling into Emily's street, I see her exiting her car and walking up her garden path. I park my car behind hers and look at the clock on the central display of my dashboard. 19:18. Hopping out of my car, I notice Emily standing in her doorway waiting for me and I smile in her direction.

"Lasagne!" I say, holding up the tray I have just purchased. "Oh super. I was beginning to think I would need to order a take-out" she smiles. Emily's fridge is always reliably low on food, I'm convinced she lives on a diet of cereal and coffee when I am not around.

As we walk in her house, I ask if she has been anywhere nice, since she usually leaves the office at around 17:30 and it is only a fifteen minute drive to her house. "No, I decided to stay late at the office, it was almost 19:00 by the time I left. I was looking to see if I could uncover any more information."

"Ah that's great!" I respond hopefully.

I was eager to ask more, but first I wanted to get the Lasagne in the oven. The measly protein bar I had eaten early morning had done nothing to curb my appetite for the rest of the day. Emily switches the kettle on and gets a couple of cups out of the cupboard, as I lean against the kitchen counter.

"So, did you find anything?" I ask. "Nothing!" says Emily, "whatever you saw this morning definitely doesn't exist on the network, I went through everything, including the back-ups". I frown and contemplate what we can do next. If the file really is gone, then someone must know that it had been sent to me in error and has done their best to remove all trace of it.

Sitting down with our cups of coffee, I turn to Emily. "Do you think that Daniel could have altered the file before it went to the Board?" I ask. In my mind, this is the only logical explanation. Emily shrugs her shoulders, "Why would he have changed the values?" she says, shaking her head. "Isn't his annual Bonus based on annual profit? Surely additional costs would lower that?"

Emily is right, I can't see a beneficial outcome resulting from inflated project financials. However, I always email him directly with the project financials and the only time I have to get involved again is if something isn't approved.

We contemplate this for a while, going back and forth with different possibilities. I don't feel like we are getting anywhere at all, when the beeping of the oven alerts us to the lasagne being ready, and as if on cue, my stomach growls loudly. I slide half of the lasagne onto each plate and grab a handful of salad leaves to put on the side, more for aesthetic reasons than sustenance.

Halfway through eating, I start to wonder if the financials had been altered on any other projects, so I ask Emily her opinion. "It's possible," she replies.

We spend some time detailing our plans for tomorrow. Emily will investigate the archives of prior projects, looking for duplicate financial projections and will try to get copies as evidence. Emily thinks for a minute, "Emails outside the business are audited and the printers are operated using our Company ID badges, so also traceable." she says, frowning slightly. "We will need to be careful." I agree, we do, but at least now we have some resemblance of a plan,

I change the subject to Mark's unexpected appearance as I left the office. “So, what did Mark want? Are you still admiring him from afar?” I ask her. Emily blushes and swats at me playfully, “Honestly Sarah!” she says, “You must be the only female in the office that isn’t drooling every time he passes.” she’s right about that, he does absolutely nothing for me. He’s a pretty boy with short blonde wavy hair, clean shaven and good physique. If I were to ever look for a man, he would be dark and rugged with a dad bod.

“I’m sorry but regardless of attractiveness, his personality is gross.” I laugh. “He’s not all that bad when you get to know him” Emily retorts, “He’s always been really nice to me”. “Hmm” I frown, “maybe he likes you?”. Emily swats at me again. I laugh along, but Mark’s sudden, silent appearance still sticks in my mind like a splinter. People don’t just materialise silently in empty rooms. Especially people with no reason to be there.

“Anyway, what are we going to watch?” she says, grabbing the TV remote in a successful attempt to change the subject. I laugh as I sit back and grab hold of the Grey throw that is slung across the back of the sofa.

Emily's house has always been a home away from home, it’s not unusual for me to just let myself in. We swapped house keys about two years back. We even have loungewear and slippers at each other's houses, just in case we don’t want to go home after work. We see each other out of work at least twice a week, sometimes staying overnight on weekends. I’ve never had a friendship like this before. Emily is family and I like it this way.

Halfway through watching an episode of ‘The Blacklist’ I notice that Emily has been messaging and glancing at her phone more than usual. “Everything ok?” I ask. “Oh yeah, fine. Just my mum asking when I will be going back to Sicily for a visit, as usual.” she replies, rolling her eyes. “She’s been nagging me for weeks and I’m not sure how much longer I can put it off.”

I envy Emily for having a home somewhere sunny she can go back to whenever she wants, but for some reason she always seems a little reluctant to commit to flying over. She says that she doesn't like hot weather. Personally, I can't think of anything nicer than being able to work from abroad, surrounded by fruit trees and endless sunshine.

As the credits roll, I notice Emily looking slightly uneasily at her phone. "Are you sure everything is ok?" I ask. Emily stiffens. Her thumb hovers over the screen a beat too long before she clicks it off, before responding, "Yes, all good" with a smile that falters slightly as she lets out a low sigh.

I gather the discarded dinner plates and take them to the kitchen. As I pass the dining table, I notice Emily's laptop bag on one of the chairs. I wonder if she's planning to do some more investigation later tonight?

"Hey," I call from the kitchen, "are you planning to do some more digging later? Noticed you have brought your laptop back." I question. "I need to be quick," Emily says. "They're doing a quarterly system refresh at the end of the month, if anything's buried in the archive, it could be gone really soon."

My stomach knots. This just went from important to critical. If the archive gets wiped, so does our proof. Suddenly, we're racing against the clock.

~ 5 ~

I spend the night tossing and turning. No matter how I lie, the questions won't stop flickering, a hundred explanations running through my head, none of which are good. As the dark of night changes to the grey of early morning, my head starts pounding and I resign myself to the fact that I'm not going to get a wink of sleep.

Mushu grumbles as I climb out of bed, disturbed but unbothered. He stretches and sinks back into sleep, as if he's mocking my restlessness.

I drag myself downstairs, grab painkillers and a glass of water from the kitchen. Sitting on the sofa I look at the clock across the room. 5:37am. My alarm isn't due to go off for at least another hour yet.

I'm grateful that today is my therapy session with Dr Voss. God knows I need someone to talk some sense into me, especially when I have so much work to get through. I can't afford to have my mind elsewhere, I need to focus on the project and secure the promotion.

One thing that I have been unable to get out of my mind is James Turner, who a little over a year and a half ago took his own life, it was a devastating time for all who worked with him. James was NexTech's long-standing Finance Director and had grown visibly on edge in the months before his death. Hiding behind his screen and scribbling into his notebook, always looking over his shoulder.

Dr Voss had spoken to us all and offered counselling to anyone who needed it in the aftermath. She spoke of a much loved man, who had developed paranoia due to issues in his personal life. But now I am wondering if that is the case, or if he knew something he shouldn't have.

I'm not inclined to state this theory openly to either Emily or Dr Voss, but I will do some digging and see if my theory has any substance.

After my third cup of strong coffee, I drag myself into the shower and set the temperature to cold. I need the shock of the water to wake me up fully. And at least the extra time I have this morning will give me the chance to have breakfast and pack a lunch for a change. Now, even if I am booked up with meetings, I can eat at my desk or on the go. Sleepless nights at least have that benefit.

I have decided that today I need to focus on my project and make sure that everything is how it needs to be. I will map out the bones of my presentation, so I can easily edit where necessary. If I get that done, I have one less thing to worry about. And I can stay after hours to investigate. It wouldn't raise any suspicion, I often stay late when a Project deadline is approaching and with the office being quieter, I can likely snoop without raising any questions.

I land at the office and follow my usual morning routine and head straight to get a cup of mocha. Emily is standing by the water cooler with Mark, who is leaning in towards her. As they see me, Mark steps back and straightens his jacket, before walking past me with a quick hello. It's a jarring shift, from sleepless dread to office gossip, but I manage a smile. "That seemed awfully cosy" I tease as she blushes.

"I think you may be right about Mark liking me." Emily says, still rosy cheeked. "What did he want?" I ask. "He was just asking if I had done anything nice last night" she pauses before quietly adding, "And if I was free for Dinner tonight" she giggles.

It's nice to see Emily happy and if it hadn't been for my terrible night, I would have been calling her late tonight to get the gossip. But I already know that I will just want to get home and crash. "Well enjoy yourself" I smile back, "And check in with me first thing tomorrow." Emily all but skips out of the door and I can't help but let out a little laugh. Maybe I had it wrong last night with Mark, maybe he was just trying to catch Emily alone to ask her out.

I add an extra caffeine shot to my mocha and make my way to the project room. A couple of the team members are already sitting at the conference table, with headphones on. This can mean one of two things, they are in an early online meeting, or they are listening to music. I'm never sure which, so I wave silently just in case, before sitting at my usual desk in the far corner of the room, facing the conference table and switch on my laptop.

At 10:30 I make my way down to Dr Voss' office on the lower floor and sit outside waiting for her to open the door, allowing the previous employee to leave. To my surprise, as the door opens, Daniel Reed walks out. If Daniel's confiding in her too... What else might she know? And would she warn him, if I said too much?

"Good Morning Sarah" Daniel says, nodding in my direction as he passes. My eyes follow him across the office. "Come on in" says Dr Voss, bringing me back to the moment.

"How have you been this week?" Dr Voss asks before I've even sat down. "I know that this is a stressful time for you at the minute, with the project getting ready to launch" she follows. "All good on the project front" I respond, "I'm prepared and I know my subject matter well." I nod to emphasise my confidence, maybe a little too enthusiastically.

Dr Voss narrows her eyes at me, probing, "You look tired Sarah, are you sure you're ok?" I want to tell her about what has been happening, but something is stopping me. Something about seeing Daniel exit her office makes my stomach twist. Rationally, I know therapy is confidential, but suddenly, I'm not sure who's safe. Or what anyone knows.

"I'm fine, I just didn't sleep particularly well last night." Dr Voss cocks her head to one side, wanting me to go on. "Nothing to worry about, it was just a little too warm to sleep" I say, shutting down the line of questioning as fast as possible.

"How are you feeling about the promotion possibility? Are you feeling confident your project will be well received by the Board? It's a fantastic opportunity for you" she asks, "Yes it really is and yes I feel confident at this point" I reply.

After my therapy session, I consider if I should just forget about everything and concentrate all my efforts and mental capacity on the project and the promotion, but I can't shake the thoughts from my head, they don't seem to want to release their grip.

The rest of the day goes quickly and I'm thankful that there have been no further surprises. I watch from the project room window, as the office slowly empties and silence settles in, I wait, biding my time.

As soon as the opportunity arises, I leave my desk and make my way downstairs. The lights to the offices are off and the only people I pass are making their way out for the night.

The hallway to the archive room feels darker than usual. The motion lights flicker once, then fade. Every footstep echoes like a warning. It's too quiet, like the building is watching my every move. My chest tightens as I remember James's hunched figure, scribbling in that notebook. Tonight, I'm determined I will find it.

~ 6 ~

I take one last look behind me before I open the door to the archive room. There is a small window in the door, so I leave the overhead lights off and flick on my phone's torch, so as not to draw unwanted attention to my presence.

I move slowly through the ramshackle shelving. Dust coats everything, like the air hasn't moved in decades. Forgotten files and crushed boxes crowd the aisles, their labels faded or missing entirely. Much to my disappointment, but not surprise, there seems to be little to no organisation in here, making this a longer task than I intended it to be. "Of course it's disorganised, why would this place be easy to search?" I think to myself, while rolling my eyes.

As I search through dozens of folders stuffed with outdated reports, I wonder why we have kept any of this stuff. I pick up another jam packed folder and finally see a box that holds promise. It has Finance scribbled in marker across the top. My pulse quickens. I ditch the file in my hand and pry the box open.

Inside are printed PowerPoint decks, scrawled with red annotations, curled sticky notes clinging to spreadsheets and graphs and finally, a black notebook, dog-eared and warped from handling. I snatch it up and start flicking through the pages. At first it seems innocuous, disjointed, notes on budgets, team names and acronyms... Then I spot it.

"Numbers don't match. Again!"

"Daniel not responded to email. Why is he sending through direct edits?"

"Conf Call at 22:45 last Friday – Wasn't on my calendar. No transcript"

"Has the bonus structure changed?"

"Investigate Z-87-CT ....

- Z = Restricted
- 87 = Fiscal Code?
- CT = ?"

I take photographs of the pages as I spot anything suspicious, when near the end of the final page there is a list. It is just initials and dates and the most recent are mine. I recoil. Why are my initials here?

My hands tremble as I photograph the page and then I freeze. A flicker. The motion-sensor light outside the room has triggered. I quickly replace the notebook and lid and retreat to a dark corner of the room before shutting off my torch. The hum of the vent is almost masking footsteps heading in my direction.

The door to the archive room opens and the floor creaks, as whoever is here, makes their way through the room. I press myself into the shadows, barely breathing. The air is thick with dust and fear. I can hear each creak of the floorboards. Closer. Closer. The soft shift of shoes on concrete.

I'm sure my heart is betraying me, thudding like a drum against my ribs. I am certain I will be found. I can see their shadow mere feet away from where I stand, my heart growing louder in my ears, when suddenly the figure turns and walks away, back out of the door and down the corridor.

I crouch down, head in my hands. That was too close. Adrenaline surges through me, hot and sickening. I feel my heart still beating at an astonishing rate, but I have what I came for and now I can get the hell out of here.

I wait what feels like a little more than long enough, for my unexpected visitor to be gone, then creep toward the door of the archive room, but as I pass the shelf where the box once sat, my blood runs cold. It's gone. Not hidden. Not moved. Just gone. The only evidence of it ever being there is a square where the dust has been unable to settle. Someone took it. I need to get out of here, and now. This cannot be a coincidence!

I shuffle quietly back down the dim hallway doing my best to avoid triggering the motion sensitive light. When I see light from a small lamp glowing in Dr Voss' office. I am certain that the light was off when I first came down here, or maybe I just didn't spot it. Is it her that has taken the box? What does she know?

I don't have time to work it out right now, first I need to get out of here without being spotted and then home to try and decode the pages I have managed to capture.

***

As I walk through the door I almost fall over Mushu in my rush, as I realise I have missed his dinner time. I throw my bag on the sofa and make my way to the kitchen with Mushu in hot pursuit. The way he is yowling as I fill his bowl, makes it seem like he hasn't eaten for a week.

With Mushu munching happily away, I pass my office, pick up a notepad and pen, before making my way to the sitting room and grabbing my phone. First I want to work out what the initials and dates relate to, not to mention 'Z-87-CT' . "Restricted. Fiscal code. CT? CT... Could it be a location code? Or a department?
No... that doesn't fit.
What about... Confidential Transactions?"

I open my phone and start to copy out the initials and dates from the photograph. I gasp. In my rush earlier I didn't notice that my initials had appeared twice, the first being '20230914 SM' whilst working on another large project and the last entry being '20240704 SM'.

I go into my work emails and look at the date of the project kick off meeting, June 3rd the first Monday of the month. I look for other project milestones with none particularly standing out, but then I spot it, what I was already dreading and my breath catches. July 4th that was the day the project finances had been signed off by the board. Anxiety spiking, I scroll back, looking at my earlier project, the same, the date is the day the finances had been approved.

There are almost two dozen other codes. What the hell is this list? What on earth have I gotten into here?

And how far down this rabbit hole did James go? No wonder he was on edge and paranoid, but what pushed him so far to take his own life... if he did take his own life, I don't remember anyone ever mentioning a suicide note, I suddenly think, shaking. "No..." I whisper. "No, I can't think like that."

But the thought is already there. Rooted. Growing.

I close the curtains tighter than usual. Lock the door. The shadows from the archive room have followed me home.

~ 7 ~

I wish I had brought my work laptop home with me, but I left it at the office in my rush to get out of there. So I grab my tablet and type *'James Turner death'* into the search engine. It's not one of the top results. Strange, for something quite recent, but it only takes a little digging to find what I'm looking for.

LinkedIn: Posted by Daniel Reed

'It is with great sadness that I write to inform you of the passing of James Turner. James sadly passed away following a personal battle.

James has been a valued employee of the Company since 2013 and he will be sadly missed by all who worked with him.'

Accompanied by a picture of James and an article about Mental Health Awareness.

Facebook: Posted by Susan Lewis

'There are no words for the pain we are feeling. On Tuesday, my husband James passed away. The love of my life. My best friend. The most devoted father to our beautiful girl. We are completely shattered.

They say he took his own life. But I don't understand. There was no note. No warning. No goodbye.

I will forever miss the way he kissed my forehead before bed every night.

I'm sharing this not because I want pity or attention, but because I need people to remember the man he really was, not just the headline or the whispers. He deserved better than this ending, and I will spend the rest of my life trying to understand what happened.

If you or someone you know is struggling, please talk to someone. Don't suffer in silence. Don't let it end this way.

Rest in peace, James. I will never stop loving you.'

I stare at the post for a long time, scanning the comments, Blue heart emojis, Prayers and Condolences from people who knew him. But it's that line. "*there was no note*" that keeps ringing in my ears.

No note.

And Susan doesn't believe he meant to go. She's not saying it outright, but it's there in the spaces between her words. In the disbelief. The grief that doesn't quite fit the official story.

I scroll back up to his picture. It looks like it was taken the winter before his death. He's smiling, with his arms wrapped around his wife and daughter, he looked *truly* happy.

Something isn't right.

I click into Susan's Profile and notice that there are very few recent posts. Hesitating only for a moment, I hit the 'Message' button and type

'Hi, you don't know me, but I used to work with your husband. I was hoping that we could have a chat, if you're able? I am so sorry for your loss.'

Then I press send before I lose the courage.

Heading to the Kitchen, I grab a glass of water, then make my way upstairs to bed. Mushu plods behind me, watching intently as I brush my teeth. It's still early, but I am completely shattered and there's not much more I can do tonight.

Sliding into bed, I plug in my phone and select a guided meditation. It usually helps to stop my thoughts spinning. But tonight, I don't even need it, my head hits the pillow and I fall asleep instantly.

***

I wake up at 7:00am and reach for my phone, expecting to see a message from Emily, but to my surprise, there are two messages on my screen. One from Emily and one from Susan.

I sit up suddenly wide awake and tap on the message from Susan.

'Hi,

Thank you for reaching out. I really appreciate your message, it means more than I can put into words right now.

I'm sorry, I don't remember all of James's colleagues by name. It's been such a blur since I lost him. But if you worked with him, I'm sure you knew what a kind and generous person he was. He really loved his job, even when things got stressful, he never brought it home. Or... he tried not to.

I still don't understand what happened. There were no signs, no warning. He kissed our daughter goodnight like he always did. He made our dinner. We even laughed at something silly on TV. And then...

If you noticed anything at work, anything that seemed off or unusual, I would be grateful to know. I keep thinking maybe someone saw something I missed. Maybe there's something in the days before that could help me make sense of this.

Sorry, that's probably too much to unload on someone I don't know. I just... I want to understand.

Thanks again for messaging me.

Susan'

I read her words once. Then again. I wasn't expecting this much. Not this raw, aching honesty. A lump rises in my throat and for a moment, I wonder if I'm in over my head.

I don't know how much I can help Susan, after all, I didn't know James very well, but I know I need to meet her and see if there is anything else she is able to tell me. Though it's not looking likely, she seems as confused as I am.

I begin typing, uncertain at first, but the words come easier than I expected.

'Hi Susan,

Thank you so much for replying. I can't imagine how hard this must be for you and your daughter.

I did know James, though we weren't close. But I always admired the way he carried himself. Calm, respectful, the kind of person you knew you could rely on.

I understand if it feels strange hearing from someone you've never met, but I'd really like to meet in person if that's okay? Even just for coffee and a quick chat. Sometimes it's easier to talk face to face, and I'm happy to come to you or meet somewhere that's comfortable.

I'm not claiming to have answers, but I can share what I saw in the last few weeks we worked together. If it helps, even a little, I'd be glad to listen or talk.

Warmly,

Sarah'

After I click send on the message to Susan, I flick to Emily's message, it sounds like she had a nice night with Mark, nothing much else, just that she will tell me all the details when I see her at work later. I smile, shaking my head, whilst thinking, *Rather her than me.*

As I am getting into my car, my phone chimes, Susan has responded, She would like to meet at a café near work, over lunchtime.

I start the car, but for a moment I just sit there, the engine humming, my fingers frozen on the wheel. My stomach tightens. It's just coffee, I remind myself. Just a conversation. But something about this feels heavier than that.

I reached out for answers. But now it feels like she's hoping *I am* the answer. I don't want to disappoint an already devastated person. There's something in Susan's words that I can't shake. A quiet urgency. The same feeling that's been creeping into the corners of my thoughts ever since I read the words '*No note*'.

~ 8 ~

As I walk into the Café at 12:05, the door chime sounds loud and clear over the midday rush, people idly look over before going back to their conversations over the hum of the espresso machine. I look around and spot Susan towards the back of the café, sitting alone in a booth.

I recognise her from the photo she posted, but she looks a lot smaller and frailer than she did back then. It's amazing what a toll grief takes on those left behind. I slide into the seat opposite her. “You must be Sarah” she says in a quiet voice, offering a small smile, but her eyes remain saddened. “Yes, it's lovely to meet you” I respond, before the silence between us opens like a gulf.

A barista comes over to take our order, which briefly relieves the initial tension, before he wanders off.

Susan starts talking before I do. Her voice, when it finally comes, is soft and stunned, as though speaking the words are transporting her back.

“I remember I was sitting on the edge of the hospital bed, my fingers curled tightly around the wool of his favourite sweater. The room smelled faintly of antiseptic and something colder, something hollow.”

“They said it was suicide,” she whispers, eyes fixed on the table between us. “But there was no note. Nothing.”

Her gaze drifts toward the window, where the sky is dim, streaked with a tired grey that matches the weight in her chest. “He wouldn’t just... go. Not like that. Not without telling me. Not without..." Her voice cracks, and she turns her face away as if ashamed of the tears she can't hold back.

"We talked about everything, we argued about the stupidest things" she said with a small laugh "but we never left anything unsaid. And they're telling me he was in pain? That he chose this?" She shakes her head, fiercely, her hair falling around her face. "No. No, that wasn't him."

She looks up then, eyes red but blazing. "He loved me. I know that sounds simple, but it was the most certain thing in my life. Whatever he was going through... he would've said something. He would've fought. For me. For us."

There was silence for a moment, broken only by the faint chatter in the background and the dull throb of her grief.

"I don't know what happened," she says at last. "But I don't believe that was a choice he made. I don't believe he left me."

I reach out and take her hand across the cold table. My gaze can't quite reach her eyes, her grief is too raw. I'm not entirely sure what to say. Nothing I can say will likely help her. "I can't imagine how you feel" I start, "I don't think I can help much, but I wondered if he ever mentioned anything to you about work, anything that was troubling him?"

Susan exhales, long and slow, before responding. "No matter what was happening at the office, he was always so good at compartmentalising, it was as if he walked through the front door and work was a distant memory. His time at home was what he lived for, work was just there for stability"

She paused, her eyebrows creased.

"But for a few months before... before his death, he had been working late more often, even staying up late, head down at his laptop. I had no idea what he was working on, but I do have this, if it is of any use to you?" She reached into her bag and pulled out a small, silver thumb drive. "I don't know exactly what's on it, I only briefly looked to check if it was work or personal" she says, "but he kept it locked away in the safe at home."

The barista returns just as Susan places the thumb drive on the table between us. It sits there like something fragile, something dangerous.

My first instinct is to push it back across the table. Whatever secrets James had locked away, maybe they were meant to stay buried. But instead, I reach for it, fingers trembling slightly, betraying what I didn't want her to see. I was afraid of what I'd find.

"Here you go," the barista smiles, setting down two coffees, hers dark and steaming, mine pale with milk and too much sugar. He gives a polite nod and moves on, leaving us alone again. The rich scent of roasted beans drifts upward.

"Thank you," I say quietly, wrapping my fingers around the warm ceramic mug. "For this. I know it probably wasn't easy to hand over."

Susan shrugs, but her eyes shimmer with the weight of what she's just given me. "You might see something. Something that explains any of this."

I nod, carefully picking up the thumb drive. It feels cool and ordinary, ridiculously ordinary, considering it might hold answers to a man's death.

"I'll look through it tonight," I say. "I'll let you know if I find anything."

She gives a small nod, gaze distant. The coffee steams between us, untouched. Outside, the clouds have thickened, and the light filtering through the café windows is beginning to turn a dull silver.

"He wasn't the kind of man who left unfinished things behind," she says after a moment. My mind flashes back. 'Just like I hadn't planned to leave Gen22 in ruins. But sometimes you don't get to finish your story. Sometimes it gets rewritten for you.'

Susan brings me back to the present as she continues "Whatever this is... it mattered to him." I reach for my coffee again, needing something to hold, needing the heat. "Then I'll find out what it was." She gives me a look I can't quite name, hopeful, scared, grateful, all at once.

We don't talk much after that. Just two women sitting across from each other in a small café, each with our own version of the man who was now gone. When we finally stand, she offers a quiet thank you and leaves without looking back.

I stay a moment longer, the thumb drive secure in my pocket, the smell of coffee clinging to my coat.

I don't owe James anything. We weren't close. But now his story has landed in my lap and it feels like I am the only one who hasn't looked away.

I have no idea what I'd just agreed to uncover, but I'm starting to wonder if it is more than either of us are ready for.

~ 9 ~

I walk back into the office, overly aware of the Thumb Drive in my pocket, as if it's trying to announce itself to everyone I pass. Even without knowing its contents, I know I can't let it out of my sight, so back in the privacy of the Project Room, I remove it from my coat pocket and secure it to my work lanyard.

Just as the clasp clicks, the door is flung open. I quickly drop the length of the lanyard down the inside of my top, out of sight, as Emily comes in, eating from a plastic tray of blueberries. "Hey, where have you been?" she asks. "I've been trying to catch you all day, you free?"

'Oh god, the date! I forgot to message back. I'm such a bad friend', I think to myself. "Hey Emily, yeah come in!" I respond, trying to sound as enthusiastic as possible. "Soooo" I drag out the word "How was your night?" I smile, as Emily pulls a chair from the conference table, over to my desk.

"It was amazing" Emily starts enthusiastically, her cheeks flushed. "We went to that amazing new restaurant in town, the one with the huge fish tank" I don't think I have ever seen Emily as animated, I muse, as she stretches her arms out to depict the sheer scale of the tank. "wow, he must be keen to impress you to take you there on a first date." I respond, as Emily giggles.

"Then we went for a walk through the gardens at the park" she gushes as I smile and nod enthusiastically. I'm happy for her, I really am, and I know that she wants to have a conversation with me, as we normally would, but I just can't focus my mind on anything but that Thumb Drive.

"I know you're not his number one fan" Emily says, misinterpreting my distraction as disinterest, "But you'll see he is a great guy, if you give him a chance" she follows, with a tilt of her head, almost begging me with her eyes to like him. I laugh and shake my head, "Fine! I'll give him a chance"

"Come over later, we will have a proper catch up." Emily breezes "And don't worry, I've not forgotten about the 'other' thing. We can order take out!" and with that she gets up and almost skips out the door. I'm glad she hasn't forgotten about the reports, but this 'Mark' distraction has come at the worst time.

As the door clicks shut behind her, I release a long, slow breath. The silence that follows is almost deafening after Emily's whirlwind of energy.

All day I feel the thumb drive against my chest, the weight of it pressing into my skin like a secret trying to burrow deeper. At first, I tried to ignore it, buried it under meetings, fake smiles, small talk, even the ceaseless drone of inbox pings.

But as the minutes of the afternoon drag by, I begin to crave its contents, like an addict craves the bottle, or the blade, or the thing they know will hurt them, but reach for anyway. It scares me. Truly scares me. Because I know I can't go back to who I was before I knew too much.

There's no 'before' anymore. Not really.

By the time the office thins out and the buzz of conversation dims to background noise, I've stopped pretending. I can barely sit still. Every time someone walks past the project room door, I flinch, afraid they'll see it on my face, that I'm hiding something. That I'm watching the edges of my world begin to peel back.

As soon as I am able, I leave the office and head home. I didn't dare use my work laptop to look at the thumb drive, I don't know if anyone would be able to trace my activity and I am not about to take any risks.

I get home just after 6:00pm, Mushu greets me with his usual yawn as he rubs against my lower legs and for a moment I stand in the hallway, keys still in hand, wondering if I've made a mistake. What if there's nothing on it? What if there's too much?

I drop my bag by the stairs and make my way to the kitchen table where my laptop eagerly awaits. I sit down and stare at the thumb drive for a long time before plugging it in. The soft click echoes in the quiet. The little light on it flickers to life.

I spend a long time opening and closing mundane folders, financial projections, commission models, and a few other spreadsheets I can make head nor tail of.

Then there it is. Hidden. Buried in a subfolder titled System Backups.

I open it.

Inside are half a dozen documents and one video file. No thumbnails, no previews, just a list:

- Observations.pdf
- Personal_Log.txt
- draft_letter.docx
- Record_01.mov

I open the Personal_Log.txt first.

Most of it is ordinary. Brief notes, dates, meetings. Some lines clearly written in haste. But then, about halfway down the file, I see a line that makes my stomach flip.

They know I've seen something. It's subtle, but it's there. Changed behaviours. Sudden decisions. Something's wrong. I think it's bigger than I realised.

Another entry a week later:

I've started backing everything up, just in case. If anything happens to me, this isn't an accident.

That line stops me cold. Everything stills, the air, the sound, even my thoughts

I sit back in my chair, pulse quickening. There's more, small mentions of 'meetings off calendar', and 'SLT discrepancies', but nothing concrete. He doesn't name names. It reads like someone who *wanted* to document something but was too afraid to write it down plainly.

The next document I open is draft_letter.docx.

It's half-finished, addressed not to his wife, but to someone named 'A. Mallory', a name I don't recognise.

'You once told me that the truth only matters if people believe it. I hope, one day, someone does. I know this will sound paranoid. Maybe it is. But something's happening at the top. I'm not sure who I can trust anymore. If this reaches you, then maybe I didn't get far enough. I'm sorry. I really tried.'

My breath catches.

This wasn't just a man under pressure. This was a man who thought he was in danger.

I click into the last file, Record_01.mov.

It opens to a grainy video. James is in a dim room, the camera angle slightly off. His face is drawn, his eyes tired. The video quality is poor, but his voice is unmistakable.

"If you're watching this... then I was right."

It cuts there, just a few seconds. A corrupt file, maybe. Or intentionally edited. I sit frozen, my heart thudding loud enough that I can hear it in my ears. I came looking for clarity, but all I've found are fragments. Warnings. Shadows. This wasn't a man who planned to die. This was a man trying to say something, and someone made sure he couldn't finish.

A week ago, I wouldn't have ever opened someone else's mail. Now I'm cataloguing the last thoughts of a dead man, chasing shadows in file names

I glance around the empty kitchen room, suddenly hyper-aware of how quiet it is. There's more here. I can feel it. And whatever James was onto... it didn't die with him. This isn't just a question of whether James died by suicide. It's a question of what he died *for*.

I should take this to someone. The police. The board. Someone with authority.

But something inside me resists.

Because I no longer know who to trust. I don't even want to drag Emily further into this, she is my best friend and I don't want to put her in any danger, but keeping this to myself is already eating me alive.

I gather my things and head for the door, the audio file still ringing in my ears. I can't be alone with this. Not tonight. By the time I reach Emily's house, the sun is low on the horizon and the sky has turned that dull, bruised blue of early evening.

I sit in my car for a long moment, watching the glow from her kitchen window, listening to the soft tick of the cooling engine. Inside, she's probably setting out glasses, maybe already laughing at something on the TV. Normal things. Safe things. Things that, just a few days ago, were part of *my* world too.

Now, it all feels... distant. Like a memory I can't quite hold onto.

I reach into my bag and feel the thumb drive again. Still warm from my palm. Still heavy with everything I shouldn't know. My fingers tremble as I draw them away.

I could lie. I could pretend everything's fine. We could eat noodles, gossip about Mark, and talk about nothing until I almost convinced myself I imagined it all. But I can't lie to Emily. Not about this.

I get out of the car and walk up the path. Her porch light flickers once as I reach it, just enough to make my stomach twist. My hand hovers over the doorbell for half a second longer than it should. Then I press it.

Emily opens the door almost immediately, barefoot and smiling, holding a glass of wine in one hand and waving me in with the other.

"There you are! You're late, but I forgive you," she teases, stepping aside. "Dinner's en route and I even got your weird dumplings this time." Her smile falters. I must look like a ghost. "Wait. Are you okay?"

"I need to talk to you," I say. My voice sounds far away to my own ears. "About James. About what he left behind." Emily sets the wine glass down without a word. She knows me too well to ask if it's serious. She just closes the door behind us, flicks the lock, and says quietly"Tell me everything."

~ 10 ~

Emily listens without interrupting. She sits cross-legged on the couch, her wine forgotten, her hands loosely clasped in her lap, are perfectly still. The files, the note to A. Mallory, the video, everything spills from me in uneven bursts. I don't plan the order or try to soften the impact. I just speak, letting it out before I lose the nerve.

When I'm done, the room is heavy with silence. The only sounds are the low hum of the fridge and the faint crackle of the fire. Emily just stares at me for too long, the expression on her face a careful mix of concern and confusion, like someone trying to piece together a puzzle that doesn't quite make sense.

Finally, she leans back, exhaling like the weight of the story has settled somewhere behind her ribs. "Jesus," she murmurs. "That's... a lot."

I nod, watching her carefully. She looks genuinely shocked. No flicker of recognition at the name *A. Mallory*. Just the wide-eyed disbelief of someone processing something vast and unexpected.

"You're sure it's real? Not something he... made up under stress or paranoia?" she asks gently, her voice low.

"I thought that too," I admit. "Until I saw his face in the video. He looked terrified. And the files weren't just thoughts or theories. They were organised. Backed up. Hidden." I hesitate. "He wasn't just spiralling, he was documenting something."

A thought blooms, dark and sudden: *I wonder where the backups are?* The drive was only a piece of the story. If James was truly scared, truly trying to protect something, then there might be more. *Maybe Susan has an idea?* She knew him better than anyone.

Emily rubs her hands over her face, dragging her fingers through her hair, then sighs. "And this name, A. Mallory. Any clue who that might be?"

"Have you ever heard that name before?" I ask. "Before I got to NexTech?"

She frowns and shakes her head slowly. "No," she says. "I've never heard of them." Something flickers across her face, a brief hesitation, but it's gone before I can pin it down.

Then she pauses, her eyes narrowing. "There's something else. Something that happened last night... with Mark." My pulse jumps. "What?"

"I didn't think anything of it earlier, but now ... I don't know, maybe I'm just spooked," she says, folding her arms. "We were walking near the park after dinner. Everything was going great. We were laughing, holding hands. Then he got this call. I don't know who it was, he didn't say. Just stepped away. For a long time."

"Did he say anything when he came back?"

She shakes her head. "Said it was work. But he looked different. Tense. Like whatever was said... rattled him. He tried to play it cool, but I could tell something had changed."

A chill skims my spine. James's voice echoes in my mind: *They know I've seen something.* "Do you think Mark could be involved?" I ask, forcing my tone to stay level.

Emily shrugs, but there's tension in her jaw. "I don't know. But you said James was suspicious of people acting strangely, right? Making odd decisions?" Her voice dips. "God, just when someone has actually paid me some attention..." Her shoulders slump. "I don't want to think I've misjudged him."

I reach for her hand. "Look. He might not have anything to do with this. Don't throw this away until we know something for sure."

Emily exhales hard, She bites her lip, glancing at the fire like she's weighing something. Then says "Well... if he is involved...At least I can do some digging. See what I can find out for you. But I really hope not, I like him Sarah"

I raise an eyebrow. "You'd be okay with that?"

"Please. If he's up to something shady, I'd rather know. I can flirt and dig at the same time. Besides, if something's off, maybe he'll let something slip."

The thought of Emily walking into something dangerous because of me, makes my stomach turn. But I also know she might be the only person who can get close enough to Mark unnoticed.

"You don't think I should go to the police?" I ask. Emily gives a small, rueful smile. "You could. But you said it yourself, you don't know who to trust. If someone on the inside was involved in whatever this is, reporting it too early could backfire. You'd risk tipping off the wrong person."

I bite the inside of my cheek. She's right. As awful as it feels to wait, I need more.

"Before you do anything official," she continues. "You said there was a name. Maybe that's the next step. Find this A. Mallory. See what they know."

The fire pops quietly in the hearth and a sudden gust of wind rattles the windowpane. "Promise me you'll be careful," she says, reaching over and squeezing my hand. Her grip is warm, steady. "Don't do anything reckless."

`"I won't," I reply, hoping it's not a lie.

We eat in companionable silence after that, dumplings and spring rolls, half-watched TV flickering in the background. For a little while, we pretend everything's normal. I even laugh once, when Emily accidentally spills soy sauce down the front of her shirt and blames the universe.

But even as I smile, my thoughts are elsewhere. With James. With the files. With the question I haven't stopped asking since I plugged that thumb drive in: *What did he find?*

By the time I leave, the sky has turned velvet-dark and the air carries that late-night stillness that feels like everyone in the world is tucked up safely in bed.

I drive home with my windows cracked, one hand on the steering wheel, the other clenched in my lap. I keep checking the rearview mirror, convinced for no reason that I'm being followed.

At home, I kick off my shoes, pour myself a glass of water, and sit at the kitchen table. The laptop waits silently, screen dark. I reach into my pocket and run my thumb across the edge of the drive. Still warm. Still too heavy for what it is.

Then I open the laptop, The search bar stares back at me.

I type the name slowly, letting the letters form like an incantation.

"A. Mallory."

No title. No context. Just a name. Then I press enter. I'll find them. Whoever they are.

~ 11 ~

It takes longer than it should to find her. *A. Mallory*, just a name, clean and forgettable. No profile photo. No listed company. No links to NexTech or anywhere else. Just one thin breadcrumb. A single-page website for **Mallory Consulting**, filled with vague corporate jargon and zero personality. No contact number. Just a secure submission form under the heading: "*For Inquiries: Serious or Sensitive Only.*"

It looks like the kind of site designed not to be visited. A professional ghost town. I sit there for several minutes, fingers hovering over the keyboard, weighing whether to type anything at all. The longer I stare at the screen, the more irrational it feels, like I was about to yell into a tunnel and hope something yelled back.

But I can't let it go. Not after what I'd found. Not after James's voice. Not after Susan's eyes, brimming with disbelief and grief and the weight of too many unanswered questions. So I type.

I'm not a client.
I believe you knew James Turner.
I think he trusted you.
Please. I need to understand what happened to him.
I'm not here to expose you. Just... to know the truth.

I don't include my name. I just hit send, close the laptop and wait. I half expect the reply to never come. Or worse, to come from someone else entirely. Someone watching. But less than an hour later, I receive a response.

Come alone. No electronics. No car.
Southwest corner of Carlton Gardens. Tomorrow 17:00. Wear green.
I'll find you.

No greeting. No sign-off. Just instructions, precise, cold, like someone who's done this before. Something about the clipped tone makes my heart drop into my stomach. This isn't an invitation. It is a warning disguised as a meeting.

***

I spend the day trying to work, luckily I am working from home today. There is nothing I can do until 17:00 so I try my best to concentrate on my upcoming presentation and make sure the project is still running efficiently.

As 16:30 rolls around, I can feel my anxiety starting to build, starting at the pit of my stomach, until finally it lands and settles in my chest.

I leave everything at home: my phone, my laptop, even my usual handbag. I am wearing the dark green coat with deep pockets that Emily bought me last Christmas. In its pocket sits my key on a simple key-ring. I leave my house with an ever-growing sense that I am following James's footsteps too closely and maybe too blindly.

Carlton Gardens is deceptively calm this afternoon. The light has softened into that cool pre-evening gold, stretching shadows across the gravel walkways. The breeze carries the crisp hint of autumn, shaking the leaves just enough to fill the silence with soft movement. It is the kind of day that tries to lull you into peace.

But I am too aware. Too raw. My eyes scan every passing face. My ears pick up every rustle. I walk the perimeter twice, slowly, trying to look casual.

Then I see her. Sitting on a bench like she belonged there, paperback in hand. Sunglasses, scarf, grey coat, no obvious attempt to hide, and yet everything about her posture says *invisible*. Not drawing attention is an art form. And she is a master.

I walk past once.

Then again.

She doesn't look up either time. But on the third pass, she turns a page and says softly, without looking:

"You're late."

My breath catches. I sit down slowly beside her. "You're Mallory?"

"Not exactly," she replies.

Her voice is low, measured, familiar in a way I can't place, sending a jolt through me. I turn to her fully, studying her face more carefully. And that's when it hit me. Not in a flash. Not all at once. More like a slow, sinking tide of recognition.

The angled jaw. The stillness. The way she never quite makes direct eye contact unless it was necessary. I *know* her.

I have seen her before. Spoken with her in passing. Heard stories. Emily and I used to joke that she haunted the audit floor like a shadow, '*the ghost in the glass office*'. Always present, never included. Then it clicked.

"Alex," I whisper, like speaking her name aloud might fracture the moment. "Alex Monroe."

She doesn't flinch. Doesn't deny it. "I was," she says. My chest tightens. "Why the name change?" I ask. "Because it's not enough to leave. You have to make sure no one remembers why you mattered in the first place."

I swallow. "Why agree to meet me?"

She finally turns her face fully toward me, no sunglasses now. Her eyes are older than I remember. Not in years, but in experience. There is a shadow in them. The kind that doesn't come from grief. The kind that comes from surviving something you're not supposed to walk away from.

"Because I saw a look in James Turner's eyes the last day he came to me. It's the same one I see in yours now." The bench feels colder than it had a moment ago, and now I wonder. did he feel this exposed? This powerless? Or did he just feel the tide turning beneath him, too slow to name until it was too late?

"He had found something," she said. "Deep in the finance systems. A code. **Z-87-CT**." I nod. "I saw it in the files. What is it?"

"A slush fund," she says. "But far more advanced than any normal discretionary spending. CT stands for *Confidential Transactions*. It's a financial blind spot. A code that lets money move where no one's supposed to look. The kind of money that builds things no one's allowed to talk about."

"Black budget?" I ask. She looks down and shakes her head. "Worse. This wasn't just hush-hush innovation. This was manipulation. Ghost vendors. Employee approvals forged. Bonuses skimmed. Entire departments marked as funding sources for things they'd never touched."

I swallow the lump rising in my throat. "And the list of dates and initials? Mine were on there." She nods. "Those are the approvals James flagged. If your name is on there, you're being positioned. Slowly."

"I tried to stop it. Quietly. I flagged inconsistencies. Escalated to the wrong people. And then one day my access was gone. My calendar cleared. HR booked me a farewell lunch I never showed up to." She turns away from me. "I got out before they could give me a worse option."

"What happened to James?" I whisper. She hesitates. Then says, without emotion. "I believe he died because he didn't stop digging. Because he believed the truth would protect him. It didn't. I tried to warn him, told him to stop..."

A silence settles over us. The hum of wind in the leaves, the distant rumble of traffic. Then, softly, she adds, "Before he died, James said something strange. 'If anything happens to me, look under the fox'."

"The fox?"

She nods. "He wasn't poetic. If he said that, it was literal. Something at home. A figurine. A hiding place?"

I stare at the ground. My thoughts spin. "I've spoken to his wife, Susan. I will go to see her and try to make sense of it." Alex grabs my lower arm, startling me. She looks deep into my eyes. "Be careful. The deeper you go, the less likely you are to get back out." She warns before releasing her grip and looking away.

Alex pulls a small envelope from inside her coat and presses it into my hand. "Burner number. Use it if you're followed. But don't call unless it's urgent. You can get me through the website. James set it up so we could communicate. Use it if you find something you can't explain. I'm not on anyone's radar right now. I plan to keep it that way."

"Who's behind this?" I ask, my voice barely audible.

She shakes her head. "I don't know. But maybe the answers lie under the fox."

Then she stands and walks away, not fast, not like someone running. But like someone who knows the route and who isn't looking back.

I sit there, long after she's gone. And all I can hear in my head are James's final words.

'If anything happens to me, look under the fox'

~ 12 ~

When I return home, I pick up my phone from the table and open the last message from Susan. Our first encounter seems longer ago than just yesterday. I start to type, unsure how much to say over messages.

'Hi Susan,

I'm sorry, but could we meet? I need to talk to you. Preferably at your house.

Sarah.'

It doesn't take Susan long to reply.

'Hi,

Of course, you've found something?

I live at 133, Sycamore Street, I'll be home all evening.

Susan.'

I try to imagine her tone from the message alone. Resigned? Curious? Distant? None of it feels right, and yet all of it feels true.

***

When I pull up in front of Susan's house, I look, watching the curtains. No movement. No lights. Just the soft, sleepy stillness of a suburban street beginning to wind down for the night.

Susan answers the door with a tired smile and shadows under her eyes. She doesn't say hello, or ask how I am. She simply steps aside and motions for me to come in.

"James's study is this way," she says quietly, as if raising her voice might disturb something. Maybe it would.

The house is dim and still smells faintly of him, aftershave and coffee and something warmer, like the scent of old pages or sunlit furniture. Grief has not yet faded him from the walls.

We walk down a narrow hallway and into a small room at the back of the house. It is sparse, neat, with clean lines and a desk by the window. The chair is tucked in, a pair of reading glasses folded beside the keyboard. Nothing has been moved. I wonder if Susan ever comes in here, or if she keeps it untouched to preserve what little certainty she has left.

"I have to ask you something," I say, pausing in the doorway. "Before he died, James said something strange. He told someone to 'look under the fox.' Does that mean anything to you?"

Susan's face stiffens. Her mouth slightly parts, but no words come. She blinks, then turns slowly toward the bookshelf. "Fox?" she repeats, voice thin. "There's one... but I never thought..."

She steps past me and runs her fingers along a middle shelf, brushing lightly across the books and knickknacks. Then she pauses.

A small fox figurine sits nestled between a paperweight and an old hardcover notebook. It is ceramic, russet and white, with glassy eyes and a curling tail. One of those delicate, overly polished souvenirs from a craft fair or a gift shop.

"He bought this at a market, years ago," Susan says, touching its ear. "Said it reminded him of our daughter. Clever, stubborn. He liked things that meant something, even if no one else saw it."

"May I?" I ask. Susan nods, not taking her eyes from the figurine. I reach out and gently lift the figurine from its spot. It is heavier than it looks at first. Dense. Not hollow. I tilt it, listening.

Something shifts inside. Turning it over, I run my thumb along the base and feel it. A seam.

I glance at Susan, who is watching with wide, unblinking eyes. Then I press along the edge, and with a quiet click, the base shifts. I twist it gently, and the underside pops open to reveal a small, padded compartment. Nestled inside is another thumb drive.

Susan sucks in a breath. "He never told me..."

I pull the drive out, cradling it in my palm like something sacred. "He didn't want anyone to find it unless they knew exactly what to look for."

She nods slowly, then sits on the edge of the desk, visibly shaken.

I close the base of the fox, set it back on the shelf. "I'm sorry Susan, but I think James was being watched. And he knew it."

Susan doesn't cry, but her eyes brim, her lips trembling. "What do you think is on there?"

"I don't know. But I'm getting closer"

A long pause follows. Then she stands and hugs her arms around herself. "Be careful, Sarah. I can't lose anyone else."

I didn't respond. I couldn't promise that. Not anymore. I thank her again and leave quietly, the second thumb drive now a weight in my pocket, heavier than it should be.

***

By the time I get home, the sky has gone charcoal-grey. Distant streetlights cast long, reaching shadows across the sidewalk and the wind has picked up enough to rattle the branches outside my house. I lock the door behind me with practiced fingers, double-checking the deadbolt before turning on the hall light.

"Mushu?" I called softly, kicking off my shoes.

Silence.

He usually comes running at the sound of the door, ready to wind between my legs and complain about the time. But tonight, the apartment is still, too still. I find him eventually, curled under the sofa, blinking up at me with a look I can't place, anxious, alert. His ears twitching.

"What's gotten into you?" I whisper, reaching down to stroke his head. He doesn't purr. The hair on the back of my neck lifts.

I stand slowly, scanning the room. Everything looks normal. The cushions on the sofa, the unopened mail on the counter, the faint tick of the wall clock. But something is wrong. Not obvious. Just... wrong.

I walk into the kitchen. One of the drawers, second from the left, is slightly ajar. Just enough to show it had been opened. I always closed them.

The smell is different too. Nothing strong, just an impression, like a breath of scent I don't wear or the faintest trace of someone else's skin on the air. It passes almost immediately, but the chill remains.

I walk through the house with deliberate steps, checking each room. Nothing disturbed. Nothing stolen. But my laptop, which I'd left off and closed, now sits open on the desk. The screen is still on. A soft, pulsing glow.

I move toward it with my heart pounding in my chest. The mouse has been moved. The screen saver is off. I tap a key and the screen brightens.

No files open. No programs running. But the list of "recent documents" is empty. I never clear it.

A wave of nausea rolls through me. Someone has been here. They haven't stolen anything. But they have looked. I back away from the desk, trying not to panic. Mushu is still under the sofa, eyes fixed on something just over my shoulder. The urge to flee is sudden and strong.

Instead, I cross the room, pick him up gently and carry him into the kitchen with me. I set him on the table, where he jumps to a window ledge and stares outside.

The new thumb drive is still in my coat pocket, alongside the other one. I place them on the table. Two identical objects, side by side. Two very different questions. I don't plug it in. I sit at the table instead, the laptop closed, the flat dim surrounding me.

Someone has been in my home. Not to threaten. Not to leave a message. To see what I have. Which means they know I have something worth seeing.

I pull a throw blanket around my shoulders and stare at the two drives. The silence stretched, interrupted only by the occasional tick of the heating system or the soft rustle of Mushu shifting behind me.

I want to call Emily. I want to tell her someone has been here. That they are closing in. But I can't shake the idea that maybe they are listening. My phone is face-down on the counter. My laptop is still on the desk. Both are capable of being compromised.

James had said, 'They know I've seen something'. Now they know *I* have. The apartment feels smaller than it had before. The walls are closer. The windows are thinner.

I pick up the drives and carry them to the bathroom, wrap them in a towel, then tuck them into a plastic container beneath the sink. It isn't high-tech, but it isn't obvious either.

Then I sit on the bathroom floor, legs curled beneath me, staring at the closed door. I don't even bother trying to sleep. I just stay awake, letting the silence wrap around me like wire.

Because the thing about knowing too much isn't just that you become a target. It's that you stop trusting the silence. It stops being peace. It starts being a pause before something breaks. And whatever James had uncovered, it wasn't finished. Not even close.

Alex's words echo from the walls "The deeper you go, the less likely you are to get back out."

~ 13 ~

I don't sleep.

The few hours I spend lying down are filled with shallow breaths, wide eyes, and every creak of the floorboards pulls me into full alertness. I stay wrapped in a throw blanket on the bathroom floor, the two thumb drives tucked away beneath the sink and Mushu curled beside me like a sentinel. Every time he twitches in his sleep, I flinch.

At some point around 4 a.m, I convince myself I hear footsteps outside the door. Not the creaky kind, but deliberate, measured. I hold my breath for over a minute, staring at the strip of light beneath the bathroom door, waiting for the shadow of a foot.

Nothing comes. But even that nothing feels like a threat.

By morning, I know I can't use any of my devices. Not the laptop. Not my phone. I don't know how they got in, but I know one thing for certain:

I am already compromised.

***

At 8:47 a.m., I pick up my phone for the first time since the night before. Every instinct screaming at me to throw it in the bin, but I need it, for one last call and one final message.

I call work first, scrolling through my contacts with a strange sense of detachment until I find the reception number. My fingers tremble slightly as I hit call. When they answer, I force a rasp into my voice.

"Hi, this is Sarah Mitchell. I'm feeling unwell. I won't be in today."

A pause. Then a polite, professional tone. "Would you like me to inform your department or just mark you as out?"

"I've already let my team know," I lie. "Just mark me out."

"All right. Hope you feel better soon."

I end the call and immediately open my messages.

Hey, I'm not coming in today. Not feeling right. Please stop looking into anything, just for now. I'll explain when I can.

I send it to Emily. Her reply is almost instant. "*What? Are you okay? What happened?*" I hesitate, then type. "*Please, Em. Just let it go. For your safety.*"

Another beat. Three dots, then none. Then again. "*Okay... I trust you. Please be safe. Let me know how you are later.*"

I don't reply.

I stare at her message, guilt twisting into something sharp inside my ribs. Emily doesn't deserve to be dragged into this. Not any deeper.

***

By 9:12 a.m., I am out of the house. I bring only essentials, my passport, cash, a scarf to tuck around my face, the tote bag I've used a handful of times, the one with a broken side seam, patched with a safety pin. And the two thumb drives.

I drive without the radio on, windows cracked just enough to hear the world outside. One eye always on the rearview mirror. Mushu is breaking the silence now and again, meowing quietly from his crate on the back seat. I drop him off with my parents, "a last minute work trip, just for a few days." I say, kissing them both goodbye, before rushing back to my car.

Driving away, I'm not sure if I'm being followed. I'm not sure of anything. But I feel like a wire stretched too tight, waiting for one sharp pull to snap. Every red light is a test. Every car that stays behind me for more than three turns feels like a tail. I change routes twice, take a roundabout detour through a petrol station, then pull into a car wash just to see who waits.

No one does. Still, the feeling doesn't lift.

I don't go to any of the usual shops. No big-box chains. No stores with loyalty cards or facial recognition at the door. Instead, I find a tired strip of independent retailers on the edge of town, quiet enough not to attract attention, unremarkable enough to be forgotten.

The electronics store is run by a man in his sixties with a faded rugby polo and glasses thick enough to start a fire. He doesn't ask questions. He doesn't blink at my face half-hidden behind my scarf. Just leads me to a shelf lined with plain black laptops. No smart integration's. No pre-loaded apps that would ping data back to some unknown server.

"I need something clean," I tell him. "Local storage only. No automatic backups. Fast, secure. Cash purchase."

He nods and points to three different models. I pick one with a decent processor and solid encryption capability. Reliable. Nondescript.

He rings it up and asks, "Need anything else?"

"Yes. A phone. No SIM."

He blinks. "No SIM?"

"I already have a number. I just need the handset."

He pulls a basic smartphone from a locked drawer behind the counter. No frills. Just calls, texts, and the internet. Black, compact, forgettable.

"That'll do."

He packs the boxes without another word, and I pay in cash, then I walk out without looking back.

A few streets over, I find a café that looks like it hasn't updated its décor since 1994. Lace curtains. Chunky wooden chairs. A chalkboard menu with half the words rubbed off. Perfect.

I pick a table in the far corner, back to the wall, view of the door. I order a cappuccino from a waitress who looks like she's worked there her whole life, then open the new laptop. The hum of the fans, the glow of the fresh screen. It feels sterile. New. Safe.

While it loads, I set up the new phone. Manual setup. No Google account. No syncing. No cloud. I take out the envelope from my pocket and input Alex's burner number, then open a blank text message. I stare at it for a long time, thumbs hovering.

No name to attach. No trust to lean on. Just one chance.

Then I type

It's Sarah. I think I'm being watched. Someone was in my house last night. They didn't take anything, but they were looking. I haven't touched the second drive.
What should I do?

I hit send. The message doesn't bounce. But no reply comes. I stare at the blinking cursor, that single mocking line like it was breathing with me. Time crawls.

By mid-morning, I'm still there, my coffee cold, the laptop shut. I keep watching the front door, flinching every time the bell above it jingles. I count the staff: two. The customers: six. No one stands out. No one lingers. Still, I can't shake the feeling I'm being watched.

I think about James and everything I know so far. Head down. Sleepless. Had he done this too? Sat in places like this, watching the door, waiting for answers that came too late?

I reach for my bag under the table and touch the old phone. Powered off, double-wrapped in plastic bags like something contagious. I don't dare smash it yet. Part of me thinks I might need it. But the rational part of me wants to drop it in a river.

At 11:26, the new phone buzzes. One new message.

Don't go home tonight. I'll send a location at 19:00. Come alone.

No signature. No greeting. But I know it is Alex.

Her voice echoes in my head. 'The deeper you go, the less likely you are to get back out'. I stare at the message until the screen dims. Then I turn the brightness up again, just to read it one more time.

Don't go home tonight.

I hadn't planned on it.

The afternoon drifts by in fragments. I move cafés. Then spend an hour inside a bookshop I used to visit on weekends before I got my job at NexTech. I pretend to read. I smile at a staff member I don't recognise. I buy a cheap paperback just to give myself an excuse for being there.

Then I drive to a quiet park which I used to pass on my way to therapy. I park facing the trees and sit in the car with the engine off. Children play in the distance. A dog chases after falling leaves. A man pushes a stroller past my passenger window and doesn't even glance my way.

No one notices me. And still, I feel hunted.

The new phone sits in the passenger seat, screen lit. No new messages. I check the time. 17:42. I still have over an hour to wait.

I think about calling Emily. About saying just one thing. Just enough to let her know I haven't lost my mind. But I can't. Every call. Every word. Every misplaced sentence might draw someone closer.

19:00 can't come fast enough.

And yet, a part of me never wants the next message to arrive. Because once it does, there will be no turning back. I would follow it and whatever comes next, whoever was really behind this, would finally step into the light.

But I already knew one thing for sure. I wouldn't be going home tonight.

~ 14 ~

At exactly 19:00, my new phone buzzed with a message.

Carlton Vale, by the old water tower. 19:45. Park two streets away. Walk the rest. No one follows.

Still no name. No sign-off.

I lock the screen and slip the phone into my coat. I don't reply.

The drive to Carlton Vale is quiet. My chest tightens the closer I get, lungs refusing to fill all the way. I take a roundabout route through residential side streets, watching the rearview mirror obsessively. No headlights follow. No tail cars. But paranoia has long since stopped waiting for proof.

I park on a tree-lined street a few blocks from the coordinates, just as instructed. The old water tower looms above the darkened skyline, rust streaks running down its stone belly.

I check my watch. 19:42 and start walking.

The footpath that curves past the tower is cracked, weeds growing up through its seams. I pass two men smoking near a bench and a woman in a red coat walking a small dog. Otherwise, the street is empty.

She is already there.

Alex leans against the passenger side of a battered 4x4, arms folded, hood pulled low over her face. She doesn't wave. Doesn't speak. Just unlocks the door and slides in. I climb into the seat beside her. The interior smells faintly of metal and woodsmoke.

"Do you have your phone or laptop?" She questions. "I have a new phone and laptop. Not traceable... and my old phone, but it's powered off"

"Give me the old phone" she says, holding out her hand.

I take the phone out and hand it to her, still wrapped in its plastic bags. She removes the phone and steps back out of the car, placing it beneath her car wheel.

When she gets back in the car, she says simply, "We can't take any risks Sarah."

As she puts the car into reverse, I hear the crunch of glass and metal against stone.

We drive in silence for a long while, heading west through residential roads, then onto quieter lanes I don't recognise. She keeps the headlights on low beam and the music off. Every turn seems deliberately chosen.

Finally, I speak. "Where are we going?"

"Somewhere no one listens," she responds. I wait for more, but it doesn't come.

Eventually, buildings give way to blackened trees and open stretches of dark grassland. The air through the cracked window grows colder, sharper. We turn onto a gravel road hidden behind a crooked wire fence and drive for another fifteen minutes before a cottage comes into view.

It is small. Wooden. Unassuming. Not derelict, not modern, just *there*, nestled into the trees like it had grown from them. There is a porch with an oil lamp. No lights in the windows.

She kills the engine and turns to me. "Bring your things."

Inside, the house is cold but dry. The fireplace is dark, but the smell of old smoke lingers. Books line every wall, some spines missing.

"Who else knows about this place?" I ask, as Alex fills the fire with wood and lights a match.

"No one," Alex responds, without looking up. "Not anymore."

She disappears into a side room and returns with a laptop, different from mine. Older. Its screen is worn with scuffs and sticky tape has been placed over the camera. She sets it on the table.

"Let's see it."

I hesitate, then pull the second thumb drive from my pocket and hand it over. She plugs it in, her face unreadable.

A directory appears on-screen. Sparse. Just three folders. All titled in cold, clinical text.

- ARCHIVE_03
- ZCT_FRACTURE
- PRIVATE

She clicks on ARCHIVE_03. Nothing happens. She tries again.

Then, after a lag, a new window opens: a spreadsheet. It looked corrupted. Cells full of gibberish and trailing symbols, as if someone has dumped code into a finance program. The first few rows seem clean, but after that, noise. Mismatched characters, some highlighted in red, others faded to near-invisible grey.

"What is this?" I ask, squinting.

"Obfuscation," she says. "Designed to hide patterns. Someone cleaned it and scrambled the rest."

She scrolls slowly, stopping at a few lines.

Names. Numbers. None I recognise.

Then one does.

S. MITCHELL — 04.07.24

But the data next to my name is blank. Just an empty row beneath a heading marked 'CONFLICT.'

I don't speak at first. I can't. Something in me recoils, like seeing your name on a grave, before you're dead.

Eventually my voice returns, "What does that mean?" I whisper.

Alex doesn't answer. She clicks into the second folder. ZCT_FRACTURE. Inside are four video files and one encrypted document. The videos have generic names—OBS001, OBS002, and so on. She clicks on the first.

The screen stays black for three seconds. Then grainy footage appears. A boardroom. A table. Eight chairs, two filled. No faces clear, the camera angle too low, or maybe tilted on purpose. I could hear voices, but they were talking in hushed tones, barely audible.

One line stands out:

"signed by Mitchell"

Another voice, louder:

"Then it's done"

Then the screen cuts to black. Alex closes the video, she doesn't open the others.

"Why record this?" I ask.

"To prove something happened," she says. "But not what, it's not evidence of anything." We sit there in silence for a moment. The fire pops behind us. A log split with a hiss. She turns to me. "I'm starting to worry he hadn't finished, the questions were never answered. He just got too close." Alex says, her voice strained. "Whatever he found, it's incomplete. These aren't answers, they're signposts."

She clicks into the third folder: PRIVATE. Password-protected.

Alex types something.

Wrong.

She tries again.

Still wrong.

She looks at me.

"Anything James mentioned? Phrases, names?"

I think back. "He said something in the video. 'If you're watching this... then I was right.'"

Alex types something. The screen flashes red. Wrong. She exhales through her nose, tries again. Still wrong. I can feel her frustration, but she says nothing for a while. I see her lock the computer screen. "I'll try to get it later," she says defeated, pulling the drive and locking it in a small metal box near the hearth. "So... what now?" Alex leans back in her chair, eyes shadowed by the lamplight.

"Now we wait. You've stirred something by looking. The fact that someone was in your flat means someone's tracking movements, maybe through internal IT, maybe through access logs. We don't know. We need to disappear long enough to see who comes looking."

"You think they'll come after me?"

She doesn't answer directly. Instead, she says, "is there anyone you can trust on the inside?"

Immediately only one name comes to mind. "My best friend Emily works in the IT department"

"And you trust her?" Alex says looking directly into my eyes.

"With my life" I reply without hesitation.

"You need to contact her, get her onside." Alex responds. "But be careful. If someone's feeding her information, or pulling hers, you'll tip your hand."

My stomach turns. "Emily wouldn't..."

"It's not about trust. It's about caution. Someone made it look like you approved financial flows tied to a black account. That someone didn't do it for fun."

I stand, my hands trembling and pace to the window. Nothing but trees and mist. No headlights. No sounds. "You knew James," I say. "Better than most."

"I knew what scared him," she replies.

"And what was that?"

She pauses. "Silence," she says. "He said it once. Not the accusations. Not the headlines. It was the silence that came after, the people who looked away."

Outside, the forest groans in the wind. Alex pushes back from the table. "You should sleep. Tomorrow we start pulling threads. One at a time." And without another word, she walks into the hallway and flicks off the lamp, leaving the room in firelight and shadow.

I stand there in the dim, listening to the creaks in the roof, the whisper of wind against the glass. The thumb drive is safe in the box. The laptop shut. But in my head, the voices from that footage play on repeat.

And for the first time since James's files found me, I'm not sure if it was a mistake. Maybe it had been a warning. But from who?

~ 15 ~

I memorised Emily's number ages ago. I never thought that would matter. But this morning, in a cold kitchen with only birdsong for company and no safe devices, it was the only thing that did.

I step out onto the porch of Alex's cottage, the wind sharp against my face and dial her number on the burner phone. My thumb hovers before I hit the green call button. It feels wrong, using a number so familiar on a phone so foreign.

She answers on the third ring.

"Hello?"

"Em," I say softly. "It's me."

Silence.

"Sarah?"

"Yeah. I... I'm safe. But I need your help."

A beat.

"Where are you? Are you okay? You vanished, your phone's off and no one at work's heard from you. Mark's been asking questions."

I ignore that last part. "I can't say much, not over the phone. Can you meet me? Somewhere public."

"Of course. When?"

"Today. Late morning. I'll send a location."

I pause, glancing over my shoulder. Alex has stepped outside, watching me. She gives a small nod.

I relay the café name, neutral ground, quiet. We've chosen it for its anonymity. A secondhand bookshop sat beside it and the windows always steamed up just enough to blur the faces inside.

"I'll be there," Emily says. "Please tell me what's going on."

"I will" I say before ending the call and standing there for a moment, breathing in cold air, the phone still warm in my hand.

***

Alex drives us into town an hour later. She keeps her hood up and her eyes moving, never parking near entrances, never staying in one lane longer than necessary. She doesn't speak until we reached the café.

"I'll stay at the next table," she says. "She doesn't need to know me."

"You don't trust her?"

"I don't trust anyone. That's different."

We entered separately. Emily is already there, wrapped in her green scarf, fingers curled around a chipped mug of tea. Her eyes light up the moment she sees me, but her expression falters as she takes in my appearance, exhausted, unwashed, haunted.

"Sarah..." she stands, half-hugging me. "What the hell's going on?"

I sit. She follows.

"I can't stay long," I say. "And I can't tell you everything."

"But something's wrong."

I nod. "I've found something else. From James Turner. Remember him?"

Emily blinks. "The Finance Director, the one with the video?..."

"Yes," I cut in. "He left something behind. I have part of it. I need help accessing a folder. It's encrypted."

Emily leans back, her expression shifting from concern to calculation. "Okay. You brought it?"

I reach into my coat, slip the thumb drive into her palm beneath the table. "There's a folder marked PRIVATE. That's the one I need. Don't touch anything else."

She raises an eyebrow. "You're being dramatic."

"I'm being cautious."

She sighs, then opens her bag and pulls out a tablet and a small external module I didn't recognise. It had a matte black shell, a tiny screen, and ports on every side.

"What's that?"

"Password breaker. Brute force tool I use for field recovery testing," she says casually, as if she hadn't just revealed she carried military-grade kit to cafés. "I adapted the scripts a little last year. For forensic simulations."

"Is that... legal?"

She smirks. "Depends who you ask. And who you're trying to protect." She connects the drive to her tablet, then routes it through the device. Lines of code scroll across the screen too fast for me to follow. Her fingers move without hesitation. Too fast, maybe. Like she'd done this before... too many times.

"It's a basic hash lock," she murmurs, eyes narrowed. "Probably salted, but not salted *well.* If he didn't use a multi-key encryption, this'll run a list of custom passphrases. Dates. Internal project names. Security questions."

"You can just... do that?"

"I've done worse," she says, and the ghost of a smile flickers across her lips.

I glance sideways. Alex has taken a seat by the window, sunglasses still on, reading a newspaper upside down.

Emily's screen flickers.

"There it is," she said. "041372. One of his fallback patterns. Looks like a reverse date, probably something from childhood."

A chime.

The folder blinks open.

Emily exhales. “We’re in.”

Inside were four files. One video. Two documents. One compressed archive.

Her hand hovers over the video file

“Wait,” I say sharply.

Emily freezes.

“I want to open that later. Alone.”

Her grin fades into a puzzled frown. “Okay... but Sarah, what’s in this? What are you chasing?”

I hesitate. Then, quietly, “I think someone got him killed.”

Emily doesn’t speak for a moment.

“Do you trust me?” I ask.

She nods. “Always.”

“Then don’t ask. Not yet. Not until I’ve had time to read everything. Watch everything. This... it’s dangerous, Em.”

She closes the tablet, slides the drive back to me under her palm.

“I won’t look further. But if you want backup copies made, secure ones, I can help.”

I touch her hand. “Thank you.”

“Just... come back, okay? Don’t do, whatever this is, alone.”

I don’t answer, I just stand up and hug her, before I walk out of the cafe to the meeting place me and Alex had agreed on. I wanted to tell her more. I wanted to stay. But safety had no room for comfort. Not anymore.

***

Back at the cottage, Alex is already at the fireplace, warming her hands. I place the drive on the table between us.

“She cracked it.”

Alex doesn’t look surprised. “Good.”

“She didn’t look.”

"Doesn't matter if she did. She probably wasn't ready to understand it anyway."

I sit down slowly, tension crawling up my back.

"I need to watch it," I say.

Alex nods once, then walks over and pulls the curtain across the windows. The fire crackles behind me. Outside, the trees groan under the weight of autumn wind.

I insert the drive into the laptop and double-click the video file. It opens with a long stretch of darkness. Then static. Then James's face, lit by a flickering desk lamp.

His voice is low. Hoarse. Measured.

"If you're watching this, you found the second drive. That means I didn't make it."

He looks to the side, off camera. As if listening for something.

"They're not just covering their tracks. They're rewriting them. The approvals, the payments... they're building something from inside NexTech. Not just software. Not just black budgets."

A pause.

"It's *people*."

My heart skips.

"I've seen the payroll entries. Ghost hires. Entire departments with no desks, no logins. Just names, recycled from terminated staff. Old pensions. Old claims. They're using the structures to funnel something out. I don't know where." He blinks. Rubbing his eyes. "I made a list. You'll find it in the archive folder. But be careful. If you try to expose it directly, it will bury *you*."

The video flickers, before James continues. "There was a name, at the beginning. Mallory. She tried to stop it. They erased her access. Rewrote her out. If she's still alive, find her."

I turn to Alex, before turning back to the screen, which fuzzes again. His final words are faint, like they are pulled from a dream. Or a nightmare.

"Don't trust anyone who asks too many questions. I don't know if this is one, two or ten people ... I just know they are in deep. And they are dangerous. If they find out I've sent this... they'll bury me. Bury *everyone* I spoke to. "

The screen goes black.

I don't move for a long time. My mind drifts to Mark. The way he probes in meetings. Always asking one question too many. I used to find it annoying. Now, I'm not so sure. And Emily? Would they come for her too, just for knowing me?

The fire cracks behind me. The wind howls outside. My reflection stares back from the darkened screen. Silent. Small.

~ 16 ~

The fire is burning low by the time I force myself to move. The room is dim, cast in hues of amber and smoke, like the truth James left behind has altered the light. Alex says nothing. She just waits, arms folded, her gaze fixed on the flickering shadows the fire throws against the walls.

"He said there was a list," I finally say.

She nods, already pulling the laptop back toward her. "Archive folder." I watch as she navigates into the compressed directory Emily hadn't opened. "This one is large," Alex says, "Several gigabytes."

I nod, but I'm not really listening. My mind is still stuck on that final line from the video. '*Don't trust anyone who asks too many questions.*' My stomach twists. Mark. His constant probing. The way he lingers over technical details that aren't his domain. The pointed questions, the timing of them.

I hope I'm wrong for Emily's sake. She likes him. And she's not stupid. But people are blind when they have feelings for someone.

Alex taps the keyboard, before a soft chime echoes from the speakers. The file unzips. A new folder blooms on the screen.

Z-Audit_Thread_46

Inside it, are half a dozen spreadsheets, four audio files, and a document labeled simply, *Crossref Notes - J.L.* Alex opens the document first.

I half hope it will be answers, but it isn't even coherent in the traditional sense. It reads like a mind unraveling slowly, trying to hold on to sense through raw notation. Cross-references to payment cycles, strange strings of initials. Jumbled data dumps, half-masked variables. Every so often, a short line in all caps:

'Z-87-CT CANNOT BE ACCIDENTAL.'

'LOOK FOR 'SHADOW' LINE ITEMS. ALWAYS QUARTER 2.'

'REDUNDANCIES AREN'T REAL.'

My mouth goes dry. "What does he mean 'aren't real'?" I whisper.

Alex doesn't respond. She clicks on the first spreadsheet. It loads slowly, like it is reluctant to be seen. Dozens of tabs. Each marked with initials and numeric codes. The data inside means nothing to me at first, just numbers, percentage allocations, departmental budgeting jargon. Then I noticed something.

The totals never matched.

Every sheet ends in a discrepancy. Not enough to trigger immediate alarms, just enough to quietly disappear into quarterly write-offs.

"We were looking at the top-level budgets," Alex murmurs, her brow furrowing. "But underneath... Someone was replicating staff profiles. Assigning shadow identities to real ones."

"Like ghost employees?"

"Worse. These aren't even fully fabricated. They're copied, twinned. But then the copies are moved... into entities that don't technically exist."

She flips open another spreadsheet. It shows employee IDs. One of them is mine.

SM-0487 / Group PM Director / Active Dual Status (Flagged)

"What does that mean?" I ask, my voice small.

Alex zooms in, scrolling past columns until we reach the notes field.

Assigned: 2024. Cross-dept. Flag mismatch. Billed hours exceed ceiling. Merge: profile reassignment flagged 07/04 (budget cycle match)..

07/04. The date the board signed off the budget. The date James had written beside my initials in his notebook. A lead weight sinks into my chest. "I didn't approve of any dual status..."

"They made it look like you did," Alex says, calmly. "It's not about the money. It's about identity obfuscation. They need your position as a shell. Your title gives cover to move funds under a different umbrella."

I feel like I am watching my life being rebuilt around me, piece by piece, by hands I couldn't see.

"What about the audio files?" I ask, already dreading the answer. Alex clicks one. It is scratchy. Poor quality. A phone call, recorded on an old system. Two voices, both sound electronically altered somehow, almost robotic. whoever is behind this has certainly done their best to cover their tracks.

"She's not compliant."

"Mitchell?"

"Too clean. Too careful. We can't seed her directly."

"Then we duplicate her profile. Thread it through OPEX. Have it routed by Monroe's old chain."

"She's already connected to Lewis. Too close."

"Keep her distracted, promise of a promotion?"

"In progress."

The file cuts out. My heart slams into my ribs. I stare at Alex, unable to form words. She doesn't look surprised. "I think James got this just before he died," she says softly. "He never told me how."

Keep her distracted. Promise of a promotion. They know my past, know my ambition and they've tried to use it against me. I reach out and close the laptop, unable to look at the screen anymore.

I sit, head in my hands trying to understand how I got wrapped up in all of this. The wind outside has picked up. Somewhere in the trees, an owl calls out, once, then nothing.

"I need to talk to Emily," I say finally. "Not tell her everything. But enough to see if she notices anything off."

"Do it in person," Alex says. "I know you're not going to like this, but I think you need to get back into NexTech, Search for answers from the inside"

"What?" My voice sharpens. "Go back to NexTech?" Alex, places a hand on my shoulder. "I think you have to," says Alex gently "and if you trust Emily as much as you say you do, we have to bring her in on this, every detail."

I stand, arms wrapped tight across my chest. My own name echoes in my mind, hollow and foreign. There is something else in those files. Something we haven't opened yet. I can feel it pressing against my thoughts like something moving just out of frame.

"They're rewriting identities," I say, more to myself than to her. Alex nods "And when they're done, you're not you anymore."

Outside, a branch scrapes the window. A low creak sounds from somewhere in the beams and I jump. I don't even trust the wind anymore. Somewhere in the data James has left behind, I am being hollowed out.

~ 17 ~

The plan is simple, in theory. Go back. Act normal. Watch everything.

I don't like it, but even I admit I can't hide forever, not if I want to unravel what James has started. My reappearance at NexTech has to look spontaneous. A brief illness, nothing more. No drama. No explanation. But in reality, I am stepping straight back into the lion's den.

It is just after 8:30 a.m. when I walk into the building. My security pass still works. That detail alone feels like a trap. Either they haven't noticed I was gone or they want me back inside.

The reception staff greet me with a smile that spoke of normality. I smile back. Forced. Polite. Watching everything.

The elevator ride up is silent. A woman I don't know checks her watch three times in the span of thirty seconds. The moment the doors slide open, I see him.

Mark.

He is standing by the coffee machine, deep in conversation with one of the legal analysts. He saw me before I saw him, his expression unreadable, his eyes too still.

When I pass, he says nothing. But I feel his gaze following me. Not hostile. Not curious. Something else entirely.

I step into the project room and exhale slowly. It is exactly as I had left it. My desk is untouched. My notes are still pinned to the corkboard. My chair is even swiveled at the same lazy angle I'd left it in.

Emily arrives fifteen minutes later, holding two coffees and a blueberry muffin. She smiles when she sees me, relief and warmth in her eyes. "I brought you the good one," she says, setting it on my desk.

"Thanks." I take it with a shaky hand. "I needed it."

She leans in close. "You okay?"

"Define okay."

Emily doesn't laugh, but her hand briefly touches mine in solidarity. "Glad you're back. Mark's been twitchy since you vanished."

I raise an eyebrow. "Twitchy?"

She nods. "After you called out sick, he started asking questions. About project files. Audit trails. Way more than usual. It felt like he was... looking for something."

My stomach twists. James' warning returned in full force: *Watch who's asking too many questions.*

Emily moves to the door, sipping her drink. "He's acting weird," she says over her shoulder. "I don't trust it. But ignore me, I'm looking at everyone differently since we met." Then the door closes behind her, leaving me alone.

I spend the rest of the morning scanning old emails, comparing archived versions of the financial statements with what we had on record. Nothing looked off. Nothing looked like anything at all. It was clean. Too clean.

At 11:02, I receive a calendar invite. 'Weekly Strategy Sync'. Sent by Daniel Reed.

I hesitate before I accept the invite.

Ten minutes before the meeting, I duck into the bathroom. The fluorescent lights buzz overhead, casting everything in too much detail. I splash cold water on my face and stare at my reflection. It stares back like a stranger.

When I return to the project room, Mark is waiting by my desk.

"Hey," he says, his voice low.

"Hey," I reply, not sitting.

He hesitates, before leaning in. "Are you... okay? I mean really. Something's going on, isn't it?"

I stare at him, unsure what to give away. His eyes were tense, probing.

"I'm fine," I lie. Mark hesitates. "Just... be careful, okay?"

I'm not sure if I'm being ordered or asked. Before I can figure out which, Emily walks in the room abruptly. "Sarah," she calls from across the room, "did you see the test server errors that came in when you were off? There's a weird IP pinging internal logs."

Mark looks sharply towards her, then back at me. I excuse myself, walking over to Emily. She places her laptop on the conference table, angling her screen so I can see. Then she watches Mark as he heads out the door. They smile at each other, in the way new couples do.

'Sorry for the dramatic entrance" Emily says, "I wasn't sure if you would want to be alone with anyone right now." I reach out my hand and put it on top of hers with a grateful squeeze.

'Thank you" I say, before Emily continues. "No problem, but I wasn't joking about the server errors, look..." There was indeed a flagged access log. A single IP, located just outside the building perimeter. No user tag. No authentication protocol.

"They've been bouncing in and out of the test network," she whispers. "Whoever it is... they're good."

"Did you trace it?" I ask. Emily gives me a grim look. "It routes through a hidden subnet. Internal. You'd need administrator access to set one up." I stare at the address.

"Could it be Mark?" I ask, unsure if I even meant it. Emily doesn't answer immediately, I can see she is torn between what could be possible and what she wants to believe. Then, softly she says, "He has clearance."

My strategy meeting with Daniel is superficial, though he is smiling too much. Talking about performance. Promotions. He thanks me for "sticking it out" through a rough few weeks. No mention of my absence. No questions or fake concerns disguised as leadership.

But the moment that sticks came near the end. Daniel leans forward, fingers laced together on the desk. "I know things can get stressful. If you ever need to talk, Dr. Voss has open slots this week. It's a good time to reset."

Reset. The word clings to the inside of my skull like a warning label. Not recover. Not heal. Just—wipe. Reformat. Disappear what you remember and return to default. Their version of me. I force a smile and thank him.

When I return to my desk. A note is stuck to my screen.

'Can't do lunch. Meeting in the sub-basement server room. IT audit. Emily x'

I blink, she never mentioned it. I stared at the note until the edges blurred. Instead, I sit in the break room, stirring sugar into a coffee I won't drink. Alex's words echo like a whisper through the static of my thoughts.

"Someone made it look like you approved financial flows tied to a black account. That someone didn't do it for fun."

***

17:00 comes around without incident, but I still don't return to my own house, I drive the long way around, back to the cottage. That night, I sit by the fire as Alex reviews another file that James had hidden inside the unzipped folder. She says nothing for a long time.

When she finally does, her voice is tight. "There's a note listing people he didn't trust. His key suspects I think."

I turn to her. "In the notes," she clarifies. "James said not to trust Daniel, Mark And..." She pauses. "Dr. Julia Voss." The wellness therapist.

I sit back, cold creeping into my bones. I remember the way she has always pressed just a little too hard. Asked just a little too many follow-up questions. Not to mention Daniel being in her office... and the light in her office the night the box went missing. And now our suspicions coincide. She is on the list.

"I'm being boxed in," I whisper, feeling sick to my stomach. "Mentored. Managed. Treated. Something by each one of them"

"Controlled," Alex corrects.

~ 18 ~

I sit across from Alex in the cottage's narrow kitchen, looking past her to the window. The sky is black and cloudless. We both nurse cups of instant coffee that taste more like burnt paper than anything drinkable. The fire has long since faded, leaving only the echo of warmth behind.

"I think it has to be Voss," I say, breaking the silence. "She's connected to both Daniel and Mark. She was already in James's orbit. If someone was feeding information upward, collecting mental health profiles, tracking employee behaviour, she'd be the perfect funnel."

Alex doesn't disagree. She just nods once, then says, "Your session is tomorrow, right?"

"10:30."

A pause. She taps her fingers against her mug. "Then we use it. You go. See what she says. See if she slips. But you need to act normal. Don't push. Let her think she still has control."

I force a smile. "So, just another therapy session where I'm being psychologically dissected, by someone who may or may not be feeding information to the people rewriting my life."

"Exactly," she says, with a hint of something close to humour. "Just don't let her see you flinch." I nod, but my stomach is already in knots of anxiety. Something about Voss's voice has always unsettled me, too soft, too smooth. Like someone trying to calm a dog just before it's put down.

***

The next morning, I leave for work earlier than usual. The roads are still quiet. My return yesterday hadn't triggered any red flags that I could see, but I don't like how that feels more like strategy than oversight.

The office is already humming by the time I arrive. The familiar smell of mocha, the clicking of the jelly bean dispenser, the low murmur of phones ringing and fingers on keyboards, it all feels unnervingly normal. I take the stairs to avoid the elevator. It gives me a few extra seconds to steel myself.

When I walk into the project room, Emily is waiting at my desk. She's holding her tablet, face lit with a mix of triumph and something else I can't quite name. She has that look that I see on her sometimes, like a cat that's dragged something through the door and wants you to be impressed, not horrified.

"Morning," she says, lowering her voice. "I've been busy." I raise an eyebrow. "I can see that."

She flicks through a few screens and then turns the device so I can see. At first, it's just code, server logs, time stamps. Then I see it, unauthorized access attempts, audit trail inconsistencies, and buried deep in a document recovery log, two names.

Daniel Reed.

Mark Bishop.

I blink, trying to process it. "Where did this come from?"

"The audit cache," she says simply. "Old server backups. Things no one ever checks unless they're bored or suspicious." I glance around the room, making sure we're alone. "Are you saying they tampered with the files?"

"I'm saying," she whispers, "there's a log entry showing Mark accessed the project financials folder the same morning you found the altered report. And Daniel approved an internal transfer that doesn't exist on our end."

I sit down slowly, heart racing. "Why didn't you tell me this yesterday?" Emily shrugs. "I needed time to confirm it wasn't just noise"

I turn to Emily, giving her my full attention, when I ask my next question. "How are you feeling now Mark is most likely implicated in all this?"

Emily smirks. "Sometimes the best way to learn what someone's hiding is to let them think you're not looking." I stare at her, unsure how to feel. She's always been clever. Ten steps ahead when she wants to be. But this? It feels cold. Calculated. Like the version of Emily I know is being slowly replaced by something sharper.

"You don't think he suspects anything?" She shakes her head. "He's too focused on covering tracks to notice what's in plain sight."

I nod slowly, trying to keep my thoughts straight. There's a tangle forming, one that won't loosen no matter how many threads I pull. Mark is on the radar. Daniel too. And now, Voss. It's like a triangle closing around me.

Emily steps back. "I'll keep digging," she says. "Quietly." She says it too easily. Like she's forgotten what it costs to be wrong.

"Be careful," I tell her. "If they're watching me, they might start watching you too."

She laughs, just once, under her breath. "Let them try." Then she's gone, back out into the corridor, her footsteps light as ever.

The first hour is a blur. Emails. Polite small talk that feels more like theatre. I don't retain any of it. Every word I speak feels like it belongs to someone else. Every smile I give is a decoy. The work I'm doing on the project is merely for appearances, now I know the promotion is just 'a distraction'.

Before my 10:30 session with Dr Voss, I escape to the rooftop garden to prepare myself. It's windy up there, leaves swirling as fast as my thoughts. I sit on the same bench James used to frequent, back when he still smiled. Back when he didn't know what shadows could look like in daylight.

My phone buzzes. A message from Alex. Just two words that should be simple, but are so much more. "Good luck."

I stare ahead until the wind starts to sting my eyes.

When I return to my desk, there is an appointment reminder flashing quietly in the corner of my screen. 10:30 a.m. Dr. Julia Voss. I close the notification and press my hand against the top of the desk. The veneer feels warm beneath my skin, almost as if it's trying to convince me everything's fine.

But the truth is... I will walk into that office and sit across from a woman who may be helping to erase me.

And I have to smile while I do it.

~ 19 ~

The waiting area outside Dr. Voss's office is quiet, unnaturally so. Even the ever-present hum of printers and clicking keyboards feel dampened. I sit, palms damp, legs crossed tightly, while the soft tick of the wall clock counts down the seconds.

At exactly 10:30, the door opens. Dr. Voss steps out with her usual smile, too serene to be comforting. Her hair is immaculately pulled back, her eyes sharp behind delicate glasses that catch the artificial light like blades.

"Sarah," she says, her voice smooth. "Come in."

I rise, each movement deliberate. After what Alex and I uncovered, James's list, the tampered files, the danger buried inside the company, this office feels less like a safe space and more like a cage.

The room is pristine, staged like a magazine spread, soft white walls, a minimalist desk, two armchairs arranged like old friends. A diffuser hums gently, lavender mist curling into the air like a sleeping threat.

I sit. Dr. Voss mirrors me, notebook in hand, pen uncapped with a subtle click. "So," she begins lightly, "you've had quite a week."

"I'm managing," I say. My tone is flat, but I force a smile. She nods. "It's been a demanding quarter for many. You're not the only one under pressure, but I imagine with your project, there's additional weight, especially with talk of promotions."

The word lingers. I keep my smile in place. "Sure. Deadlines. Team management. The usual." She studies me. "You took some time off. That's not like you."

I tilt my head. "Didn't realise my patterns were being tracked." I start too sharply, before correcting myself. She laughs, too rehearsed. "Not tracked, just observed. I've always admired your consistency. It's what made you a great candidate for... everything."

Everything. It wasn't just about the job. My pulse quickens. "You've never said that before," I say. "Haven't I?" she replies too quickly. "Well. It's true." There it is. A flicker in her control. Small, but unmistakable. Her mask doesn't slip, but it cracks.

The session trudges on, each question a scalpel, stress, burnout, internal relationships. Her voice is neutral, but there's a current beneath it, like she's pressing for weakness.

Then: "Have you spoken to Mark much since returning?" I blink. "I've seen him around. Why?"

"Oh, nothing," she says, too breezy. "You two just seem... divisive sometimes."

My breath catches. We'd never spoken about that. Not here. Not with her. Only Emily knew. That was the slip.

"I could use some water," I say. She pauses, just long enough to betray herself. "Of course." She rises, smoothing her blouse. "I'll be just a minute."

The door shuts.

I move fast.

I head to her desk first, quickly opening and shutting the draws, looking for the notepad. Nothing. But the corner shredder hums softly, still warm. The bin beside it is half-full. I kneel, fingers sifting through the strips. Most are nothing. But then...

A scrap of handwriting. Slanted. Familiar.

"Merge – 04/"

My blood turns cold. I should feel vindicated. I don't. I feel sick. Because now it's real. Everything James feared, it didn't just outlive him. It's watching me.

As I dig down, I see black weathered paper. The remnants of a black notebook. James' notebook. Then I spot more fragments. Another piece: "Lewis—see item Q2." Then, chillingly, "S.M."

It's his handwriting. James's notes. Or what's left of them. What else did she destroy? What did she read before she did? I shove the largest pieces into my pocket and stand just as the handle clicks. Heart pounding, I drop back into my chair, breathing fast and silent.

Dr. Voss re-enters with a water bottle, her smile intact. But something's changed. Her eyes sweep the room with subtle precision. "Sorry," she says. "Intern chaos."

I take the water. Drink. Smile. But I see it now, the slight tension in her shoulders. The way her gaze flicks to the shredder, then back.

She knows.

The session winds down with a pointed remark from Dr Voss, "You seem more guarded lately," she says, smoothing her skirt. "Be careful, burnout can sneak up on even the most resilient." I don't respond, just look into her eyes as she stares back, unblinking.

At 11:00 sharp, she stands. "Let's touch base again next week." My jaw clenches, I hate that phrase, it's too rehearsed, too cliche. "Of course." I reply. Her smile doesn't waver. But I feel her watching me as I leave, she's likely already rewriting what she'll say in her notes.

Outside, I walk fast, not stopping until I'm deep in the stairwell. I pull out the fragments, press it flat against the wall.

"Q2 / Merge / S.M. / Monroe not responding"

The floor seems to shift beneath me. She was watching James. Watching me.

I don't go back to my desk. I head straight to the IT room to find Emily. She looks up. "You okay?" I scan the room to make sure noone is close enough to overhear.

"I need you to see something." I show her the note. Tell her where I found it. Her eyes widen. "She had his notes?" Emily breathes. "She shredded them?"

I nod. "But not all of them. She slipped. She's in this." Emily's expression hardens, as I feel the walls closing in.

~ 20 ~

Walking back through the offices, something has shifted, not outside, but in me. I feel the residue of her gaze, like invisible fingerprints on my skin. The project room greets me like a museum of normalcy. My desk. My chair. The pin-board with my timeline of milestones, so neat it almost looks staged. I sit down and stare at my monitor. The login screen waits for my credentials, but I hesitate.

What if they're watching this too?

I log in anyway.

Alex texts me only two words: "It's ready." I don't need to ask what she means. I know what she's been working on.

***

Back at the cottage that evening, the fire is already crackling when I arrive. Alex has turned one of the walls into a pin-board of digital printouts, Post-its, and red string connecting names and Pound signs. It's almost absurd in its intensity and the longer I look at it, the more surreal it becomes.

"You were right," she says before I even take off my coat. "There's something consistent about the payments. One name keeps showing up."

She points to a column in a printout, her finger tracing a series of high-value transfers routed through vendor codes. The name jumps out like a scream.

ZettaCore Consulting.

"Doesn't sound familiar," I murmur.

"It shouldn't. It doesn't exist. Not in any registry, not even in off-the-book circles. But it's listed as a preferred contractor across four internal departments. The same departments Daniel had temporary oversight of."

My throat goes dry. "You think it's one of the ghost vendors James mentioned?"

"I think it's *the* ghost vendor."

We stand staring at it, the flames whispering behind us. I feel a pressure in my skull, like something just behind my eyes is trying to rearrange my perception. The deeper we dig, the more we find, like someone peeled back the wallpaper and found something alive underneath.

"Let's cross-reference it with the payment logs," I say, already reaching for my bag.

We spend hours combing through files, deep into the night. Metadata, time stamps, invoice chains. We draw lines. We find patterns. And then we find something else.

My name.

"What the hell? Not again" I say, as I feel a mixture of tears and anger rising. "Did they pick me because they thought I'd already been broken? That the shadow of Gen22 still hung heavy enough to make me pliable? Easier to erase?"

I feel like running outside and screaming into the silent dark of night, until my throat can take no more. But Alex places her hands on my shoulders and looks straight into my eyes. "If they did, they underestimated you. They thought you were still licking your wounds. But you're already bleeding them dry."

I take a few deep breaths before she lets me go and turns back to the board. I join her with more determination to solve this than I ever have before.

One of the invoices is linked to an approval code bearing my credentials. The date is two weeks ago. I was in a strategy meeting that day. The timestamp doesn't match... It puts me in two places at once. And not one person flagged it.

Alex leans in, jaw tight. "They're doing it in real time now. Using your identity." The thought clings to my brain like rot. I don't remember approving anything. I never saw this vendor. And yet my digital fingerprint is everywhere.

"They're not just hiding the money," I say. "They're laundering it through me." Alex says nothing. Her silence is enough agreement. Outside, the wind howls. Inside, my reality fractures. Every step I take now isn't just dangerous. It's evidence. Every email. Every login. Every keystroke. I am a walking liability. A perfect scapegoat.

And the worst part? It's working.

That night, I don't sleep. I sit by the window with a blanket around my shoulders, watching the trees sway like they're whispering secrets to each other. My thoughts loop endlessly. Was James sitting like this before he died? Waiting for proof? Watching shadows move outside his window, wondering if they were real?

***

The next morning, I wake up with the taste of metal in my mouth and a certainty in my chest.

They want to erase me. But first, they have to believe I'm still playing along.

I get dressed. I go to work. I smile at Emily. I nod at Daniel. I avoid Mark's gaze, though he seems to linger too long at the edge of every room I enter.

And when I sit down at my desk, I open a blank file.

I title it simply.

ZettaCore: Thread 01.

And I begin to write.

Because if I don't tell the story before they finish writing mine, there won't be anything left of me to save.

~ 21 ~

Emily arrives at my desk just after ten, balancing a takeaway cup in one hand and her tablet in the other. She looks tired, less put-together than usual. Her ponytail is loose, and there are shadows under her eyes that even her concealer can't completely hide.

She doesn't say anything at first, just places the coffee beside me and takes the chair across the desk, turning the tablet off with a soft click.

"I've been thinking about that scrap you found," she says finally, her voice low. "From Dr. Voss's office." I glance up. "Me too."

Emily chews her bottom lip for a moment. "I'm worried, Sarah. That piece you showed me 'Merge,' 'Monroe not responding,' your initials... That's not just stray notes. It's part of something. If Voss had it, and shredded it..."

"She knew," I finish. "She was either complicit or trying to cover her tracks."

Emily nods, her expression drawn. "Exactly. And if she's involved, we don't know who else might be. You're in this deeper than we thought."

Her concern feels genuine, and that makes it harder to bear. "I can't walk away from this," I say. "James didn't just write this stuff down for fun. He died trying to reveal it."

Emily leans forward. "I get that. I really do. But you have to think about your safety too. James is gone, Sarah. What if chasing this only gets you there too?" I study her. She's trying to look calm, but I can see the tension in the way she grips the cup, her knuckles pale.

"Maybe it's time to let the James stuff go," she says carefully. "Or at least slow down. Focus on what's happening now, your project, the promotion? You've already uncovered so much. Maybe someone else can pick up the trail." There's a flicker in her tone I can't quite place. Is it fear? Guilt? Or just genuine concern?

"Letting go of James's legacy isn't an option," I say. "Not yet." Emily exhales slowly. "Then promise me you'll be careful. I'll keep looking through logs and vendor approvals, quietly. I'll keep an eye on the compliance team too. But Sarah... don't get reckless." I nod. "Thanks. I'm not trying to be a martyr. I just want the truth." Emily gives a tight smile. "You and me both."

She lingers for a moment before standing up, brushing invisible lint from her sleeve. "I should get back to my desk. Mark's been hovering around the server logs again. I don't know if it means anything, but I'll let you know if he finds something, or if he's too interested."

"Thanks," I say, watching her walk away. After she leaves, I sit staring at the cup of coffee for a long time. Something about her reaction feels just off enough to echo. Like she's afraid of more than just what Voss did. Emily is scared, but of what?

Is it because she suspects Mark? I should have asked her if keeping up appearances with him is becoming too hard for her. She offered help. She always has. But I don't want to put her in a position she's no longer comfortable with. And the silence she left behind is louder than anything she said.

I open a new browser window and pull up the internal vendor directory with one name in mind. "ZettaCore Consulting." that Alex had flagged. I type it into the system and wait.

No results.

I try again, narrowing the search to older contracts. Still nothing. That in itself is suspicious. No vendor just vanishes completely, not without deliberate deletion.

I pull out my notebook and look at the file name Alex had also mentioned 'ZCT_FRACTURE' and cross-reference the timestamps with project approvals during Q2. Several authorisations show my name, or rather, my initials. I wasn't even in the office for one of them.

Another ghost trace.

I scroll back through email archives, flagging any correspondence between me and Daniel or Mark during the same time frame. I find one, a short chain about revising milestone budgets. Mark's reply is terse, businesslike. Daniel's response is too eager, like he wanted the changes implemented fast.

The financial document attached is no longer downloadable.

Deleted.

I lean back in my chair, feeling the weight of it all. I'm standing in a minefield, and every step is sounding an echo of someone else's plan. The coffee Emily brought has gone cold. I sip it anyway, needing the bitter sting.

Around noon, I head down to the server room under the guise of needing to review archived compliance data. I don't stay long, just long enough to confirm what I suspected. Recent access logs from the past week are incomplete. Someone has been tampering with the logs.

When I return to my desk, there's a sticky note on my monitor:

"Call me when you can. – E"

I don't call. I need to think. The image of the shredded notebook paper burns in my mind. So does the uneasy look in Emily's eyes. I trust her. I've always trusted her. But something's changed, she looks too... haunted.

By the end of the day, I've compiled a new list, vendors, flagged users, deleted approvals. And at the centre of it all, the same initials. Mine. Whoever is behind this, they have purposely targeted me. And if Emily's right, and I am in deeper than I thought? Then I need to be even deeper still, so I can see who's waiting at the bottom.

~ 22 ~

I ignore Emily's warning. Not because I think she's wrong, but because the fear she voiced only confirms what I already know, I can't stop now. Every lead we uncover knots tighter around something huge, something intentional, methodical. James didn't die for a whisper of suspicion. He died chasing something solid. And I owe it to him to finish what he started. And Alex agrees.

We're back at the cottage, the blinds drawn, laptop screens lighting our faces in a pale blue glow. The air smells like burnt coffee and damp wood. It's close to midnight, and we've been at this for hours. "Got something," Alex murmurs. She turns the laptop toward me.

A payment record, buried deep in an archived financial directory. "ZettaCore Consulting," I say. The name feels radioactive. Alex nods. "This one's clever. It's disguised as an HR development program. The memo says it's for onboarding psychological support training, signed off by Daniel Reed. But the bank route is wrong." I squint at the routing number. "That's not internal."

"Exactly. The transaction leaves NexTech, bounces through two international clearinghouses, and lands in an account tied to a holding company registered out of Liechtenstein." I exhale slowly. "That's not onboarding. That's laundering." Alex is already digging deeper. She traces the origin tag on the requisition form.

"This is where it gets better," she mutters. "The HR profile that filed the requisition? It doesn't exist in the main employee database." She pulls it up. A profile labeled Maria H. – Department: Personnel Development. Senior onboarding coordinator. Employee since 2021. The photo is a stock image, the metadata still tagged from a public image archive.

"Jesus," I whisper. "A fake profile."

"Fully fabricated," Alex says. "But inserted cleanly into the HR system. Whoever did this had real access. And it looks like Maria H. approved at least five similar transactions in the last eighteen months." I stare at the payment timeline. All Q2 disbursements. One matches the date tied to my credentials, 07/04.

"We're staring at the shell," Alex says. "This is how they moved it, through HR, masked as wellness or training." My stomach churns. I think of Dr. Voss. Of the shredded paper. Of how easily someone could manipulate health records to justify dismissals, replacements. How easily I could be written off.

I cross-reference the account numbers with older files James left behind. One pops. "Here," I say, pointing. "James flagged this number in the last thumb drive. It's linked to a shell vendor he marked as untraceable. Back then, he didn't know about Zetta-Core. But it's the same trail." Alex sits back. Her expression is tight, jaw clenched. "We have to move faster." Staring at the screen, I quietly say "I know."

Outside, wind presses against the cottage walls. A branch taps at the window like a code I don't know how to read. We document everything, screenshots, hash keys, data chains. A mirrored copy is uploaded to an anonymous drive, buried in noise. "We should prep this for the board," Alex says. "If anything happens..."

"It won't," I say, too quickly. "Not yet. We need more. We can't go in without tying this to Daniel directly." Alex raises an eyebrow. "You don't think this is enough?"

"I think if we show our hand too early, they'll bury it faster than we can explain it. We need to find who created the Maria H. profile. And who else she worked with." Alex exhales, nodding. "Then we chase the login trail next. Whoever built her would've had to spoof credentials or override admin protocols. Either way, it'll leave residue."

"And when we find it?"

"Then we drop it like a bomb."

I sit back, heart pounding. James had left a road-map. Twisted, fragmented, but real. And now, step by step, we're walking it.

Maria H. doesn't exist. But whoever made her does. And we're close.

By the time we break for air, it's well past one in the morning. I step outside, phone in hand, needing a moment away from the electrostatic of our search. The night is sharp. Cold enough to sting. Above, the stars are muted by low clouds, their light struggling to break through.

I dial Emily. She picks up on the third ring. "Hey," she says. Her voice is groggy, laced with sleep. "Sorry for calling late. I just... needed to hear a familiar voice." There's a pause. "It's okay. Are you safe?"

"For now. I think we're close to something. We found a fake HR profile. ZettaCore. Routing funds internationally through Liechtenstein." Emily doesn't respond right away, there's a pause, longer than I expected. When she finally speaks, her voice is steady. "Be careful," she says "If you're right, you're dealing with professionals. People who know how to disappear."

"Yeah," I murmur. "Or how to make others disappear." A beat of silence follows. "You're not alone, Sarah," Emily says. "Just remember that." I want to believe her.

When I return inside, Alex is typing furiously. "They logged in from an old admin credential set," she says without looking up. "Guess what name it's under?"

Without taking a beat, I say one name. "Daniel?" Alex turns the screen. The name glows.

D. Reed — Admin — Credential Override ID#7712B

I stare. "He's not even hiding it."

Alex shakes her head "Because the system masks the access path if it's run under a credential set with override privileges. It would've been invisible unless you were looking in the back-end server mirrors."

"How did James even find this?" I ask. "He didn't," Alex says. "He built a watcher script. It recorded every privileged login, archived and encrypted them. He must've known he wouldn't live long enough to see the end."

I sit down slowly. My fingers tremble. We're close. But that closeness feels more like a cliff edge than a finish line. And I know someone else is always watching, waiting for a misstep that will send me over the edge.

~ 23 ~

A message arrives just after 8 a.m. A quiet ping in the inbox of Nex-Tech's Internal Compliance Office.

The subject line is innocuous: "Concerned Staff Tip." But the contents are anything but.

"There may be irregularities in billing and vendor approvals related to the Horizon Initiative. One of the team members, female, director-level, is involved. Check Q2 disbursements. Start with ZettaCore."

No name. No signature. Just a breadcrumb dropped into the blood-stream of the company, designed to trigger alarms.

By 8:15, the message has been flagged as "Priority Two" and routed to Legal for review.

By 8:30, someone in IT is pulling access logs from the Horizon team's shared directory.

***

At 9:02, I feel it... something off.

I head to the IT office and Emily is already at her desk when I walk in, headphones on, tapping at her screen like nothing's wrong. But the atmosphere in the office feels heavier, like the oxygen has thickened. People glance up more than usual. Conversations stop when I pass. I can feel eyes on me, but no one says anything. There's a quiet tension to the air, the kind that clings to skin and makes your stomach tighten for reasons you can't yet name.

Alex messages me at 9:13.*"Something's coming. I can feel it."*

I respond quickly *"Same. You think we triggered it?"* seconds later, Alex replies. *"Or someone wants us to think we did."*

I'm still responding when the email pops up on my phone.

Subject: Internal Review Notification **From:** Compliance Operations **Time:** 9:21 AM

Sarah,

We're conducting a routine review of Q2 financial authorisations tied to the Horizon Initiative. Please be available for a brief discussion with HR this afternoon at 2 p.m.

Regards, Compliance Office

Routine. Nothing at NexTech is routine. Especially not this. I glance up. Emily is watching me now, her expression unreadable. She blinks once and removes one headphone. "You okay?" I nod slowly. "Yeah. Just got flagged for a meeting. Something about Q2 finances." Emily's eyebrows twitch slightly. "Weird. You're probably fine, though. These things pop up every so often." I look at her. She sounds casual. Reassuring. But her eyes are too still. "I'm sure," I say, forcing a smile. "Thanks."

The rest of the morning passes in fragments. I try to work, but every click of the mouse feels hollow, performative. Eyes flick toward me every time I leave the Project Room. I catch whispers that stop the moment I appear.

By lunchtime, the hallway near Legal is unusually active. I spot two members of the internal audit team walking with purpose. One of them is holding a printout with my name on the front.

Alex calls me when I'm in the break room at 13:10. Her voice sounds tight. "It's planted," she says without preamble. "What is?" I say. "The tip. I heard from one of my old contacts in compliance. It came in early this morning. Anonymous, vague, but pointed. *Horizon Initiative. Q2. Female director-level staff.* It's got you written all over it."

I sit down hard. The chair creaks beneath me. "Someone's framing me." Alex sighs. "And doing it well." The line goes silent, neither of us knowing quite what to say. The implications spiral out around us, widening with every beat of silence.

"You need to stay calm," she says eventually. "Go to the meeting. Say as little as possible. Let them talk. Make notes if you can. But don't defend yourself too early. If this is what I think it is, they're trying to bait you into overreacting." I swallow hard. "What about the files we've been compiling?"

"Don't bring them in. Not yet. If they're watching you, anything you carry will be flagged. Even a thumb drive. Play dumb. You're just as surprised as they are." She hesitates. "And one more thing..."

"What?"

"Be careful around Emily."

I blink. "Why?"

"I know she's been helping. But think about the timing. She knew about the audit trail. She saw what you pulled from Voss's shredder. Now this shows up? Just... don't tell her everything. Not yet." My mouth feels dry. I reply slowly. "Okay." I know Alex doesn't know Emily like I do, doesn't trust anybody, but I really need my friend to tell me everything is going to be ok. This is exactly what she was trying to warn me about. The reason she wanted me to stop.

The meeting with Legal is worse than expected. Three people. Two from Compliance, one from HR. All smiling, all polite. The kind of politeness that makes you feel like you're already guilty.

They walk me through the tip, never naming me directly, but always circling the obvious. They ask about my approval process, about vendor verification, about ZettaCore.

"I don’t recognise that vendor," I say truthfully. I want to scream. To demand a forensic audit. But all I do is smile. "I don’t handle those approvals directly. We have layers for that." They nod, taking notes. "And your access logs from Q2, were you working off-site during the budget approval week?"

"No, I was in-office. But I didn’t make any final budget sign-offs without Daniel or Finance." I say. One of them responds with a smile, "We understand, This is just preliminary. We appreciate your cooperation." Then they dismiss me like a witness. Not a suspect. But not quite innocent either.

When I return to my desk, my computer is locked. Emily appears at my side a minute later. "They locked your system?" she says, too fast. "Yeah." I sigh, raking my hand through my hair. She hesitates. "Look, I’m sure it’s temporary. I’ll talk to someone in IT. Maybe it’s just standard during investigations."

I watch her. Every word she says is right. Supportive. But there’s something tight behind her eyes, I know what she's probably thinking. ‘*I told you so*’.

"Thanks," I say. "I appreciate it." She smiles. "We’ll get through this." But I don’t answer. I don’t know what to say, or what I can say to her anymore. I want to believe her. But I can’t tell if she’s trying to calm me, or herself.

The rest of the day drags, slow and heavy. I have brought my burner phone, so I find a quiet corner in the lower stairwell to sit with my thoughts. It’s cold. The hum of distant air vents buzz against the silence. My fingers tremble slightly as I type a note to Alex:

"Confirmed. compliance is after me. Meeting was all surface. But they're watching. If they start revoking access, we lose the trail. We need to finish tracing the Maria H. logins before that happens."

By the time I leave the building, the sun has dipped below the skyline. Shadows stretch long across the parking lot. I glance over my shoulder as I walk to the car. A car idles across the lot. Lights off. No driver visible. Just the glint of a screen inside, flickering once, then dark. Someone is still watching me. I can feel it.

But now, I'm watching them back.

~ 24 ~

The moment I walk into the cottage, the air feels heavier. The fire is out and Alex is already at the table, her screen glowing in the dim room, the usual halo of cold blue around her. She looks up when I enter, jaw set.

"Emily got us access," she says before I've even taken off my coat. "You're not going to like what we found". My pulse jumps. "You asked Emily to help?" I say, concern etched on my face. "I had to. She's the only one inside the system who could get past Nex-Tech's firewall without raising alarms. And now we dont have your access..."

She turns the screen toward me. On it is a cache of appointment records. "Dr. Voss's private system, decrypted and accessed through a masked protocol. Emily helped get in, said it was part of a corrupted internal audit record. She didn't ask too many questions."

Alex points to a row of entries. "These are prescriptions. Voss keeps her medical scripts separate from clinical notes. Maybe she thought it was more secure this way. Less oversight."

I lean closer. The name at the top of one entry stands out in bold: J. Lewis. "James?" I whisper. She nods. "Look at the date." My stomach knots. The prescription was written two days before he died.

"She logged it as an anti-anxiety medication, Tramadol." Alex says. "But I ran the doses she prescribed and they are extremely high." She looks at me, eyes wide. "It also has a dangerous interaction profile. Especially with SSRIs like the one already on his records." I look at the logs before finishing what Alex has already seen. "She was fully aware that his own Dr had been prescribing those for at least two years."

Alex clicks open a tab in her browser. "I looked it up. This drug has been flagged in several studies. In combination with common antidepressants, especially SSRIs, it can increase the risk of serotonin syndrome. And in higher doses, it has been linked to impulsivity, emotional blunting, and suicidal impulses."

My breath catches. "She prescribed this to him? Knowing it could push him over the edge?"

Alex scrolls down. "And here's the worst part. It was entered manually. Not through the company script portal. Hand-typed. No pharmacist routing. No digital trail. It's like she wanted no one to see it."

There's a note attached. I read it aloud.

'Patient exhibiting heightened paranoia. Recommend temporary pharmacological support to mitigate workplace disruption. Dosage tailored to reduce reactivity.'

"That's not treatment. That's containment." Alex's expression hardens. "And she flagged it under a custom diagnostic code, bypassing red flags. She knew how to game the system." She clicks open another file. James's final session note. It's clinical. Hollow. A postmortem weapon in disguise.

'Patient demonstrates psychotic thoughts. Claims of fraud conspiracy. Believes internal surveillance is targeting him.'

"She was framing his mental state," I say. "So if something happened to him, no one would question it." Alex leans back. "This isn't just unethical. She used therapy as cover to build an official record of delusion, then dosed him with a cocktail of drugs designed to make him mentally unstable or kill."

"We need to show Susan," I say quickly. "She might know more about James's final day. Maybe he mentioned the prescription. Maybe she knows what medication he was already taking." Alex nods. "If he was taking the SSRIs already, even a moderate dose of Tramadol could have tipped him into a spiral. It wouldn't have needed to be direct. Just enough to make the wrong thoughts louder."

The wind rattles against the windows. I can hear the trees outside swaying, against the silence that has filled the room. I sit stunned for a moment, then speak again. "I need to know what else she's done. Who else she's treated. Who else she might have targeted."

Alex's fingers move across the keyboard. She pulls up a search window and runs a filter. Voss's sessions over the last twelve months. A dozen names surface, including employees I know. Including mine. I lean closer. "Wait. That's... my session from a week ago."

Alex opens the record. The note is brief. "Subject shows signs of latent anxiety, resistant to vulnerability. Recommend observation." I feel anger rising in me. "That's not what she said to me," I say. "She told me I was stable. Focused." For one insane moment, I want to scream, to smash the screen and make the whole thing stop. But I don't. I breathe. Because if I fall apart now, they win.

Alex's voice is low. "She's writing profiles, Sarah. Ones that can be used later to support discreditation. The same thing she did to James." I stare at the screen. My name. My mind, slowly, methodically rewritten under someone else's control.

Alex clicks into my file, enlarging the note tied to the session. A small symbol flickers in the corner. "Wait," I say. "What's that footer?" Alex squints, leaning in. "Hidden notes field," she murmurs. “Buried under the User Interface. I almost missed it.” She extracts the text and reads aloud:

“Directive: Q2 - SM authorisation mirrored. Subject response pending. Maintain narrative integrity. Backchannel to DR.”

My stomach turns. “SM. That’s me. She cloned my authorisation, used my credentials to greenlight something. And ‘DR’... that has to be Daniel.”

Alex’s expression hardens. “She wasn’t just treating people. She was building a behavioral paper trail, engineering justifications. Feeding Daniel whatever he needed to manage risk from the inside.”

“She was laundering people,” I say. “Their careers. Their mental profiles. Rewriting them until they fit the narrative.” Alex nods slowly. “James must’ve discovered it. The prescription wasn’t a treatment... it was a silencer.”

“And she’s doing the same to me,” I say. “Setting me up for a fall. Or a breakdown.” I start pacing, the room suddenly too small. “It’s not just the medication. What if she’s using evaluations to shape HR actions? Blocking promotions? Approving quiet terminations?”

Without a word, Alex flips open another tab. She digs into HR’s internal flagging system ‘Psych Eval Exceptions.’ There they are. Dozens of internal cases. Low performance alerts. Emotional instability flags. Sanctions for burnout, erratic conduct, leadership unsuitability. All signed by: Dr. Julia Voss. I scroll through the list, heart pounding. My name isn’t there. Not yet.

Alex doesn’t speak. Neither do I. The screen glows between us like a loaded weapon. Finally, she says, “We go to Susan. Tomorrow. She needs to confirm the prescription was real. And then... Then we go to the board.” I nod before saying. “If this gets buried... We get buried with it.”

The fire in the hearth remains cold. Shadows crawl longer along the floor. There’s a weight in the room now, like something watching from just beyond the edge of the light. Outside, the wind starts to howl. Inside, everything sharpens into place.

Dr. Voss didn't just cover up a crime. She designed it. Controlled it. And now, she's aiming it at me.

~ 25 ~

The wind stirs as we walk up the narrow garden path, gravel crunching under our shoes. Susan's house is unchanged since the last time I visited, tidy, modest, a little too still. The curtains are drawn even though the light outside is soft and pale. I hesitate at the door, then knock.

Susan opens it within seconds, like she was waiting. Her eyes widen when she sees me, then shifts to look at Alex behind me. "You're back," she says. Her voice is gentle, but the tension in it is unmistakable.

"We found something," I say. "We need to talk. About James."

Susan steps aside without asking questions, ushering us in. The living room is the same as before, framed photos on the mantel, a vase of dried flowers on the coffee table. But now the air inside feels as if grief has soaked into the wallpaper.

We sit. I pull out the printout from Alex's folder and place it gently on the table between us. "What is this?" Susan asks, reaching forward. Her hand trembles slightly as she scans the document.

"It's from Dr. Voss's private files. A prescription she wrote for James two days before he died. Tramadol." I pause, watching her face. "Do you recognise it?" Susan frowns. "He never mentioned that name to me. He was on citalopram for anxiety, he had been for years. But nothing else."

Alex leans in. "We researched it. Tramadol is dangerous when mixed with SSRIs. In high doses, it's been linked to disorientation, hallucinations, depressive spirals. Sometimes suicidal ideation." Susan looks at me, stunned.

"But he was doing fine on citalopram. He'd started running again. He'd wake me in the middle of the night just to talk about what we were going to do once things at work had quietened down. He was obviously worried about something, but I just thought it was normal work stress... I had no idea. But suicidal? No. I told you, there were no signs."

I nod. "And now we know why. He wasn't spiraling. He was pushed right at the last minute. Dr Voss prescribed him something that made things suddenly too much." Susan puts a hand over her mouth. For a long moment, she doesn't speak. Then she whispers, "She's no Doctor, she's a killer. She murdered him. She didn't push him to the edge, she walked him off it," and breaks into a sob.

Alex is quiet, her expression dark. "Voss didn't log it through the normal channels. She manually entered the script into a side system. No pharmacy records. No oversight. She covered her tracks."

Susan leans back, staring at the ceiling like she's searching for answers hidden in the plaster. "He kept saying he was researching something whenever I asked. I thought... I thought he was just busy. He was always more intense when an audit was going on, so I didn't press him. But now... if only I had asked..." She turns away, trembling, as the tears flow freely.

"I thought he was being dramatic," she whispers. "The way he talked... He said someone was feeding false data into the system, but I didn't really understand all the intricacies of his job. So I just told him to slow down. He said he was exhausted, but I put it down to him working more late nights."

I move over and take her hand, and she squeezes it back. Her fingers are cold. "You don't know what it's like to live thinking the person you loved gave up. That they chose to leave you. I lived in that silence for months. I hated him for it." She swipes at her face. "But he didn't give up. He was fighting. And now... I see that." There's a pause, the quiet kind that grows roots and anchors you in the past.

Alex clears her throat gently. "Susan, we're taking this to the board. We have evidence tying Dr. Voss to James's death and to broader fraud within the company. We believe she was working with the CEO, Daniel, possibly others. We needed you to confirm that James wasn't on anything else. That he didn't hide anything from you."

"He didn't," she says firmly. "He told me everything. At least... well, everything he could." Her gaze drops to the floor, then to the printout again. Her thumb traces the edge of the paper, as if the touch alone might let her rewind time.

"There was one night," she says slowly, "just days before he... before it happened. He was in his office, muttering about 'Q2 authorisations' and something about 'mirrored credentials.' I barely understood him. He kept writing things down, crossing them out, scribbling in that little notebook. He said he had nearly finished it, whatever 'it' was."

I glance at Alex. We both know what he meant. The second drive. The notebook. The notes we have seen and scrutinised, night after night.

"Do you still have anything he left behind?" I ask gently. "Anything he might've hidden?" Susan shakes her head. "After... after it happened, NexTech sent people over to collect his company belongings. Files, equipment. They said it was protocol. I thought they were just cleaning up, clearing out his digital access. I didn't know they were erasing him."

"You've helped more than you know," I say softly. The fire is unlit, but the room feels warmer somehow. Maybe because something long frozen in Susan is finally beginning to thaw. Susan reaches for my hand as we are walking out of the door "Thank you for not letting them bury him." she says softly "Finish what he started." I give her a single nod and step over the threshold.

Outside, the wind has picked up, sending leaves scattering across the street. Alex and I walk in silence for a while. "That was harder than I thought it would be," I finally say. "She needed it," Alex replies. "She needed to know it wasn't in her head. Just like James did."

I tighten my coat. The world feels different now. Sharper. Like the truth itself has weight. Like it occupies physical space in the air we breathe. "You think she'll be okay?" I ask quietly. Alex shrugs. "I think she's been living in a kind of purgatory. This gives her something real. Something to hold on to."

We reach the car. I pause with my hand on the door handle, staring at the pale reflection of myself in the window. "He was right," I say. "Everything James feared... It wasn't paranoia. It was a certainty. And Voss made sure no one would believe him until it was too late."

"That's how she works," Alex murmurs. "She doesn't just manipulate data. She manipulates people. Thoughts. Emotions. Sanity."

I get in, buckle up, Alex doesn't turn the engine on right away. She looks out into the distance, letting everything that's happened sink in. "You said there were other patients," I say. "People flagged with emotional instability. Burnout. Leadership concerns. All signed off by her."

"Dozens," Alex confirms. "It seems that is how she maintains the illusion of clinical legitimacy. Paper trails that support the next dismissal, the next denied promotion. And no one questions it because she's the expert."

"But she's not treating anyone," I say. "She's *curating* them. Grooming mental profiles to match corporate needs. To make threats go away." Alex nods slowly, "And now she's doing the same thing to you." The words settle between us like stones.

I think about the notes in James's file, the psychological triggers Voss marked, the chemical she used, how she constructed the illusion of psychotic delusion to silence him. And I feel it, deep in my chest. She's doing it again. This time, to me. And this time, I won't be so easy to erase.

Alex finally breaks the silence. "Next stop: the board." Alex starts the engine. I nod. "Time to see what happens when the lights come on."

Behind us, the wind howls again. But this time, I don't flinch.

~ 26 ~

Emily meets me in the storage alcove behind the server room. Her idea. It's early, before most staff have arrived, the building still wrapped in that eerie hush of motionless air and half-lit corridors. She ducks inside without a word and closes the door behind her.

"I brought everything you asked for," she says, handing over a thumb drive, her expression tight. "Encrypted backups. I ran a blind crawl through Voss's system. Found a set of flagged archives that don't match her standard file structure."

"Thank you," I say. "You're sure it won't trigger an alert?" Shaking her head, Emily replies, "I spoofed the request from one of the retired asset IDs," she says. "No one's watching those I assume. But we can't go back in that way again. If anyone audits the logs... it won't hold up long."

Alex is at the cottage still compiling our evidence for the board. I needed someone on the inside today. And Emily, despite her warnings, hadn't hesitated when I asked.

We walk together to the side stairwell, then peel off in opposite directions to avoid drawing attention. I take the long way back to my office, every footstep echoing louder than it should.

When I slide the thumb drive into my offline laptop, I hold my breath. The file directory opens like a vault, folders nested within folders, each one dated according to session logs. They look ordinary at first, standard backup names, innocuous enough. But there's one labeled 'INTERNAL_DO_NOT_DISTRIBUTE', buried three layers deep and tagged with a Voss-specific identifier.

I double-click. Nothing. It asks for a password. I text Emily:

'Found a locked file. Starts with INTERNAL.'

She replies instantly, Try 'MARLOWE2020' that was her emergency encryption key last time we ran compliance checks. I enter the password. It works.

A single PDF loads. It's titled 'PSY-EVAL_CHRON_M-V_FINAL'. There's a delay, almost like the file itself is reluctant to be seen, before the first page renders. I scroll.

Page one is a memo. Internal, unsigned, but authored from Dr. Julia Voss's admin console. The language is dense, clinical, and chilling.

In accordance with Q2-Retention Protocols, the following profiles are to be monitored for signs of instability, burnout, and leadership misalignment. Termination recommendations are justified via psychological rationale under evaluation codes 49B and 62J. All incident reports are to be submitted directly to Risk, no HR flagging required unless escalation is mandated. Subjects who question procedural intent are to be monitored more closely. Compliance is not always overt.

Then, beneath it, an email routing table. Not just internal storage. These weren't just kept. They were *sent*.

Primary Recipient: CEO Daniel Reed – CONFIDENTIAL
CC: D. Voss, Risk Subcommittee Review Queue (Black Label Routing)

My breath catches. Daniel knew. He didn't just approve of her methods, he *requested* the reports.

I scroll again. A table loads: dozens of names. Some I recognise, engineers, support staff, a few team leads who had left under vague circumstances. Some I don't. Each name has a session log ID. A diagnostic code. And an outcome: Exit. Exit. Reorg. Early Leave. Discreditation. Each word feels sanitised. But I know what they mean, careers destroyed, people broken. All made to look voluntary.

Voss wasn't just a gatekeeper, she was Daniel's filter. The company's reputation manager. Quietly pruning out dissent, instability, or what they decided "instability" looked like.

Alex calls just as I finish compiling the names. "How did it go with Emily?" she begins, and I can already hear the tension in her voice, "did you get anymore proof?"

"You won't believe what we found...," I say. "Voss didn't act alone. These reports were routed directly to Daniel. He's not just enabling her, he's using her." There's a beat of silence. "I just ran a parallel search," Alex says. "At least four of the people flagged in her reports had their bonuses suspended days before their exits. Guess where that money went?"

"ZettaCore?"

"ZettaCore. Every time."

I forward the decrypted file to Alex using our secure relay, then call Emily. She picks up on the second ring. "You found it?"

"It's worse than I thought," I say. "It's not just a cover-up. She's weaponising her position. And Daniel is behind it, he's been receiving her reports for months." Another pause. "Does it mention you?" I scroll to the very bottom.

There it is.

Mitchell, Sarah — Monitored since Q2 FY. Flag: Overcompensatory Behavior, High-Stakes Project Risk, Elevated Suspicion Threshold. Recommendation: Soft Exit Strategy if Threat Profile Escalates.

The world stops spinning for a second. "She's building the same case against me," I whisper. Emily's voice softens. "Sarah..."

"She's not just diagnosing," I say. "She's not diagnosing, she's scripting. Giving Daniel a clean excuse to erase people. If we hadn't found that prescription, if we hadn't followed the trail..."

"You'd be next," she finishes. I sit back. My hands are cold. "She knew James was close. So she prescribed him something to accelerate the outcome. She did it quietly, through channels no one watches. And she's doing the same thing now, only this time she's using policy." Emily is quiet for a second. Then she says, "You have to go to the board."

"I will," I say. "Soon." Another beat of silence. "I'm sorry," Emily adds quietly. "For not seeing this earlier." I smile slightly, even though she can't see my appreciation, I hope she can feel it. "You helped today," I say. "That's what matters." She doesn't answer at first. Then, "Just... be careful. Okay?"

I reassure her before I hang up and stare at the screen. There's something sacred about the way Voss wrote her reports. Detached. Precise. Surgical. As though what she was doing wasn't corruption, but curation. A controlled burn to protect the ecosystem. But people burned in it. People like James. And if she's left unchecked, people like me.

I pull open a side window and begin drafting the board report. Alex and I had agreed: when we go to them, it has to be air-tight. It can't just look like whistleblowing. It has to look undeniable.

It's almost noon when Alex calls me from the cottage. "Got your message," she says. "Jesus, Sarah. This is the kill file."

"She's gatekeeping the psychological records," I say. "She's the silent hand behind every unexplained termination. Every red flag in HR that no one can trace. And Daniel... he signed off on it."

"I've cross-checked ten of the names so far," Alex says. "Half of them left within a month of their last session with her. Most without formal exit interviews." I feel nauseous at the thought. "She rewrote their legacies," I say. "Turned personal struggle into professional threat."

"She's trying to do it to you too." Alex says gently. "I know." Alex exhales on the other end. "You ready to burn the house down?" I nod with conviction. This isn't just evidence. It's ammunition. And I'm the one holding it. "More than ready! Let's light the match."

~ 27 ~

At 3pm I have a meeting scheduled with Daniel, our usual weekly catch up. Usually I attend these sessions with a sense of achievement, ambition and opportunity, but today I walk across the office feeling like I am stepping into a trap.

The conference room feels colder than usual. Not physically, temperature-wise it's the same climate-controlled sterility as always, but something about the air feels sharper, more calculated. The windows are drawn, the artificial lights overhead casting a harsh glare across the polished table.

Daniel is already seated when I arrive. He's alone, reviewing something on his laptop. His expression is unreadable, as always, a picture of composed efficiency. When he sees me, he smiles. It's a good smile. Rehearsed. Professional. A mask I now know hides much more than indifference.

"Sarah," he says smoothly, gesturing to the chair across from him. "Glad you could make it." I nod and sit, setting down my notes even though I already know this meeting isn't about any real project milestone. It's about power. Proximity. Pressure.

"This won't take long," he says. "I just wanted to check in on your projections for the Q4 rollout. I know you've had some... unexpected resource strain."

His tone is light, but I catch the edge. *Unexpected resource strain* is code. The compliance inquiry. The missing files. The ghost vendor flags. The weight of it sits just behind his smile.

"I've adjusted the budget model," I reply, careful to keep my tone steady. "Built in risk buffers for the dependencies flagged last cycle." Daniel leans back, fingers steepled. "Good. It's important we stay agile. I appreciate your ability to adapt. Though I have to admit, you seem... tense."

Adapt." A word that had appeared in Voss's notes. I used to think it meant flexibility. Now I hear it as compliance.

I meet his eyes, whilst responding. "Long few weeks." He gives a quiet chuckle. "Of course. These things tend to come in waves. But you've always been one of our more... resilient contributors." There's something about the way he says '*resilient contributors*' that turns my stomach. I hear Voss's voice behind his, clinical and cold, *Overcompensatory behavior. Elevated suspicion threshold.* He's quoting her without quoting her. Echoing her diagnosis without the formal paperwork.

He knows. He's seen the reports. He's *using* them.

"You know, if you ever feel overwhelmed... We have resources for that." Daniel says, I dont know how to respond, but just as I am about to speak, the door opens. Mark steps in, late but not flustered. He gives a slight nod to Daniel, then sits beside me with a quiet, "Sorry."

"Good timing," Daniel says. "I was just asking Sarah about the updated rollout plans." Mark doesn't look at me right away, but I can feel his presence like static. When he does glance over, his expression is thoughtful. Curious. But something about the way his gaze lingers on me sends a spike of tension down my spine.

"I had a few follow-ups," Mark says, directing it to me. For a second, he looks at me too long. Not with suspicion. With something like a warning. But it passes.

"The figures you approved last quarter for the bonus reconciliation, do you have a clean version of that model? There were some gaps I wanted to review."

I blink. "Gaps?" He shrugs. "Just timing stuff. Dates versus approvals. Some of the vendor entries seem misaligned. I figured since it came from your team..."

"They weren't routed through me," I say, maybe too quickly. Daniel glances between us, watching, I think I see him shuffle as if uncomfortable in my peripheral vision, but I can't quite be sure.

Mark smiles slightly. If he's protecting himself, I understand. But if he's protecting Daniel... then he's already chosen his side. "Right. Still, I figured if anyone had the original... it'd be you." There's something too practiced in his voice. Too precise. I suddenly can't tell if he's fishing for information, or planting something. Either way, the temperature in the room drops another five degrees.

We finish the meeting with hollow formalities. When I stand, Daniel reaches across to shake my hand again. "Thanks, Sarah. Keep up the good work." His grip is just firm enough to feel performative. I return the pressure without blinking.

As I step into the corridor, I hear Daniel murmur something to Mark behind me. I don't catch the words. I don't need to.

Outside, the hallway feels too bright. Too exposed. I pass one of the black glass panels near the conference rooms. My reflection walks beside me, calm on the outside, hunted underneath. I move quickly down the side stairwell, ducking around the corner just to get my bearings. "Hey," a voice says. I turn. It's Emily.

She's leaning against the door to the server room, arms crossed, tablet in one hand. She looks calm. But there's something in her eyes I haven't seen before, a warning, maybe?

"You okay?" she asks. I nod too quickly. "Fine. Just a long meeting." She tilts her head slightly. "With Daniel?" I nod weakly, "Yeah. And Mark."

At the mention of Mark, something shifts in her expression. It's quick, too quick to name, but it's there. A flicker of something not quite surprise. "You're playing with fire," she says. I pause, blinking. "What do you mean?"

Emily glances around before answering. "Just... he's the CEO. You're poking around in things most people would walk away from. I know you want answers, but this kind of pressure changes people." Her words are vague, but her tone is specific. It's a warning, not just about Daniel, but about how close I'm getting.

"Mark was asking questions too," I say. "About financial approvals. Bonus reconciliations. Stuff he wouldn't normally be looking at." Emily's jaw tenses, but she doesn't look surprised. "He's been... nosy lately," she admits. "I've noticed him snooping into older log entries. Accessing backup systems he doesn't usually touch. But that doesn't necessarily mean he's part of it."

I study her. "And you didn't think to tell me?" She shakes her head quickly. "I was waiting to confirm it wasn't just routine. He's in Risk, after all. Technically, he can look at anything."

"But why now?" I ask. Emily's voice softens. "I don't know. Maybe he's trying to figure out what you know. Or maybe he's covering his own tracks." I don't respond. The silence between us stretches. "You and Mark are still...?" I ask, leaving the rest of the question unspoken. Emily's face is unreadable. "Yeah. We're still seeing each other. It's casual. Mostly."

Mostly. That one word is doing a lot of work. "Does he ever talk about the project?" I ask. She hesitates. "Sometimes. But he's careful. Vague. Like he's trying to find out what I know without giving anything away." I close my eyes briefly, trying to take everything in, before responding. "So you think he is involved?" Emily looks down at her tablet. "I do, but I'm still trying to confirm it."

There's a long pause. Then she looks back at me. "Just be careful, Sarah. And I'm not just talking about Daniel."

I nod slowly, not sure what to say. "Thanks for telling me," I say finally. She gives me a quick nod, then slips away down the corridor. I watch her go, then turn and walk in the other direction, the hallway stretching out before me like a gauntlet. The meeting was supposed to be about progress, milestones, strategy.

But it wasn't.

It was a warning. Wrapped in politeness. Laced with menace. Daniel smiled while checking for cracks. Mark asked questions he shouldn't have known to ask.

And now I'm left with the feeling that the walls are closing in faster than I expected. And someone, somewhere, is counting on me to break.

~ 28 ~

Back at the cottage, I'm greeted by the familiar smell of dust and coffee, the scent soaked into every beam and curtain like old secrets. Outside, the trees hiss with wind, their branches whispering things I can't quite hear. Inside, the world has shrunk to the dim glow of screens and the relentless tapping of keys. The air feels weighted, like it knows what we're trying to do.

Alex sits across from me at the table, sleeves rolled up, jaw tight, her expression honed with surgical focus. She's always been precise, methodical, but this is different. There's urgency now. Each click of her trackpad is a cut through the lies we've unearthed. Her eyes flick rapidly between lines of code, emails, files.

The data sprawled across our screens forms a brutal map of intent, spreadsheets, screenshots, internal memos, call logs, time-stamped session notes, prescription entries, and the decrypted audit trails from both thumb drives. The digital anatomy of a corporate weapon, designed not just to hide fraud, but to discredit and dismantle the people who might see it.

"This version is almost clean," Alex says, tapping her trackpad once more. "I've pulled metadata into footnotes, nested references, even included cross-linked hashes from the thumb drives. If they try to deny any of it, the checksums will hold under scrutiny."

I nod, scrolling through the master file we're building, *ZettaCore: Thread 01 - Risk, Manipulation, Collapse.* The title reads like an obituary more than a report.

"You think it's too much?" I ask. "Too detailed?"

"No such thing," she says. "We don't just want to expose Voss and Daniel. We want to make it impossible for anyone to explain it away. We have to flood the system with truth."

We work for hours, stopping only for refills of bitter coffee and the occasional splash of cold water to the face. As we go, each piece of evidence tightens the noose. The prescription logs. The ghost HR profile. The shell vendor payments routed through Liechtenstein. The therapy notes that are rewritten to justify termination. And most damning of all, the internal routing table showing Daniel's direct receipt of those psychological evaluations.

I pause at one point, staring at a scanned PDF. James's final flagged entry. There, buried in the corner of the image, is his handwriting. We hadn't noticed it before, faint, almost overwritten by system text. Just seven words: *If I disappear, they'll call it instability.* It's not a confession. It's a warning. And he was right.

Around midnight, Alex saves the compiled file to an encrypted partition, then backs it up onto two mirrored thumb drives. She hands me one in a plastic sleeve, the metal warm from her hand.

"This doesn't leave your sight," she says. "I'll sleep with it under my pillow," I say, trying to smile. She doesn't laugh.

We run through the checklist one more time. Board summary deck, done. Witness verification, done. Collated documentation, backed up, timestamped, redundant. The entire infrastructure of their lies now sits compressed into a file small enough to fit in my palm. It's astonishing really, how something this destructive could be so portable.

The wind outside rises, curling around the walls of the cottage. I look to the window and softly say "I think we might actually win," almost not believing it.

Alex glances at me, eyes shadowed. "Maybe. But winning has a cost."

***

I wake to silence.

Not the peaceful kind. The unnatural kind. The stillness after something breaks. The kind of silence that feels like it's pretending.

My eyes flick to the ceiling. A pale blue washes in through the edge of the curtains, dawn still unformed. I check the nightstand, laptop, burner phone, everything where I left it.

Then I walk into the main room. Alex is already there, standing stiffly by the table, shoulders square, but still. She doesn't look up at first. Just points toward the corner where we'd kept some of the older gear. Laptops, cables, backup thumb drives, spare batteries.

One of the laptops is gone. We stare at the empty space. "They didn't take anything else," Alex says. "Not the main system. Not the drives. Just that one."

"The one we used the first night?" I ask. She nods. "It had the raw dump from the first drive. We moved everything important off it, but it still had the initial cache."

I move to the window. It's closed. Locked. The door shows no signs of damage. "How did they get in?" I question. Alex shakes her head. "Back door was latched last night. I checked. This morning. it wasn't."

There's no glass broken. No alarms triggered. The lock wasn't picked. Someone got in, and out, without disturbing a thing. A ghost.

"They bypassed the external cameras," Alex continues. "But they missed the motion-triggered one inside."

She turns her screen toward me. A black-and-white still loads. A grainy figure in a hood. Average height. Gloves. They're crouching beside the stack, hand reaching toward the very laptop that's missing.

The timestamp reads **3:27 a.m.** The next frame is empty. “Ninety seconds total,” Alex says. “Too fast for anything random. Too surgical.”

I feel a cold sweat rise at the back of my neck. This wasn’t theft. This was precision. “They knew exactly what they wanted,” I say. “And exactly what not to touch.”

I rush to my coat, still hanging on my bedroom door. The thumb drives are there. But when I reach into the pocket, something else is waiting for me. My fingers curl around it. Cold. Smooth.

I pull it out. It’s small. Almost weightless. For a second I don’t know what I’m holding. Then it blinks. Soft green, every three seconds. Not a coincidence. Not a gift. A signal. A lock on my location. My life.

I carry it downstairs like a bomb that's about to go off at any second. Alex sees it and steps back. “Jesus.” she exhales. “Someone’s tracking us,” I whisper. “They planted this.”

She takes it with tweezers, drops it into a signal-proof pouch. “Could’ve been Daniel. Voss. Or someone we haven’t even seen yet.”

I turn to the still on the screen again. The figure is faceless. But not featureless. Something about the way they moved, like they didn’t worry about being caught, unnerves me more than anything else.

“What was even on that machine?” I ask again.

Alex sighs. “Cached logs. Redacted screenshots. Metadata fragments. Nothing with passwords. But if someone’s trying to reconstruct what we saw... they’re starting from the edges and working in.”

“They’re trying to erase our trail while building their own.” She nods. I start pacing, panic flickering beneath the surface. “We move faster. We don’t wait. We take this to the board.”

"I'll re-secure the backups," she says. "And scan every inch of this place. We can't afford any more holes."

"Let's assume everything is compromised from now on," I say. "Even each other." Alex doesn't flinch at that.

Outside, the sky lightens to grey. It's not a warm light. Not hopeful. But it's morning all the same. I look one last time at the empty space where the laptop used to sit.

They didn't touch the evidence. They didn't hurt us. They just took something almost insignificant. Almost.

And that makes it worse.

~ 29 ~

The office feels too normal. Fluorescent lights buzz overhead, steady and indifferent. The smell of recycled air hangs in the corridor like nothing's changed, like I haven't spent the last few days pulling apart a conspiracy that could devour the entire building from the inside out.

Every step echoes louder than it should. My shoes on the polished floor, the soft rustle of fabric when I move my arms, normal sounds, but today they scrape at the edges of my nerves. I walk with measured steps, aware of the burn behind my eyes from too little sleep and too many lies. The thumb drive tethered around my neck feels like a weight around my spine. Alex and I finished the board deck last night and after the break-in, every step forward feels more like a dare.

They know we're close. Someone does. Close enough to steal from us without leaving a trace. Close enough to drop a tracker in my coat.

I take the long way to my desk, avoiding eye contact, skipping the kitchen. I pass the IT room where Emily is usually sat without slowing down. I glance through the open door as I pass and see that her chair is empty, her screen dark. Part of me is grateful. Part of me wonders where she is, but I keep on walking, head down.

Every footstep is a calculation. Every glance a question. Every silence is a trap I might not recognise until it closes around me.

I'm halfway down the east corridor, passing the rarely used fire escape, when I hear a low voice behind me.

"Sarah."

I stop.

Mark is standing at the top of the stairwell. His tie is crooked. His brow furrowed, like he's been standing there awhile, debating whether to speak. The light above him flickers once before steadying. His presence, in this shadowed corner of the building, is somehow more unsettling.

His eyes track mine with a strange intensity, not hostile, but heavy. Intentional. "Everything okay?" I ask, keeping my voice neutral. "Come here," he says quietly.

I glance around. The hallway is empty. Cameras don't face this stairwell. It's a dead zone, by design or by neglect, I don't know. But it feels like a place where secrets go to be spoken in hushed tones.

I step inside. The door swings closed behind me with a quiet clunk. The stairwell smells like metal and dust.

Mark doesn't move aside. Doesn't smile. Just stands, arms crossed, like a man bracing for a storm. "I just have one question," he says, his voice low enough that I have to lean in slightly to catch it.

"Okay..." He doesn't blink. "Were the Q2 financial submissions, your submissions, run through the approval API, or did they bypass the risk buffer protocol?"

The words land like a slap. Technical. Precise. Loaded. My heart thuds once, hard, before it resumes its rhythm, faster now. The question is too exact to be idle. He's been digging. Deeper than I thought.

"I don't know what you're talking about," I say, but I do. And so does he. His eyes search mine. Not for guilt. For something else. Proof, maybe. Or contradiction.

"Multiple transactions. Mismatched timestamps. There's a split in the audit trail. Either it was deliberate... or someone got sloppy." he says.

I want to say something dismissive, evasive, to shut this down, but I can't. His voice is calm, but I can see it, the tension in his jaw, the crease between his eyebrows. He's not accusing me. He's testing something. A theory. A hunch. Or maybe... warning me.

"And you think that was me?" I ask, voice low. Mark hesitates. It's barely perceptible, but I catch it. The micro-stall before his reply. The way his eyes narrow, not in suspicion, but in frustration.

"No," he says eventually. "But someone could be using your authorisation chain." That stings, more than I expect. Because he's right. I know it's true. But hearing it said aloud by someone I don't trust, makes it real in a way I'm not ready for.

He steps forward, dropping his voice further. "Do you trust everyone on your team, Sarah?" I blink. "What?"

"Do you trust them?" he repeats, slow and measured. My breath catches. The way he says it, it's not a suggestion. It's a warning cloaked as curiosity. A mirror turned toward me that I didn't ask for.

Does he know something? I open my mouth to respond, deny, deflect, maybe even confess, but I don't get the chance. His head tilts slightly. A sound down the hall. Footsteps. Distant, then closer. His eyes flick briefly toward the fire escape door, as if checking something... or someone.

He takes a step back. "Wait," I say, my voice sharper now. But he's already turning, already retreating into the gray.

"I'll see you around," he murmurs, not looking back. The stairwell door creaks open. By the time I step into the hallway, he's gone. Like he was never there.

I stand for a moment, absorbing the echo of the exchange. Trying to dissect his question, understand the meaning of what wasn't said.

Back at my desk, I type in my password with anticipation, waiting to see if I will be granted access. With a quiet chime the screen lights up and I breathe a sigh of relief. I stare at the screen for ten full minutes before realising I haven't typed a single word. My fingers hover above the keyboard, twitching like they're waiting for instructions I don't know how to give.

Mark's question replays in my head, over and over. *Do you trust everyone on your team?* And the worst part is, I don't know. I no longer fully trust anyone. Not really.

Mark's question felt like a key to a door that I'd locked behind me. And now it's open, and everything inside looks different.

I scroll through the board presentation again, trying to focus, trying to believe in the finish line. But even the evidence feels brittle under my fingers now. Like it could crack with a whisper.

What if we've missed something? What if there's someone else, someone we haven't seen? Or worse... What if there's someone we have?

I need some air. I walk to the IT room, Emily is back now, seated at her desk, her face bathed in the soft light of her screen. She's typing something, but her eyes flick to me and she smiles in my direction for the briefest second. Then goes back to typing.

"I'm going to the roof for some air," I say to Emily. "Do you want to come?" I don't feel like being alone right now. "Sure" says Emily rising from her chair.

Alex once said not to tell her everything. Emily once told me to be careful around Alex. And now Mark is telling me not to trust anyone.

Paranoia is a parasite. It doesn't just whisper doubts. It burrows into memories and recreates them. I don't know who I know anymore. But I know one thing. The walls are closing in.

And someone, maybe all of them, are watching to see whether I run... or burn the whole thing down.

~ 30 ~

Emily walks beside me in silence. She doesn't ask what's wrong. She doesn't prod or press or pretend. She simply follows as I push the heavy rooftop door open and step into the cool, open air, then lets it close behind her without a sound. It's late afternoon, the light fractured and soft, turning the shadows long and thin.

The rooftop is nearly empty. A thin breeze threads through the metal chairs, rustling the leaves of a half dead potted plant someone's long forgotten. The city sprawls beyond the edges of the building, a tapestry of muted colours and distant motion. The view is still beautiful. But now it feels like a lie someone painted over a crime scene. The world is slowly moving, the same as it does every day, just as my world seems to be spiralling.

I make my way to the far corner where the concrete meets with a low wall that borders the rooftop. I lean against it, wrapping my arms around myself. Emily stops a few feet away, then slowly sits on the ledge, careful not to look at me too directly. She just sits. It's the kindest thing she could've done.

There's nothing performative about her presence. No questions. No advice. Just proximity. And in a world where every glance seems to carry hidden motives and every word is loaded with double meanings, her silence feels strangely safe.

We stay like that for a while. The wind nudges my hair across my cheek, and I don't bother brushing it away. Somewhere down below, a siren wails and fades. A helicopter hums past in the distance. Life, continuing, uncaring.

Emily pulls her knees up to her chest, her arms looped loosely around them. She's dressed simply, gray slacks, an oversized sweater I think I've seen her wear on weekends. There's no urgency in her movements, just patience. Steadiness.

For a moment, I want to tell her everything. About the break-in. About the tracking device. About the old laptop and what might've been on it. About Mark, the stairwell, the question he left me with like a bruise.

But I don't.

She glances at me once. Offers a small smile. Then looks away again. We sit until my hands stop trembling.

My phone buzzes. I pull it out, already knowing who it is. Alex. Her name flashes on the burner's tiny screen. I hesitate, then glance at Emily. She notices. Doesn't ask. Just rises quietly and gives a small nod, as if she already understands.

"I'll head back in," she says softly. I watch her leave, the door swinging shut behind her with a soft click. I wait until I'm alone before I answer. "Alex?" Her voice is tight, fast. "We were right." I stiffen. "Go on."

"I found two more profiles," she says. "Two former employees who were flagged for early exit protocols. Both filed whistleblower complaints six months before they disappeared from the org chart. You want to guess who signed off on their psychological evaluations?" I close my eyes. Voss.

"Voss," Alex confirms. "The language matches James' file almost perfectly. Same diagnostic tags, same burnout narrative, same recommendation: removal with HR bypass."

My hand grips the wall until the bones in my knuckles ache. "Their evaluations were faked," she continues. "Timestamp metadata shows edits made after the supposed session dates. She retrofitted the files to match a narrative she wanted documented. Which means those sessions might not have even happened."

"Who were they?"

"One was a systems engineer named Clara Wood. The other a DevOps consultant, Ian Crossley. Both worked on high-level compliance analytics. Both flagged the same type of anomalies James did."

"And they vanished." I ask. I hear Alex clicking at her keyboard in the background, before responding "HR records show 'voluntary leave due to stress.' Their exit interviews are blank. No final logs. No follow-up. It's like they never existed." The wind picks up. "Why target them?" I ask. "Why use Voss?"

"Because it's untraceable. Clara had submitted three anomaly reports in her final month. Ian logged over 400 hours of unpaid system tracing. Both were erased with a sentence." Alex says. "Anyone with a recorded psychological risk becomes a liability, not a whistleblower. The company protects itself under the guise of mental health concern. And Voss? She's the perfect scalpel. Silent. Surgical. No blowback." My skin crawls. "We need this documented in the board file."

"Already added it," she says. "Pulled the backups, archived the file differentials, everything. Clara and Ian are now Thread 02."

"They deserved better," I whisper. "So did James." We fall into silence, before Alex adds, "I also reran the credential audit. Daniel's name appears again. He signed off on the admin override for both terminations."

Of course he did. I stare out at the city, the sunset bleeding into the glass of nearby buildings. For a moment, I can almost see what this place looked like before I knew what lay beneath it. Clean. Efficient. Prestigious.

But it was always rotting underneath. "The board meeting is tomorrow," I say. "First thing."

"It's time." Alex replies. Then her tone softens. "How are you holding up?" I glance at the rooftop door, still shut tight. "Ask me tomorrow," I say. We hang up.

The wind shifts again. I stand there a little longer, letting it press against my skin, letting it remind me that I'm still here. Still breathing.

Emily was right to say nothing. Sometimes, the only thing more honest than truth... is silence from someone who doesn't need an answer.

~ 31 ~

The night feels still. Back at the cottage. The air is thick with anticipation, not the kind that hums with excitement, but the dense, suffocating kind that coils in your lungs and refuses to leave.

Alex moves through the small living space with practiced control, organising papers, rechecking backups, flipping through printed copies of the evidence binder like it might spontaneously rearrange itself overnight. I sit at the table, watching the cursor blink on the encrypted laptop. The final version of the board deck is open, untouched for over an hour.

The deck is done. The files are backed up. There is nothing left to add, nothing left to prepare. But still, we hover, because preparing feels safer than admitting it's time.

"You haven't eaten," Alex says without looking up. "Neither have you," I reply. My voice sounds quieter than I mean it to. She nods, sets the folder down and walks to the tiny kitchen. "Do you want tea?"

"Sure." The kettle begins to hum, the sound oddly loud in the stillness. I glance at the clock. 21:42 "If they ignore this," I say suddenly, "if they see all the proof and still look the other way... what do we do then?"

Alex turns, leans against the counter. "Then we burn it wider. Go outside the company. Media. Legal. Full exposure. But let's not assume defeat before the fight." she says, pouring hot water into mismatched mugs.

She brings one over, sets it in front of me, and sits. The table between us is cluttered with flash drives, annotated printouts, and the two pen drives that used to belong to James sit between us like ghosts. I wonder what he'd think if he knew it had come to this.

We've cross-referenced every name, every invoice, every log. The picture is clear. Corruption at the top, sanitised through layers of wellness protocols and risk buffers. Voss, Daniel, and the ghost company they've hidden behind. But clarity doesn't mean certainty. Not in rooms like the one we're walking into tomorrow.

Alex blows on her tea. "You know they might try to discredit you." I shrug, "They've already started. My file's a blueprint for it. Voss made sure of that."

"Then we lead with it," she says. "Own it. Let them see how twisted it is. Make it undeniable." We sit in silence, letting that settle.

Outside, a fox cries in the distance. Not the eerie scream of fear, but something else. a tether to its pack, a unity. Poetic in a way, I think to myself, as I look towards Alex, who less than two weeks ago was a stranger.

"Did you ever think about walking away from all this?" I ask. Alex shrugs. "All the time. But I didn't. You didn't. And that means something."

I nod, staring into the surface of my tea. It reflects nothing. A black disk of uncertainty. Two weeks ago, I was chasing a promotion. Now I'm holding the proof of something that could collapse the walls I once wanted to climb."Tomorrow changes everything," Alex says, her tone neutral, but something in her eyes flinches. Her fingers tap once against her mug. Then still..

We go over the plan again, step by step. Arrival time. The order of the presentation. When to deliver the board packets. What to say if interrupted. What not to say unless forced. The layers of truth, the scaffolding of survival.

Alex secures the drive with the final deck in a foam-lined travel case, then slips it into her old messenger bag. She tests the latch twice, then sets it on the hallway table like it's a bomb set to go off at sunrise.

I curl onto the couch, not even pretending to sleep, while Alex takes the chair by the window, eyes on the dark woods outside. She's silent, but I know she's still strategising. Watching the shadows as if they might form into figures. Preparing for angles of attack that haven't even surfaced yet. The kettle whistles again in the distance. Neither of us moves to make more tea.

I think about Mark. About the question he left hanging in the stairwell. About Emily, and the quiet way she sat beside me on the rooftop. The world doesn't split neatly into sides anymore. It never did. And if tomorrow ends in silence, or in shouting, or in handcuffs, ours or theirs, I don't know what I'll do next. But I'll do something. We don't say goodnight. We just wait for morning.

~ 32 ~

As I step into the boardroom, I notice that it feels warmer than usual, or maybe it's just my anxiety spiking my temperature.

Rows of dark leather chairs, a long obsidian table polished to a mirror sheen. Everything is too neat, too measured. The light from the ceiling panels feels artificial, like a person can be scrubbed out if the brightness is dialed high enough.

I take my place at the end of the table. Emily is beside me, here to support me with any technical questions about the project I won't be speaking about. I haven't told her my plan, not because I don't trust her, but because we're too close to the edge now, and one wrong word to the wrong person could pull us under.

Across from us sit the board: a dozen faces lined in corporate steel. Some curious. Some blank. One, Daniel, tight and still. Mark is here too, near the center. He offers no signal of recognition, but his eyes are sharp. Alert. I take a breath. No one speaks. Then I begin.

"Thank you for your time. I know this was scheduled for a project demonstration. Instead, I'm presenting a risk profile that affects every corner of this company." A few brows lift. Phones are set down. Daniel shifts in his seat.

"This is a whistle-blower report. The project data has been folded into a broader audit trail, one that exposes systemic misuse of employee identities, falsified wellness evaluations, unauthorized financial flows, and the concealment of whistle blower terminations."

I click to begin the deck.

Slide one: the ZettaCore trail. Names. Accounts. Patterns.

Slide two: Shell companies. Transaction records. Offshore routing.

Slide three: The wellness files. James Turner, Clara Wood's, Ian Crossley's. And mine.

Emily leans forward slightly as I speak. A silent cue: keep going.

"Each of these employees reported anomalies, financial, compliance, ethical. Each was evaluated by Dr. Voss shortly before being removed from their roles. The reports show signs of post-session tampering. Metadata proves the files were altered days after the sessions supposedly occurred."

I watch the board members as I speak. One woman scribbles notes. Another leans back, arms crossed. No one interrupts.

"In James Turner's case, these fabricated mental health concerns were used to discredit and isolate him. He later died due to a potential misallocation of medication prescribed by Dr. Voss.. I advise you to leave this investigation to the correct authorities."

I pause and let the gravity sit.

"And he wasn't the only one. Clara Wood and Ian Crossley, two former employees with similar roles in compliance and systems security, raised concerns and vanished from the organisational chart soon after. There were no final logs or exit interviews. Just a flat, unexplained burnout label. And silence in reality."

Slide four: Timestamp comparisons. Highlighted edits.

"The files were backdated. The language is identical. Psychological profiles that Voss reused word for word."

Now, some of the board is shifting. One man lifts his glasses to pinch the bridge of his nose. Another murmurs to the woman beside him. Daniel still hasn't blinked.

"These evaluations weren't medical. They were weapons. Used to isolate, to remove, and to protect something else."

Slide five: The ZettaCore payment funnel. Over £4.6 million routed through various programs, signed off by Daniel Reed.

"The funds moved quietly through a fake consulting vendor that had no physical presence, no website, no real work performed. ZettaCore Consulting. It's a shell. A cover for financial manipulation at scale."

Daniel finally reacts. He shifts abruptly in his seat and clears his throat. "These accusations..." he begins, his voice measured but tinged with rising heat.

A woman from the boardroom's legal team cuts him off. "Mr. Reed, you'll have an opportunity to respond after this presentation concludes. Please allow Ms. Mitchell to continue."

Daniel bites his tongue, visibly tense, his knuckles whitening around the armrests of his chair. He sits back but doesn't relax.

I glance at the back of the room. Legal has stopped taking notes. Now they're watching.

"The access logs, the financial records, the manipulated psych reports, it all ties together. A system built not just to enrich, but to erase anyone who noticed."

Slide six: emails. Redacted chains, but enough to show Daniel authorising administrative overrides. Voss confirming appointments that never happened.

And finally, slide seven: a scan of James Turner's final note. Highlighted.

'If I disappear, they'll blame instability. But this isn't madness. It's deeply woven corruption'.

His words fill the room, and for a second, I forget I'm standing in front of a dozen senior leaders. I just feel the weight of what we let happen.

The room is still. Dead still.

I straighten. "Everything I've just shown you is documented, time-stamped, and cross-verified by three independent systems. We have backup copies in secure storage. We have witness corroboration. And if needed, we are prepared to go public."

Someone near the head of the table finally speaks. "How long have you known about this?"

"I began seeing signs within the last three weeks. I confirmed it all at that time. With help."

Emily nods beside me. Quiet, present. For the first time in weeks, I felt my lungs fill fully. No lies left to carry. Just truth, finally spoken aloud. Then a voice from legal, sharp and clear, "We're going to pause this meeting." Murmurs ripple.

"Out of caution, we need to confirm this documentation and review internal protocol before proceeding. This board is now in executive recess."

Chairs scrape. Papers shuffle. But no one speaks directly to Daniel. He stays seated, his eyes fixed ahead, as if he's watching the world he built fracture in real time.

Emily leans close as people begin to rise. "You did it." I nod, but my stomach turns. Because now the machine knows we're inside. And machines try to fight back.

Legal doesn't leave the room. Instead, two representatives make a quiet call from the corner, speaking in hushed voices. After a moment, one of them steps toward the hallway and gestures for security.

The door opens. A moment passes. Dr. Voss walks in. My spine stiffens instinctively.

She's still in her cream blazer, still composed. But her eyes are scanning. Calculating. She sees Daniel first. Then the board. And then me and Emily.

For a second, something flickers in her expression. And Emily looks away. I catch it. The exchange. The shift. But I can't read it.

Voss sits, summoned but silent. The board isn't done. Not by a long shot. As the door swings shut again, sealing us in, I realise what we've done. We've cracked it open. Now we see what spills out.

~ 33 ~

Security arrives without fanfare. No slammed doors. No shouting. Just the quiet, precise footsteps of two uniformed men flanking the door, nodding at Legal, then at the board. It's all done with the cold professionalism of people who've done this before.

Dr. Voss barely blinks. Her hands are folded in her lap, perfectly still. When the head of legal gestures toward her, she rises smoothly, like she's been expecting it. No protests. No questions. She glances once at the board, then again at me and Emily. I look back, composed. Emily doesn't return the look.

Daniel, on the other hand, bristles. His chair screeches back as he stands. "This is a mistake," he says, his voice cracking in the stillness. "You're basing this on doctored evidence from a ghost. None of this will hold."

"Mr. Reed," says the head of Legal, voice low and clipped, "please comply. Further comment will be addressed during internal investigation and, if necessary, police review."

Daniel opens his mouth again, but one of the security officers steps forward. Not aggressively, just enough. Just close enough that Daniel sees what's waiting if he resists.

He exhales sharply through his nose, gathers his things with trembling hands, and follows Voss toward the door. The silence they leave behind is weighty.

Mark remains at the table. The board doesn't dismiss him. Instead, two senior members quietly request he stay for an internal debrief. There's no accusation in their tone. Not yet. But there is scrutiny.

He nods once. Calm. Composed. “I’ll answer whatever you need,” he says. “I want the truth, same as you.”

He looks at me for the first time, and there’s no anger there. No bitterness. Only a kind of quiet resignation. Like he’s known something like this was coming all along.

I watch as the room reorganises around him, Legal taking notes, board members shuffling into position. He remains poised, unflinching, as the door closes again behind the others.

Emily and I are told we’re free to go. That we’ll be contacted for further questions. That an internal review is being initiated.

I nod. I don’t know if I trust the words, but I understand them. It’s how institutions protect themselves while pretending to listen. We leave the boardroom.

Out in the hallway, the air feels different. Lighter, somehow. Not safe. Not yet. But different. We walk in silence at first. My pulse still pounds in my ears. I keep replaying the moment Voss looked at me and Emily. The flicker in her eyes. Recognition? Warning? Betrayal?

“Are you okay?” Emily asks softly. I stop walking. Turn to her. She’s watching me carefully, her expression open but unreadable. “I don’t know,” I say. “It feels like we just detonated something. I’m waiting to see what’s left.”

Emily nods, and then, without hesitation, wraps her arms around me. It’s not the tight, panicked hug of survival. It’s quiet. Steady. The kind you give someone when you know the fall isn’t over, but you’ve landed somewhere new.

“I’m proud of you,” she says against my shoulder. “You were incredible in there.” I pull back slightly, meeting her gaze. “We’re not finished.”

“No,” she agrees. “But we’re not invisible anymore either. They can’t pretend this didn’t happen.” We walk slowly to the elevators. I realise my hands are still trembling.

"They took them out of the building," I say quietly. "Voss. Daniel."

"Yeah," Emily replies. "I saw."

"I didn't think it would feel like this."

"Like what?"

"Like the beginning, not the end."

She considers that, nodding slowly. "Sometimes, justice starts in silence." The elevator doors open. We step inside. I think of James. Of Clara and Ian. Of the notebook, the thumb drives, the long nights in the cottage, the break-in, the rooftop. I think of Mark, still inside, answering questions I can't hear.

And I think of Emily. Her steady hand. Her silence on the rooftop. Her comfort now. The elevator hums downward.

***

Outside, the sun has shifted behind a line of clouds, a slow drizzle falls. . The air is thick with the smell of ozone and pavement. A storm threatens the horizon.

We walk, neither of us saying where we're going. We just walk. Half a block away, we stop for coffee. The shop is half empty, fluorescent in a way that feels too bright after the boardroom. Emily orders for both of us. I sit in the corner booth, watching the street.

When she returns, she slides a cup across to me. "You should get some rest," she says. "You haven't stopped in days."

"I don't think I can. Not yet." I sigh, "Then don't," she replies, her voice light. "But you should at least sit still long enough to breathe." I sip the coffee. It burns a little. I welcome the sensation. "I'm still not sure what Mark was doing," I say.

Emily's expression darkens slightly. "He didn't stop you. That counts for something." I mess with my fingers, contemplating. "But he knew." I say. Emily nods. "Maybe. Maybe he was waiting to see which way things would break." I look up at Emily before adding. “Or maybe he was working an angle we haven’t seen yet.” She nods again slowly. “We’ll find out. Eventually.”

I lean back against the booth, watching people pass outside. Life continues. Bus routes. Umbrellas. Phone calls. Completely unaware of the implosion just triggered behind glass conference doors.

“What if they bury it?” I ask. “What if they spin it, restructure, pay off whoever needs paying off?”

“Then we go wider,” Emily says. I agree. “Alex already prepared for that. Press kits. Dead man’s switch. Full release if things go quiet.”

“Jesus.” Emily laughs, “Welcome to whistleblowing 101.” We finish our drinks in silence. Outside, thunder rolls far in the distance.

***

Later, back at the cottage, the air feels lighter. Alex is waiting at the door when I arrive. She greets me with her usual nod, then steps aside so I can enter. “Well?” she asks. “They called security,” I say. “Voss and Daniel were escorted out.”

Alex exhales, the closest thing to relief I’ve seen from her. “And Mark?” I shake my head. “He was still inside. Being questioned. I wonder if he’s telling the truth. Or waiting for the right moment to trade one.” Alex raises an eyebrow. “I think that he’s playing a long game. Maybe not ours. But not theirs either.”

I sit on the edge of the sofa. My muscles ache like I’ve been holding a heavy weight for too long. Maybe I have. Alex drops a thick folder onto the coffee table. “Media prep,” she says. “Just in case.” I nod. But I don’t reach for it.

***

That night, I lie awake. The wind has picked up again. Outside, trees sway. Alex hasn't gone to bed yet.

I stare at the ceiling. There's a future now. That much is certain. But what kind of future, and who gets to write it, that's what comes next.

They'll circle the wagons. They'll try to manage the fallout. Maybe Voss and Daniel will take the fall and the rest will be quietly reshuffled. Or maybe the truth will break wider than they can contain. And maybe, just maybe, something good will grow in the space we've burned clean.

I turn on my side. I think of James's final words. "*Not madness,*" *I whisper.* "*Not paranoia. Just truth. Truth that lived long enough to be heard.* Not for me, but for him. And for whatever comes next.

~ 34 ~

The announcement comes the next morning.

The board meets in a closed-door emergency session. When I'm called back in, this time alone. I'm already numb from the weight of anticipation. Emily waits outside, calm but alert, her phone clutched in both hands like a tether.

Inside, the atmosphere is different. The room is smaller, the lighting dimmer. A different kind of quiet, less ominous, more deliberative. Legal is present, but silent. The chair of the board clears his throat and addresses me directly.

"Effective immediately," he says, "we are appointing you as acting CEO." For a moment, the words don't register. I blink. The air feels too thin. "Me?"

He nods once. "Pending full investigation and restructuring, we believe your oversight and integrity are what the company needs. Your leadership in crisis, your clarity under fire, it's more than any of us showed. You're the only one who didn't flinch."

I almost laugh. Integrity. After everything. But I don't argue. I nod. I thank them. I leave the room with legs that feel like paper, arms heavy as stone. Emily is waiting in the hallway. She stands when she sees my face.

"Well?" I take a breath. "I'm the acting CEO." Her smile is immediate. Wide. Genuine. "Are you serious?" I nod, barely able to say it again. The words stick to my tongue like glue.

She throws her arms around me, pulling me into a tight hug. "You did it. You actually did it." I stand stunned. "It doesn't feel real." I say. She pulls back, eyes shining. "Believe it. I'm so proud of you, Sarah."

We leave the building side by side. Outside, the sun has broken through the storm clouds. It doesn't feel like victory, not exactly. But it does feel like the first step into something new.

We stop for coffee on the way back. Emily insists. She orders a celebratory latte and jokes that I need to start drinking overpriced espresso now that I'm an executive. I let her talk, let her tease. I don't know what I would've done without her.

The barista calls our names and we settle into a quiet corner. People pass by us, unaware of the tectonic shift that just occurred upstairs. Emily stirs her drink with the kind of idle calm I've come to envy.

"Do you think they'll actually follow through?" I ask. "They have to," she says. "You gave them no other choice."

"It still doesn't feel like enough. Not yet." She leans forward. "Then make it enough. You're in charge now. Burn out the rot."

Her words are firm but gentle. She believes in me. Maybe more than I believe in myself at this moment.

***

Later, I return to my own house for the first time in days. The building is still familiar, but it feels strange now, like stepping back into a version of myself I've outgrown. I walk up the path, key poised in hand, and unlock the door.

Mushu is waiting just inside, tail flicking lazily before springing to life. He pads toward me, meowing in bursts, head-butting my shin with practiced affection. I drop my bag and sink to the floor, letting him nuzzle into my lap. His fur is warm, his purr thunderous and grounding. "Hey, Mushu," I whisper. "Miss me?" He presses his head under my chin in response.

Emily steps inside behind me, setting her bag down gently. Mushu immediately darts toward her, but instead of his usual affection, he stops short. His tail stiffens. He lets out a soft, uncertain chirp, then backs away, ears twitching.

Emily crouches slowly, extending a hand. "Hey, buddy," she says softly.

Mushu doesn't hiss, but he doesn't approach either. He stares, blinking slowly, then pads back to me, jumping onto the couch and curling into a wary loaf. Emily watches him, amused. "Guess he missed you more." I shrug. "Maybe he's just in a mood," I offer, trying to smile.

We settle in. The apartment is quiet but no longer eerie. Just lived-in. Familiar. I light a candle in the kitchen while Emily makes tea, and for a moment, it almost feels normal.

Later, while we sit on the couch with Mushu curled between us, Emily shifts slightly and looks at me. "Hey," she says. "I've been thinking. I'm going to visit my parents." I pause, surprised. "Oh?"

"Just for a week," she adds quickly. "I haven't seen them in over a year. And... I think we both need a break." I study her face. She's not running. There's no urgency in her voice. Just... relief. A door opening to air that doesn't carry the stench of cover-ups.

"You deserve it," I say. "Go. Rest. I'll keep the ship from sinking." She smiles. "I know you will. You've already done more than anyone could've asked."

"When are you leaving?" I ask. "Tomorrow. First flight out." I nod slowly. It all feels too fast, too soon. But at the same time, it's been a lifetime since we've breathed freely.

"Bring me back something Italian," I say. She laughs. "Only if it's not wine. You'll just spill it during your next dramatic reveal." We share a quiet moment of laughter. It doesn't solve anything. But it softens the edge of what's still ahead.

I ask her about Sicily, where her parents live, what the weather's like. She talks about citrus groves and ceramic rooftops, about the warmth and the sea air. Her voice is soft, almost wistful. She's already halfway there in her mind.

Later, after she's gone home to pack for her trip, I sit alone at the dining table, staring at the title page of the interim operations report. I don't touch it. I just look. I realise I'm not afraid anymore. There's uncertainty, yes. But fear? No.

We made it through the fire. Now we see what survives the smoke.

***

I wake early the next morning to take Emily to the airport. She is already standing in her doorway when I arrive at her house, suitcase by her feet. She looks fresher than I've seen her in days.

"Taxi for Emily?" I call, laughing. She jumps in the car and settles in for the short drive. The journey is nice, fun and full of laughter, the conversation feels light. I realise how much i've missed the ease of being around Emily.

When we arrive at the terminal, Emily hops out of the car and goes to the back seat to retrieve her case. By the time she has it on the pavement, I am standing next to her. She hugs me tightly. "Take care of yourself, Sarah. Really. And don't forget to eat. CEOs have this terrible habit of pretending they're immortal."

I smile. "No promises." She lingers for a moment. "I'll call when I land. And I'll bring back something beautiful." Then she's gone. And for the first time, I'm truly alone with the weight of what comes next. But instead of fear, I feel something else entirely. Readiness.

***

Back at the house, after my first official day as acting CEO, I glance toward the pin-board I used to hang half-serious inspiration quotes on. It's different now, the quotes pulled down, replaced by process maps and deadlines. But in my mind, one line echoes. *We survived. Now we lead.*

Later that night, I hear from Alex. A message. Simple, but meaningful. "Publishing timeline's set. Starting the draft this week. I'm calling it *Sanitised*."

She's writing a book. Our story, James's story. The buried truths and the polished lies. The rot beneath the sleek exterior. She wants the world to know what happened. And who let it happen.

I write back: "I'll send you the foreword." Then I curl up on the couch, Mushu purring on my chest, and close my eyes.

For now, we rest. Tomorrow, we rebuild. James always said truth doesn't end a war. It begins one. I think... he'd be proud we chose to fight anyway.

Part Two

~ 35 ~

EMILY

The engine hums beneath me as the plane cuts through the clouds, steady and distant. I watch the land blur beneath me, shrinking into irrelevance. It's strange how silence on a plane feels different, less absence, more insulation. A perfect place to disappear.

This wasn't the plan, not at the start. Five years ago, I wasn't thinking about vanishing. I wasn't thinking about Sarah. I was thinking about the numbers, columns of opportunity and the way money moved when no one was really looking. NexTech practically begged for someone to take advantage of it. No one questioned the wellness budget. No one understood the layers of automation I built to save time, to bypass manual checks. They called it efficient. I called it a canvas.

I remember the first reroute, just a small adjustment to a disbursement file. I masked it under training reimbursements, bounced it through an inactive vendor account and let it sit in an offshore placeholder. It was too easy. Almost disappointing. But when the system didn't blink, when no one checked the numbers... I knew I could do more.

The hum of the engine deepens as we tilt slightly. I stare down at the clouds. I haven't cried. Not for James. Not for Daniel. Not even for myself. But Sarah...

She was the variable I never accounted for. I used her. At first, before I knew her, she was just another funnel. But over time, I started to care. Genuinely. Her laugh, her loyalty, her unshakable belief in doing the right thing. She once brought me soup when I lied about being sick. No questions. Just trust.

I should have stopped. I should have rerouted to someone else. But I didn't. I was too far in. She trusted me. She let me in.

I think about her face when she gets my confession, which is sitting in my Drafts, ready for me to press send. The confusion. The betrayal. I hate myself for that. I wish I had been someone else. Someone who could have deserved her trust.

The seatbelt light blinks on. The captain says something in a low drawl I barely register. We're descending. I close my eyes. There's a new name waiting for me. A new system to build. I won't do this again. I say it like a promise. But I'm not sure I believe it.

Goodbye, Sarah. You were never supposed to mean anything. But you did. And I will miss you for the rest of my life, even if you never think of me again.

Maybe especially if you don't.

~ 36 ~

TWO WEEKS EARLIER

The IT room buzzes with the usual low hum of pre-9am chaos when my phone rings. 8:40. Sarah. I don't hesitate before answering. She rarely calls this early unless something's wrong.

"Emily," she says, breathless. "All the project files are gone. Everything. They're just... not there."

"Ok, calm down," I say. "We can retrieve the documents from the backup servers." There's a pause on the other end. I imagine her gripping her phone, knuckles white. After I have calmed her down, I wave over the new Graduate IT Tech,"Jameson," I call across the floor, keeping my tone breezy. "Hey, can you help retrieve some files from last night's backup? All Horizon project folders, top level and any child directories."

He nods without question. Coming back on the line, I say, "Ok, it will take about half an hour for the files to be recovered, but then you'll need to check all documents once they've been received."

"Thank you so much," she says, some of the tension draining from her voice. "If you weren't already my favourite person..."

A few hours later a meeting alert appears at the bottom of my screen. I am due in the boardroom to go over the project milestones, I decide to quickly check Jamesons work, to make sure that the document recovery has been successful.

My pulse starts to race as soon as I see two Financial Reports have been added back. One of them contains my inflated figures, money I have already routed out of the business.

Rushing to the conference room with my laptop, I can only hope that Sarah hasn't noticed them yet. She hasn't called me, so that's a good sign.

Sitting surrounded by the other project members, I start to delete all traces of the file from the network. It will take five minutes to purge the file Jameson accidentally restored. Another Ten to remotely access his recovery log. I will then need to rewrite the activity trail so it looks like a standard refresh. It's not perfect, but it'll hold. Hopefully.

Sarah finally walks in the room, she's a few minutes late, which is unlike her. I smile despite myself. I should feel guilty. But I'm too busy cleaning up the mess.

Still, I can't shake the dread curling low in my stomach, I can see it on her face. Sarah's already seen the file. She has to have. And if she has, she knows the numbers don't match.

I pull up Sarah's most recent emails. I've been intercepting her threads to Daniel for months. She sends the project financials for review, trusting that he sees what she sends. But what he gets? That's mine. I intercept the attachments, tweak the budget lines, inflate values, reroute surplus. Then I send them along. Daniel never notices. He skims. He signs.

Sarah's files were perfect. Detailed. Clean. And because they were so well-structured, so predictable, they made the perfect carrier. I didn't start with her, but she was the most consistent. And once I realised no one was watching... I broadened the field.

Six other project managers. Two assistant directors. A handful of department heads who submitted requests through templated forms. I siphoned through all of them. Tiny amounts at first. A travel stipend here. A vendor invoice there. Then training programs. Wellness budgets. Initiatives no one cared to track. The money always moved quietly.

Until now. I press my fingers to my temple, exhaling slowly.

As I follow Sarah back to the Project room after the meeting has finished, I feel my heart hammering against my chest, despite knowing that I have already wiped the network clean.

As intended, when Sarah opens the network to show me, the second file is gone and I finally breathe again. Of course it is. I scrubbed it from every traceable path.

Watching Sarah stare at the screen, confused. I say smoothly. "Maybe it was just a glitch from the recovery. Sometimes temp files get duplicated during the batch restore. Especially if the server hiccuped."

"Please, just... don’t mention this to anyone. I need time to figure it out." she murmurs, still staring. She’s confused now. Doubtful, not suspicious. But it won’t last. Sarah’s not the type to let confusion rest.

I almost tell her. Right there. The words nearly leap out of me. But they don’t. Because that would mean she stops smiling. And I don’t want to be the reason she stops smiling. So I offer my help, like a friend should, knowing I can't give it.

Relief crashes over me so forcefully I almost feel faint. She doesn’t suspect me. Not yet. Not really. I can see it in her eyes, uncertainty, not accusation. She trusts me. I just hope that she leaves it alone.

She offers me a biscuit from her desk drawer. It’s nothing. But she always remembers I like the chocolate ones. I wish I’d known what she would mean to me. I wish I’d known before I chose her. Because once you know someone like that, once you *see* them... using them doesn’t feel like a strategy anymore.

I used to think the cleanest lies were the ones wrapped in kindness. But Sarah ruined that for me. She made me care. Now every kind gesture I give her feels like theft. And every smile she gives me back feels like a sin I didn’t mean to commit.

~ 37 ~

Late that afternoon, it's quiet in the IT room, blessedly, unusually quiet. The kind of quiet that only happens when the rest of the building has somewhere better to be. I'm the only one here. Everyone else cleared out early, probably riding the tail end of a long meeting day.

I've got my headphones on, my old, clunky retro pair with the worn leather pads and the coiled cable that tugs every time I shift too far. Some playlist from university is pulsing through them, synth-heavy background noise that helps me focus. On screen, lines of access logs scroll past, backup nodes blinking green. I'm not reviewing them for fun. I'm combing every last archive to make sure I haven't left any trace. Anything Jameson could've touched. Anything Sarah might stumble into.

I curse under my breath. I should have caught the duplicate earlier. I should've double-checked the rollback paths. How could I have missed something so basic? Sloppy. Reckless. I've never let things get this close before. It's not like me to panic, but the pressure is mounting and I can feel it behind my eyes like a slow-building migraine.

The sudden feeling of someone tapping me on the shoulder makes me flinch hard enough to knock the headphones askew. One ear pad slips from my ear as my heart leaps. Sarah's standing beside me, eyes wide with surprise, maybe at how startled I look, maybe at the fact I didn't hear her approach.

"Jesus, Sarah," I say, breath catching. "You scared me."

"Sorry," she says, blinking. "I didn't mean to sneak up on you. You looked... focused."

I laugh nervously, minimising the console on my screen. "Yeah. Just verifying some old backups. Making sure our systems aren't quietly dying on us."

She doesn't look convinced, but she lets it go. "That weird duplicate earlier is still bugging me."

Of course it is.

"I've rechecked," I say, scooting to the side. "Take a look. I ran a delta check earlier. No anomalies."

She leans in, close enough I can smell her perfume, that faint tropical and berry scent. Her eyes flick over the screen, but not like someone reading. Like someone remembering. Her frown isn't confusion. It's precision. Her eyes don't leave the log list, even when I speak. I pretend to focus on a side monitor, but my eyes are flicking back to her profile, trying to gauge what she's really thinking.

"And you're sure nothing else was restored?" she asks.

"Nothing that wasn't supposed to be," I say smoothly. "I even ran a file comparison. Matched hashes."

I can see her mentally filing that away. Sarah doesn't take things at face value. She never has. Her silence stretches a beat too long.

"It just felt... off," she murmurs. "Like something was there and then wasn't."

I offer a casual shrug.

"I'm here if you need anything." And I mean it. Sort of. I'm here, just not in the way she thinks.

And then, like a ghost, Mark appears. Not a sound from the door, no footsteps. Just there, behind us, clearing his throat.

"Hey," he says, his voice low and even.

I jolt again, yanking off the headphones completely and forcing a smile that I hope looks more genuine than it feels. "Mark. Hi. I didn't see you come in."

"Didn't mean to interrupt," he says, but his eyes are already on my screen. That careful, measured stare he uses when he's trying to figure something out. It's not the look of someone who's just passing through. It's the look of someone hunting.

Sarah doesn't say anything. She gives Mark a tight, unreadable smile, then turns and walks toward the door without another word. I watch her go. I know she doesn't like him, never has. And honestly, I don't blame her. He has that air about him. Like he's always storing things away for later. He's too careful. Too quiet. And annoyingly good-looking, which makes him harder to hate.

"Sarah was just checking on the backup logs," I say, closing the window quickly. "We had a weird sync glitch today. Everything's fine now."

He nods, but he doesn't look away fast enough.

"I didn't know you handled the delta comparisons yourself," he says casually.

"I like to make sure nothing's missed," I reply, just as casually.

He doesn't push it. Not now. But I can feel it, his suspicion. I'm not sure if he trusts me, and if he doesn't it's for a good reason. There's something off about him too. He notices things he shouldn't. Connects dots others ignore.

I've always known there was more to Mark Bishop than the pragmatic Group IT Director act he wears. He's never directly challenged me, most of the time I feel like he doesn't even see me. He's never recommended me. Never promoted me. Always looked through me like I was another fixture in the server room.

Its not a bad thing, to be unseen, especially when I have things to hide.

But if I can get the opportunity to keep him close, I could try and work out what he's up to, what he knows. So I give him a smile, one that hovers between polite and warm.

"Need something?" I ask.

"Just checking the server logs for that HR wellness sync," he says. "Saw a ping on the mirror node earlier. Wanted to make sure it wasn't a leak."

"It wasn't," I say quickly. "I ran diagnostics. No outbound calls. False positive."

"Good to know," he says. Then, after a beat, he adds, "Don't work too late."

He leaves without waiting for a reply.

As the door clicks shut behind him, I return to my screen, pretending to type something irrelevant. My heart is thudding. That look in Mark's eyes... he was looking for something, I'm sure of it. I used to be proud of my scripts. How clean they were. How invisible. Now I'm building a graveyard and hoping no one finds the headstones.

And if he starts really digging into logs, admin overrides, archived credentials, I may not have time to keep up with him. And if Mark and Sarah ever start comparing notes, it won't take long. I've already started erasing myself. But maybe I should be erasing something bigger.

~ 38 ~

Sarah shows up at my door around 19:15 with a tray of lasagne in her hands and that warm, casual energy that makes me feel like I might actually be a good person again. For a second, I let myself believe this could be normal. She chats as she walks into the kitchen.

“You're late home tonight, Been anywhere nice?” Sarah asks. I had intended to get here before she showed up, but by the time I left the office tonight, it was already dark.

"I stayed late," The truth, sort of. I tell her, placing my bag carrying my laptop carefully on the dining chair. "Was looking into the backups again." Again true, I did stay late to dig through the archives. But not for her reasons. I wasn’t trying to help. I was trying to cover my tracks.

She lights up. "That’s great! Maybe we can figure out what happened."

I nod, setting the kettle to boil while she slides the lasagne into the oven. My hands are still trembling faintly from the terminal purge I did before I left work. If she had shown up ten minutes later, she would’ve seen the real me. The version of me hunched over the dining table, logged into NexTech’s internal systems from an admin bypass.

"Anything look off in the archives?" she asks as we wait for the lasagne to heat.

"Not that I could see," I lie smoothly. "Whatever you saw earlier must’ve been wiped before I got there. Maybe even overwritten."

By the time we sit down, she is still questioning, trying to connect the dots. I dodge where I can, deflect where I must. I'm too practiced at this to slip. I point out that Daniel wouldn't benefit from inflating the numbers, which is true, just not relevant.

The oven timer goes off. We eat. She keeps digging and with each new question, my heartbeat increases a fraction more.

At one point she mentions Mark again, how he startled her at the office earlier. I pretend to laugh, to act like it's nothing. But my guard goes up. He's watching too closely. He's not just another clueless exec. He's not looking for proof, he's looking for patterns. And that's even more dangerous.

"He's not all that bad when you get to know him," I offer, trying to keep her calm, keep the suspicion off of me.

She jokes. I joke back. But I'm not really present anymore. I'm thinking about the laptop in my bag, about the test environment I need to spin up to check one last redundancy path.

When Sarah gets up to clean the dishes, I see her glance at my bag. For a second, watching her standing at the sink, I imagine saying it. Everything. Just blurting it all into the steam and soap and letting it be hers. But I don't. I can't.

"Hey," she calls, "are you planning to do some more digging later? Noticed you brought your laptop back."

"Yeah," I say easily, "Just in case. There's a quarterly refresh coming up. If something's still buried in the archives, it might be wiped soon."

That part's true. It's why I've stayed up half the night for the last week, scraping, hiding, deleting, moving. One wrong folder, one missed path, and everything unravels.

The clock is ticking.

Sarah thinks we're racing to save the truth.

She doesn't realise I'm racing to erase it.

And that's what twists the knife. Because part of me wants to deserve the trust she places in me, the way she still believes I'm on her side. But every backup I scrub, every log I reroute, is another betrayal she hasn't uncovered yet. I hate how easily I slip into the role. How natural it feels to play both sides. I tell myself I'm doing it for survival, for freedom. But when she looks at me like that, hopeful, trusting, I wonder if I've already lost something far more important.

By the time we settle into the sofa with 'The Blacklist,' my hands are busy clicking on my phone, which I am careful to tilt from Sarah's view, texting, masking IPs, rerouting logs through a proxy, talking to a contractor who's helping me rewire the corporate registry link for ZettaCore's wellness initiative paperwork.

Sarah notices. "Everything okay?"

"Mum again," I say with a sigh, tossing my phone aside like I'm annoyed. "Nagging about Sicily."

It's not a complete lie. If I disappear, Sicily is where she'll assume I went.

I keep smiling. I keep sipping tea. I keep lying.

Telling Sarah it's my mum texting from Sicily is effortless now, like muscle memory. Just a sigh, an eye-roll, and the conversation moves on. But behind that throwaway excuse, I'm maintaining a network of digital ghosts, shell profiles, and burner chains. Every ping on my phone is a calculation. Every reply is a risk.

I'm balancing a web of burner phones, encrypted threads, and shell identities, each one stitched together with the precision of a surgeon. A single typo, a traceable packet, and everything I've built could unravel in seconds.

I'm not proud of how good I've gotten at this. But I am good. Better than most.

Jameson's recovery job might've created more problems than it solved. I've spent the last two hours purging fragments, overwriting access logs, double-checking that nothing escaped into the shadow backups. At some point tonight, I need to ghost into one of the backup nodes from home just to delete a mis-flagged access session. But that will have to wait until Sarah has gone home.

I can't afford another slip. Not now. Not when I know Sarah is looking. She never lets anything go.

After the show ends, Sarah curls her legs beneath her on the sofa, leaning her head slightly against the cushion. The lasagne has made her sleepy, but I can tell her mind is still turning. She always gets that glassy-eyed stare when she's deep in thought. I need to try and deflect, move her attention away.

"Maybe tomorrow we pull the financials on the old 'Horizon Alpha' project," she says, eyes still on the television screen. "If it's not just my numbers that have been manipulated..."

I nod, sipping my drink slowly to mask the spike of adrenaline in my chest. Horizon Alpha was one of my earliest trial runs. If she goes digging there, she'll find subtle overages and ghost vendor invoices tucked into departmental ledgers. Nothing big. But enough.

"Don't worry, I will check them for you," I say aloud, already thinking of how to redirect her. "If anyone asks, I will say I'm checking for audit consistency. Cover story."

She smiles at me, grateful. God, that smile.

I feel like a monster.

I turn back to my phone, typing one-handed. It's time to close the loop on a shell vendor tied to Liechtenstein. I need to sever its mirrored trail and push the holding name through a faux liquidation. I've already created the tax cover story. All I need now is time.

Sarah yawns and stretches. "I should probably go soon," she murmurs.

"You can crash here if you want," I offer, because part of me still wants to be the friend she thinks I am.

"Nah," she says, stifling another yawn. "Early meeting tomorrow. But thanks."

As she heads to the door, I watch her like I always do when she's not looking. Like I might never see her again.

"Let me know if anything else feels off," I say, and I mean it. Not because I want to help. Because I want to stay one step ahead.

The second the door closes behind her, I'm back at the table, booting up the laptop.

One more sweep tonight.

Then the hard stuff begins.

~ 39 ~

It starts at the water cooler. I am sipping a lukewarm paper cup of filtered tap water, trying to look nonchalant while covertly checking server sync reports on my phone, when Mark appears beside me.

He doesn't say much at first. Just leans in slightly, close enough that I catch the scent of his aftershave. Something subtle. Clean. Like Lemons and cold sea air. It catches me off guard more than it should.

"Did you do anything nice last night?" he asks casually, eyes flicking toward mine. I hesitate, partly because I hadn't expected the question, but mostly because I am trying to decide which version of myself to offer him. The friend-of-Sarah version? The diligent IT Tech? Or the one that knows how to manipulate systems, and people.

"Nothing exciting," I say, smiling lightly. "Just worked late and collapsed on the sofa." He gives a soft chuckle, nodding like he understands. And then comes a question I'm really not expecting, but welcome nonetheless. "Would you want to grab dinner sometime? Tonight maybe?"

I blink. He plays it off so casually, like it is just an afterthought, but I can tell he's rehearsed it. Mark doesn't make impulsive moves. Everything with him is measured. "Sure," I say before I can overthink it. "Why not?"

It is just about curiosity. Saying yes is a calculated move. Getting closer to Mark could prove useful. If he is suspicious of me, and I sense he might be, then proximity is my best weapon. It's easier to control a threat when you're holding their hand.

Then Sarah appears, walking toward the coffee machine with that knowing smirk she wears whenever she is about to stir trouble.

"That seemed awfully cosy," she teases, nodding subtly toward Mark, who is walking away from the cooler and straightening his jacket.

I roll my eyes, but I can feel the flush rising in my cheeks. "I think you may be right about Mark liking me," I admit, trying to play it off.

"What did he want?" she asks, clearly enjoying herself.

"Just asked how my evening was... and if I was free for dinner tonight." Sarah's eyebrows shoot up. "Dinner? Tonight?" She grins. "Emily, look at you!"

I'm still smiling as I head toward the work bathroom, I have butterflies in my stomach, and more than a few calculations running through my mind.

As I retouch my eyeliner in the mirror, I catch myself actually smiling. A real smile. That surprises me. But before I can get myself too wrapped up in thoughts of my date with Mark, I need to speak to Julia Voss.

***

As I make my way down to the lower-level offices. I feel the small object in my pocket. The bug is no bigger than a button. A passive transmitter, voice-activated. I'd programmed it myself. All I need is five seconds.

I knock on Julias door and wait for her to open it for me. As I enter I stop briefly, adjusting my bag on my shoulder, as a cover for what I am really doing. My fingers work fast, dropping the bug into a plant pot near the two chairs Julia uses during her therapy sessions. Here the acoustics will be clean. Done.

This isn't only about Sarah and knowing what she might say, it is about control. Julia has been a liability since James and I need to protect Sarah.

***

After his death, Julia swore she hadn't meant for it to happen. "I only prescribed the combination to keep him unstable," she'd said, eyes wide, voice trembling. "Just enough to make him seem unreliable. So if he did try to come forward..." Her sentence had trailed off into an apology she didn't have the courage to say aloud.

I'd believed her, then. Believed she was just playing her part. But even now, the way she avoids saying his name makes my stomach twist.

Still, that accident has concerned me. Julia has secrets now. Mine aren't the only ones at risk anymore. I need to know everything that is being said. Especially where Sarah is concerned. And if Sarah is digging, I need to get ahead of it.

***

Julia sits at her desk and picks up her mug of herbal tea. Her posture is relaxed, but her eyes as always hold that sharp intelligence she never bothers to hide when she is with me.

"Emily," she says warmly. "Sit." I take the chair across from her. We don't do therapy, not with each other. Our arrangement is too complicated for that. But we have a rapport, long-standing, tangled, mutually beneficial.

I stare at her, then slowly exhale. "Julia, I need to know what Sarah's thinking, she saw one of the old reports. The inflated financials."

That makes Julia sit up straighter. "Which report?"

"The Horizon variant. From quarter two last year."

Julia's face falls, her fingers tighten around the mug. "How? I thought you cleared it."

"So did I. But Jameson rolled back an older backup. One of the mirrors had it tucked inside a child directory."

"Christ, Emily..."

"I fixed it, I purged it from the system. Rewrote the logs. But she saw it. Even if it was just for a moment. And I don't know what she's doing with that. Yet."

Julia presses her lips together in thought. "She has a session this morning. I'll keep an eye."

"No," I say. "I need more than that. You need to steer her. Distract her. Talk to her about her Promotion"

Julia sighs. "I will speak to Daniel about it again before her session."

"That will give her something to hold on to," I say quickly. "hopefully she will forget about the report and focus on securing the position."

For a moment, Julia doesn't speak. She just looks at me with that therapist's expression that's usually reserved for clients. Like she's trying to see something underneath the words.

"I don't like this," she says finally. "It's dangerous." She presses the rim of her mug to her lips, but doesn't drink. Her hand trembles just slightly, enough to betray what her face won't.

"Everything we've done is dangerous," I snap back.

"She trusted you."

"She still does."

Julia gives a soft snort. "For now."

"I didn't want her to get caught in this."

"I know. You didn't choose her, not at first. But you didn't walk away, either." Julia says, not unkindly.

We sit in silence for a while. The quiet, oppressive weight of consequence hovering in the air.

Finally, Julia opens a drawer and pulls out Sarah's latest evaluation file. She taps it with one finger. "I'll reinforce her status with Daniel. I'll make sure she feels seen. Valuable. Not threatened."

"Good," I say, rising. "Because if she starts to pull at the threads, I might not be able to hold the whole thing together." Julia doesn't answer right away. She closes the file, then looks at me squarely. "I want to believe that you can stop this before it gets worse."

"I can't promise that," I say. She nods, once. A kind of understanding. Or surrender.

I leave the office, heart pounding. I know Julia will play her part. She always does. But I also know she is reaching her limit. The guilt is getting to her.

And if Sarah presses harder, if she asks the wrong questions in one of those soft-lit therapy sessions...

Well. That's why the bug is there. Just in case. Because I can't afford surprises. Not anymore.

~ 40 ~

At the end of the day, I bide my time. I watch the office empty out and the quiet settle in. I need to get this done quickly. In and out, no distractions, no complications. I still have to shower, change, and find something to wear that says clever but not calculating before Mark picks me up at 19:30. It's not like I'm nervous. This is still a strategy, after all. But I also don't want to show up with archive dust under my nails.

The air in the archive room is stale, warm with electronics and old paper, and the faint scent of toner clings to everything like a memory. I make sure the door closes softly behind me.

No one should be here. Everyone's either in meetings or already gone for the day. I check my watch. 17:42.

Plenty of time.

I head straight to the shelf where we keep the legacy finance boxes. The one I need is dull beige with the faded label FINANCE, scribbled on the top with marker. It's inconspicuous. Forgotten. A relic tucked beneath stacks of training audits and IT requisitions. No one touches these unless they're doing a system refresh or prepping for an external audit.

I don't know what exactly is in the box. I didn't stop to check the contents before, but I know it needs to go. Anything that might trace back to old project files, to early vendor entries, to training reimbursements rerouted through ZettaCore... it can't exist anymore. Not when Sarah is poking at threads. Not when Mark is asking questions I can't answer without revealing everything.

I slide the box off the shelf carefully, clutching it against my chest like it's something precious. It's heavier than I expected. I cradle it all the way up the corridor, nodding briskly at a passing cleaner who doesn't even glance up from her cart.

***

Julia's office is empty. Perfect.

I swipe the IT override badge and the lock disengages with a quiet beep. Julia won't be back tonight. Her schedule showed her last therapy session finishing at 15:30. She's long gone by now, probably sipping tea and pretending she doesn't have blood on her hands.

I step inside, careful not to disturb anything I don't have to. The lights are off, so I flick on the small lamp sitting on the coffee table between the two armchairs. It gives off just enough light to work by, not enough to cast shadows onto the frosted glass.

The shredder is already in place, discreetly positioned behind her desk chair. It's quiet, industrial. Fast.

I kneel beside it and open the finance box. The contents are a mess of manila folders, loose papers, and hand-clipped reports. It's worse than I thought. Sloppy. Dangerous.

I start feeding paper through without looking too closely.

First, a few nondescript folders. Expense summaries. Reconciliation reports. Standard junk. One after another, sheets disappear into the whispering teeth of the machine. I work methodically, careful not to jam the feed. I count to five between stacks, just like we were taught.

Then I find it. A soft-covered notepad shoved near the bottom of the box, nearly missed. Black, worn at the corners. No label.

I open it instinctively. My breath catches.

James Turner's handwriting.

My blood runs cold. I flip pages fast now, my pulse stuttering with each line. It's not just notes. It's a record. A timeline. A damn roadmap. It has everything if you know what you are looking at, dates, invoice numbers, names, his suspicions.

My fingers clench around the notepad. How did this end up here?

I rip each page out and shove it through the shredder as quickly as I can, as though every extra second those pages exist, is a gun pointing directly at me. I can hear my breathing now. Too loud. Unsteady. I count the seconds. One. Two. Three. Four. Five. Again.

The pages vanish. My heart doesn't slow. His voice, page by page, swallowed by the machine that already helped erase him once.

I fold up the black cover and place it in my pocket to dispose of in the larger waste bin outside. Too risky to leave anything here. Then I rush the rest of the box's contents through the shredder, financial statements, internal memos, even an unsigned approval slip I recognise from one of the manipulated training initiatives. I don't let myself stop. If I hesitate, I'll spiral. I can't afford to spiral. Not with Sarah questioning the same records. Not with Mark watching.

Every piece of paper carries weight. And guilt.

Finally, the box is empty. I wipe my hands on my skirt without thinking. My palms are damp.

I take a breath and glance around. Julia's desk is too clean. Everything is perfectly aligned. Just like it was the night we cleared out James's session records. The night she said, "He was unraveling, Emily. All I did was give him a nudge."

I remember looking at her then and feeling a flicker of something I hadn't let myself feel before. Fear and doubt. And it's back now, curling in my stomach like something living.

I close the office door behind me and step into the lift, exhaling as the soft hum encloses me. My fingers tap against my thigh. I glance at my phone. 18:13.

Still time to go home. Get changed. Pull myself together. Mark will be waiting. And I need to make sure he sees what I want him to see.

As I walk through the office, the late-daylight throws long shadows across the deserted floors. Everything feels stretched thin, like reality is papering over itself. I shove the notepad cover deeper into my coat pocket, gripping it like it might leap out and accuse me. I don't breathe until I hit the far bin near the service stairwell.

I swear I hear footsteps behind me, but when I turn, there's only the dim hallway and the soft whir of distant fans. Then, with one last look around, I toss the folded cover into the trash, then scatter a layer of rubbish over it. Gone. Finally.

I lean back against the wall for a second, the sound of my own heart thudding in my ears. That box was supposed to be benign. I thought I'd cleared every trace of James. But the fact that the notebook existed at all means there could be more I haven't seen. More he could have hidden. And if there is another one like it, If someone sees it, If Sarah sees it...

No. She won't. I'll make sure of that.

I push off the wall and keep walking.

The silence of the office after hours is almost sacred. No conversations. No interruptions. Just the quiet pulse of overhead lights and the low hum of servers deep in the walls. It's the only time I feel in control.

At my desk, I pull up a terminal and run one last diagnostic on the archive logs. The purge trail from today is clean. Untraceable. I double-check the batch timestamps. The modification entries. The clearance path through Julia's profile, re-routed through my credentials via a dummy proxy. Good.

I close everything, clear the cache, and lock the machine.

Then I head home.

Tonight I need to look like someone worth believing in.

Someone calm. Capable. Honest.

Someone Mark might fall for.

Someone Sarah will keep trusting.

And most importantly, someone who never had a hand in any of this.

~ 41 ~

Dinner is more perfect than I'd anticipated. Mark has taste. He takes me to that new place with the massive aquarium wall. The kind of place that tries hard to look effortless. Sarah would call it pretentious. I find it perfect. Expensive enough to matter, quiet enough to talk. The air feels fresh but not cold, and the lighting is dim enough to flatter but bright enough to read each other's expressions.

Mark listens. He laughs. He even orders dessert. He asks about my job, my family, my old university. Not just small talk. He isn't skimming. He is reading carefully. Trying to make sense of me. And I match him. Step for step. But beneath every conversation, there is a quiet hum of strategy. Because I know something he doesn't. I am studying him too.

I play the role well, interested, a little shy, and flattered. But the truth? I am watching him with the same clinical precision I use when combing metadata logs. Measuring reactions. Mapping blind spots. Filing away every tell.

But then there's the other truth, the one that gnaws quietly beneath the surface. I like him. More than I should. More than I can afford to. It hits me in subtle ways, how he holds the door open without making a show of it, how he genuinely listens when I speak, how he watches me like I'm a puzzle he wants to solve, not pick apart.

It terrifies me. Because I've spent so long being someone else. Wearing masks. Playing roles. And Mark... he makes me want to be real. He makes me wish I was just a normal girl on a normal date, leaning into something that feels like the start of something.

He tilts his head slightly when something surprises him. He glances to the left when he's buying time to think. His smile softens around people he respects, but with me, it seems to stay a little sharper, more controlled. There's something he's not saying. And I want to know what.

The walk afterwards feels like something out of a romcom. We stroll through the gardens that wrap around the square, soft fairy lights strung between lamp posts and trees. His hand brushes against mine before he finally threads our fingers together. For a brief moment, I let myself feel it. The warmth. The attention. The illusion of safety.

Then he gets a call.

He steps away without a word, posture rigid as he answers. I can't hear what is being said, but I watch his face change. All the softness drains out of it. His jaw tightens. His eyes flick to me once, quickly, like he's assessing something.

When he returns, he's wearing a different expression. Guarded. Calculating.

"Work," he says. But there's a pause before it. Like he's weighing whether to lie and something shifts in that moment. Not between us, not visibly. But inside me. A flicker of doubt. Or maybe recognition. Whatever that call was, it rattled him. And Mark doesn't rattle easily.

We part ways with a kiss on the cheek. At the end of the night, there is a moment, small, almost forgettable, when we are saying goodbye, and his hand lingers just a little too long on mine. And in that pause, in that stillness, I wonder if he felt it too. The unspoken calculation, or maybe something else entirely. Something almost tender. I'm not sure if it's strategy or something real. And that uncertainty terrifies me most of all.

***

The following afternoon, I step into Sarah's project room, still glowing from the night before. I can't help it. I feel light, energised in a way I hadn't in months. Even my reflection looked softer this morning. Less damaged, more disguised.

Sarah looks up from her screen, seeming a little distracted before smiling. "Soooo... how was your night?" she finally asks, voice laced with mischief.

"It was amazing," I say, grinning. And it was. It really was.

I fill her in on every detail of the night, the restaurant, the dessert, the walk through the park. I even exaggerate the way he looked at me. Sarah's teasing doesn't let up. She's practically vibrating with amusement.

"You like him," she says, nudging my arm. She laughs like there's nothing between us but trust. It makes me want to confess, even though I know I won't.

I scoff. "Maybe I just like expensive wine and handsome men in nice jackets."

Truthfully, I don't know what I'm walking into with Mark. If he knows something, if he suspects me, I have to be close enough to manage it. But there is another part of me, the part I keep buried deep, that wants him to see me. Really see me. For once.

I can't afford to fall for him. But the line between manipulation and something else is thinner than I want to admit. Sooner or later, one of us is going to slip and I honestly don't know which of us I'm rooting for.

~ 42 ~

That evening as I am waiting for Sarah to come over, I find myself scrolling through Mark's department logs. Not out of paranoia, at least, that's what I tell myself. It's due diligence. He handles systems I don't touch. The overlap is minor, but it exists. And if he's covering anything, I need to know.

But there's nothing overt. His activity is clean. No anomalies, no access outside of standard hours, no edits. But he's smarter than that. If he is digging, he could be doing it from another node, or using a mirrored profile.

I lean back in my chair and look around the room. It's too quiet. Too still. I hear my own thoughts louder than I'd like. I want to trust someone. But that instinct, however human, is a liability.

Looking at the clock, I pick up my phone and order a chinese for delivery and then get up to pour a couple of glasses of wine. Just as I am putting the bottle back in the fridge there is a knock at the door.

Sarah. Right on time. I open the door before she has got her spare key fully in the lock

"I need to talk to you," she says before she is even through the door. I study her face and the hollow feeling in the pit of my stomach returns as she finishes her sentence, "About James. About what he left behind."

I set the wine glass down without a word. and close the door behind us, flicking the lock, "Tell me everything." I say, though I'm not sure I want to hear the words I know are coming.

She talks. And I listen. Every word twists the knot in my stomach tighter. I need to get hold of this thumb drive, see everything that it contains. Who is Mallory? And more importantly, where is the trail James left behind going to take her? I need to make sure its path doesn't lead her directly to me.

I keep my face still. Concerned. Supportive. But inside, I'm screaming. Sarah doesn't know what she's found. Not yet. Not fully. But she's close. And I can't stop her without tipping my hand.

I nod at all the right moments. Offer ideas. Ask cautious, helpful questions. But my brain is racing.

If she finds out what I did... if she sees anything implicating me...

I sip my wine.

I don't have to pretend I'm as shocked and afraid as Sarah is, I am, but for different reasons. I feel my pulse thudding in my ears.

I have to stay ahead of her. Even if it means watching my best friend walk into something she'll never come back from. Because if Sarah finds out the truth, it won't just be her life unravelling, it'll be mine too.

I excuse myself briefly, disappearing into the bathroom. I stare at my reflection for a long time. My face is pale, a little too still. I splash water on it and breathe deep, slow. One step at a time. I just need to buy myself space. Time. Keep Sarah pointed in the wrong direction long enough to figure out what she knows and how to steer her off-course.

Back in the living room, I ask Sarah if she's brought the thumb drive with her, if I can see the files, but she hesitates. Trust, it seems, only goes so far.

A knock on the front door startles me, I notice Sarah looking at me as I flinch, before she stands up to retrieve dinner from the delivery driver.

We eat dumplings on the sofa like nothing's changed, but everything has. Every bite that sticks in my throat is a countdown.

If I'd just told her the truth a year ago... would she have helped me fix it instead of finding it?

When she gets up to leave, I offer to walk her to her car but she declines. I stand in the doorway and watch her go until she disappears around the corner. Then I close the door and lean against it, eyes shut.

I don't move for a long time. The wine sits untouched. My stomach churns. I should be working out the next steps. But all I can think about is Mark's voice. The flicker in his eyes. The way it felt to hold his hand. If Mark ever sees what I've done... would he still hold my hand?

There are too many variables. Too many risks.

And the most dangerous one of all is the girl who just walked out my front door.

My friend.

My undoing.

~ 43 ~

By the following morning I know I need to find out more, I need to be sure of exactly what Sarah has seen. My first call is the bug I planted in Julia's office. I listen to the recording with the volume low and my fingers curled around a chipped mug of tea I'll forget to finish. The playback is clear enough, the usual clinic mic quality, faint echo from the walls of Voss's office, but I only care about the words. About Sarah.

The file had landed in the directory sometime around noon. No alert. Just a quiet timestamp and a label: VOSS.10:30AM. I knew what it was before I clicked. And now, with Sarah's voice bleeding through my speakers, I press pause and breathe slow.

She sounds careful. Guarded. Smiling at things that don't deserve it. I can hear the tension in her voice, the way she couches her suspicion inside polite phrasing. Classic Sarah. Always playing fair.

Julia, though, she's slippery. Slips in a mention of Mark. I listen harder. Waiting for the crack.

But nothing useful comes. No names. No locations. Just the usual therapist murmurings and a few too-obvious redirections. Julia isn't dumb. She's pressing in a subtle way, but seems to be holding enough back not to raise direct suspicion.

I scrub backward through the recording and play it again.

Still nothing. No mention of the thumb drive. No files. No sign Sarah has pieced it together. But her voice, it's like flint scraping steel. She knows. She's circling it. And I'm running out of time.

I snap the laptop closed.

If she isn't going to say it, I need to see it. Which means finding that thumb drive.

I don't plan it. Not really. I just find myself putting on my coat, grabbing the spare key she gave me two years ago with a trust I never deserved. If she's home, I'll say I'm checking in after what she told me the previous night. But if she's not... well, then I will be free to look around. And I know the layout of Sarah's house as well as I know my own.

***

The street is quiet when I arrive. Her window is dark. No sign of movement. I knock anyway, wait the appropriate length, then slip the key into the lock and step inside.

Mushu is the first to greet me.

He stares from the arm of the couch like he knows exactly what I'm doing. His tail twitches once. Judging. Suspicious. I ignore him.

The place smells like cedar and chamomile and the faintest trace of Sarah's perfume. Everything is meticulously clean, of course it is, but I notice a coffee mug on the table, half-finished. She left in a hurry.

I don't know how long I have, but I move fast. I start with the obvious places. Drawers. Under the couch cushions. Behind the books on her shelves. Nothing. Her desk is locked. I pull out a tension wrench and pick, quick, practiced. Inside, papers, stationary, a passport.

In the bedroom, I lift her mattress, run a hand along the frame. Still nothing.

I try the closet next. Shoes aligned perfectly, color-coded blouses on felt hangers. It's like rummaging through a museum exhibit of Sarah's life. I kneel, press along the edges of the floorboard. There, one is loose. But inside is just an envelope of old letters and receipts.

I check behind the radiator, behind picture frames. Nothing. I even press gently along the seams of the baseboards, searching for any panel she might have manipulated. The silence feels accusatory, every tick of the clock counting down to discovery.

Either she's hiding it somewhere better, or she has it with her at all times.

I check the fridge. Nothing. I look in the freezer, a tub of ice cream. I stare at it, remembering last week, when we sat watching tv, with two spoons and the tub between us, two friends laughing, talking... I shake myself, I need to move on.

Back at the table, I open her laptop and check her recent files, network activity. There's nothing of interest. Nothing traceable.

I linger longer than I should. Just standing in the middle of the room, looking at the small pieces of her life I've always known but never studied quite like this. The throw blanket draped over the armchair. The stack of well-read books sitting under the coffee table. A small ceramic egg, with wire legs and glasses sits on her windowsill. There's a photo half-tucked behind the lamp. Sarah and I at the coast two summers ago. Sunglasses, wind-swept hair, her hand on my shoulder. I flip it face-down.

A lump rises in my throat. Because beneath the strategy, beneath the paranoia and the contingency plans, there is still a part of me that remembers when this was just friendship. When this was a second home. When I used to visit without a purpose. When Sarah's laugh didn't make me flinch with guilt.

But I need to know what she's hiding, and where she's keeping it. What files she's seen. Anything with a timestamp or metadata trail I can chase down later.

After I have exhausted all feasible hiding spaces, I walk towards the door. But I leave something behind.

Not because I'm careless. Because I want her to feel it. Just a little. The breath of someone else in the room. A drawer left open half an inch wider than before. The corner of a rug slightly curled.

A book not quite returned to the right angle on the shelf. Her search history cleared.

Let her feel watched. Let her believe the walls are closing in. Because if she starts looking over her shoulder, she might stop looking under her feet. And that's where I need to live, just beneath her line of sight.

Mushu gives a low, unimpressed meow as I step out of the front door. I crouch down and scratch behind his ears. "Keep my secret's safe, buddy."

He doesn't blink. Just watches me, sharp and silent, like he's memorising everything I touch.

I double-check the door. Everything locked. Everything set.

Outside, the air is damp. It smells like rain. I duck my head into my coat collar and start walking without knowing exactly where I'm going.

I pass the corner café where we once spent two hours debating whether The Moon Landing really happened. I cross the street where Sarah once saved a stray dog from traffic and insisted we follow it home. It all feels brittle now. Like a postcard from another life.

***

Back at my house, I make notes. Lists. What I've seen. What I haven't. Who Sarah might have shared files with. If she's found out who Mallory is, I'm already two steps behind.

The tea from earlier is cold. I drink it anyway.

On the screen, I bring up the recording again. Voss's voice this time. Smooth. Measured. I listen for cadence, for guilt, for the small inflections that might give her away. There's a part where she says, "Sarah, you're carrying a lot right now."

Yes, she is. And I'm the one who put it there.

My phone buzzes. A text from Mark. Just a smiley face and the words, "You okay?"

I stare at it longer than I should.

No, I think. I'm not okay. I'm threading needles through someone I love and hoping she doesn't realise I'm the one stitching the trap. I hover over the keyboard. He could be fishing. Or maybe he just misses me. I don't know which would be worse.

I text back "Yeah. Just tired. You?"

He responds "Same. Talk tomorrow?"

I reply with a thumbs up. Then silence.

I close my laptop and lean back, staring at the ceiling. The pieces are moving too fast and I fear that I will never catch up to Sarah.

I fall asleep with my clothes on, Mushu's cold eyes haunting me from memory. By morning, I know I'll have to do more than search her apartment. I'll have to start rewriting the game board entirely, because Sarah isn't circling the truth anymore, she's inside it and I'm running out of time.

~ 44 ~

The message comes through at 08:56.

"Hey, I'm not coming in today. Not feeling right. Please stop looking into anything, just for now. I'll explain when I can."

I stare at the screen longer than I should. The punctuation is off. No emoji. No casual sarcasm. No follow-up gif of a cat looking tragic under a blanket. Just plain text. Straightforward. Uneasy.

Something's wrong.

But the question is, *how* wrong? Is she genuinely sick, stress finally catching up with her, knocking her sideways with some psychosomatic flu? Or has she discovered something she doesn't want to tell me? Yet.

Either way, she's not in the office. That changes things. It gives me space. Space is an opportunity. And opportunity is something I can't afford to waste.

I reply with a careful balance of concern and distance.

"Totally understood. Rest up. Let me know if you need anything. x"

No questions. No pressure. Just enough warmth to sound real. Then I set my phone down and let my expression drop.

She doesn't want me to look into anything. *That* is what worries me most. Because if Sarah wants me to stop digging, it means she's already found something. Or she's waiting for something to fall into place.

I sip coffee that's gone cold and pull up the sandbox terminal on my laptop. The one I don't let connect through the standard VPN. I've used it before to test malware behavior, simulate audit traces, run invisible diagnostics. Today, it's going to serve a more creative purpose.

If the truth is coming, and I can feel it looming, then I need to make sure the story *around* the truth is shaped by my hands. I can't stop her from chasing breadcrumbs. But I *can* decide where they lead.

First step: Daniel.

The risk buffer logs from last year's Q2 cycle are easy enough to duplicate and modify. I open a secure log replica and begin inserting subtle inconsistencies, inflated approvals, erratic timestamps, just enough to suggest that Daniel may have overridden process checks manually. I keep the formatting exact. The language corporate. Routine. The kind of corruption that hides behind bureaucracy and boredom.

I tweak two signature strings, not forged, just re-sequenced. Something that would raise an internal flag *if* you were already looking. But to anyone else? Just admin noise.

Then I create a digital trace that leads to an overwritten file. Buried inside the Horizon_Q2_Review_2023 folder. I rework the permissions metadata to suggest Daniel accessed it late, on a Saturday, from his secondary terminal. It's subtle, hidden two layers deep in a mirrored audit node. But it'll show up to the right kind of search.

Second step: Julia.

This one takes finesse. I cross-reference her session records from the two-week window surrounding James Turner's final submission cycle. Then I inject a single trace, a deleted folder log tagged SessionEval_BetaReview_JTurner.docx. That filename is just close enough to real to get flagged. The deletion timestamp overlaps with a known wellness meeting.

The implication is clear: Julia saw it. She removed it. She interfered.

I log the deletion through a secondary credential, her old research assistant profile that should've been deactivated after the system refresh in January. It wasn't. I made sure of that months ago.

Then I tie both Julia and Daniel together with a subtle overlap, a single shared document stored in a deprecated collaboration folder. It's not real, but it references projects both of them have touched. I mask the authorship logs, but leave just enough signature to let suspicion creep in. It's a thread. And Sarah's going to pull it.

Breadcrumbs.

I make sure the access time overlaps with one of Julia's flagged therapy sessions. The implication is subtle but damning, she saw something, and she buried it.

***

By noon, it's done.

I sit back, the cursor blinking on a line of shell code. For a moment, I feel hollow. This isn't protection. It's a misdirection. I know that. But if Sarah keeps pulling the threads, this is the only way I survive what comes next.

I glance at my phone. No new messages. Nothing from her.

I think about texting Mark, then decide against it. I need distance today. I can't split my attention. I need Sarah to stay still long enough for the dust to settle.

I make myself a second coffee, then sit back at my laptop, I take a drink and burn my tongue. A painful reminder that i'm playing with fire

At 15:03 I get a ping, the sandbox confirms the planted logs have replicated successfully into the audit queue. It's perfect. Invisible to most. Irresistible to someone looking for irregularities.

All I have to do now is act surprised when someone finds them

***

By evening, I'm sitting in the quiet of my kitchen, dinner untouched, laptop closed. I've already memorised the story I'll tell if it comes to it. I'll act confused. Shocked. Concerned for Sarah. For the company. I could even suggest someone is trying to frame Daniel. That it must be external. That I just want to help. Or I could just sit back and let the cards fall, watching from a distance.

My phone buzzes again. I lunge for it, but it's just a weather alert. Storm incoming tomorrow.

Fitting.

I wonder if Sarah's asleep. If she's really sick. Or if she's staring at the ceiling, the same as I am, wondering who to trust.

She'll find the answer soon.

I just need to make sure it's the wrong one.

That night, I leave my laptop running. Set up a network monitor in the background to watch for any pings on the dummy file paths I've planted. If she starts digging again, I'll know.

I lie in bed with the lights off, eyes wide open, counting the seconds between each breath. I try not to picture Sarah at home, pulling apart Horizon_Q2_Review_2023, wondering why the numbers change when she runs a checksum.

I try not to picture Julia, watching everything come undone.

I try not to think about Mark at all.

But mostly, I fail. If he sees the wrong version of the truth first, I'll lose him before I even know if I had him.

I fall asleep with the sound of falsified data echoing in my ears like a lullaby made of lies.

***

In the morning, I wake before my alarm. Something cold and metallic has settled in my chest overnight. I move through the house like I'm underwater, shower, dress, brush my hair like it matters. Every motion mechanical, every moment a countdown.

The monitor shows no pings overnight. Sarah hasn't accessed anything new. But that doesn't mean she's let it go. It just means she's waiting. Maybe for someone to confirm what she suspects.

Or maybe, she's scared of what she'll find if she looks again.

I catch my reflection in the kitchen window. My face is pale, drawn, shadows under my eyes deepening by the day. It's the look of someone who's treading water to survive against an unrelenting undercurrent and I wonder how much longer I can keep this up.

Then I sit down. I log in and I start fabricating the next breadcrumb.

Just in case.

~ 45 ~

I'm standing in the kitchen, staring blankly at my mug of tea, when an unknown number flashes across my phone screen.

I answer on the second ring. “Hello?”

“Em, its me”

"Sarah?"

“Yeah. I... I'm safe.”

There's a pause on the other end, just a breath too long. "I need your help," she says. Her voice is raw and quiet. "I can't say much, not over the phone. Can you meet me? Somewhere public."

"Of course. When?" I say.

"Today. Late morning. I'll send a location."

"I'll be there."

I end the call and press my phone to my chest. I can hear my own heart pounding.

***

I walk past a secondhand bookshop and into the café. outside it is drizzling, but inside it is warm enough to steam up the windows. The decor is mostly reclaimed wood and the space is filled with the buzz of quiet conversations tucked between the hiss of the espresso machine. I order a cup of tea and take a seat. I am early. When Sarah walks in I stand up and hug her. “What the hell is going on?” I ask as she sits down opposite me. Her face is pale, tired, but she smiles when she looks at me, and for a moment it's almost enough to make me forget why we're really here.

“I can’t stay long,” Sarah says. “And I can’t tell you everything.”

“But something’s wrong.” I respond, my stomach turning. She's found something, I know it. I can tell from the look on her face.

She nods. “I’ve found something else. From James Turner. Remember him?”

My heart hammers in my chest as she says his name. “The Finance Director, the one with the video?...”

“Yes,” she cuts in. “He left something behind. I have part of it. I need help accessing a folder. It’s encrypted.”

I lean back, trying to mask my expression of terror to something more like concern. “Okay. You brought it?”

Sarah reaches into her coat, and slips the thumb drive to me beneath the table. “There’s a folder marked PRIVATE. That’s the one I need. Don’t touch anything else.” she says.

I pull my tablet and password breaker from my bag. "Password breaker. Brute force tool I use for field recovery testing" I say it casually, like it’s no big deal, and she nods, trusting me. That trust still stings.

As I plug in the cable and begin the decryption attempt, I open a separate shell window on my screen, masked under the decryption script. It’s clean, precise. Silent. While the decryption tool churns, I quietly clone the contents of the thumb drive into a secure directory on my machine. Partitioned. Hidden behind three layers of sandbox. No one would even know what I’m doing, even if they were watching over my shoulder. Especially not the woman sitting three tables back, half-tucked behind a newspaper.

I didn't notice her at first. Just a flicker of something, maybe the way she’s not reading the paper in front of her, or the slight shift in posture when I glance her way. She's well-dressed but understated, the kind of presence that’s meant to fade into the background. But there’s something too careful in the way she holds her coffee, too still.

Alex. I don't realise it's her until much later, but she's there. Watching. Blending. And she doesn't let me know she's seen me. That restraint is what confirms it.

"Here," I say to Sarah as the prompt disappears and a folder window opens on her screen. Inside were four files. One video. Two documents. One compressed archive. My hand hovers over the video file

"Wait," Sarah says sharply. And I freeze.

"I want to open that later. Alone."

Sarah notices my Frown as I respond, "Okay... but Sarah, what's in this? What are you chasing?" I need her to open up to me, to tell me what she knows, what she's seen.

She hesitates. Then, quietly, "I think..." Her voice falters for the first time. "I think someone got him killed."

I feel the bile rising in my mouth. She knows. She's closing in. Panic is wrapping itself around every bone in my body. I try to slow my breathing.

I turn back to my screen, praying that the clone operation has finalised. and is now sitting safely in my encrypted vault. I pull the thumb drive from the machine and hand it back to her.

"I won't look further. But if you want backup copies made, secure ones, I can help."

Sarah reaches out to touch my hand. "Thank you." she says, it's genuine and kind. so much more than I will ever deserve.

"Just... come back, okay? Don't do, whatever this is, alone."

The moment lingers. Then she smiles before standing up and hugs me again.

She leaves first. I stay a few minutes longer, pretending to check emails, but really I'm planning on watching the woman at the back. But Alex is gone. Just an empty cup and the paper still lying open, untouched.

I gather my things and walk out into the cold, heart thudding. Sarah has the key now.

But so do I.

***

Back at home, I lock the door behind me and pull down the shades. I move through the living room on autopilot, coat tossed, boots kicked off, laptop open before I've even boiled the kettle. I don't turn on any lights. The glow of the screen is enough.

The cloned directory opens with a password, and I watch as the four file names spill out again across my machine. It's surreal, like looking into someone else's memory and finding yourself tucked inside.

There's a copy of the audio file I almost opened. I don't listen to it. Not yet. My eyes skim the document names.

I open one of the documents, my eyes skimming the data. James had been watching earlier than I thought. He noted anomalies. Vendor inconsistencies. Even flagged one of the reroute paths I'd used during the early days of ZettaCore.

He wasn't just suspicious. He was methodical.

My name isn't mentioned explicitly, but the context hovers like a shadow. A reference to "non-compliant access reroutes" and "internal asset repointing" phrases only James would know how to phrase so precisely.

My chest tightens. I hover over the audio file. I hesitate, I don't click it. Not yet. Because if he named me, if he said it outright, this is all over.

I slam the lid of the laptop shut and press my hands to my face. This is bad. Worse than I expected. If Sarah reads this carefully, *really* reads it, there's enough here to raise questions. Not definitive proof, but enough to crack the walls I've carefully layered around myself. Enough to send her back into the archive logs. Into the hidden corners I've tried to seal.

And the audio file...

I need to prepare.

I open a text file and start writing everything I remember about James. Every detail. Every interaction. Every time I slipped and he might've seen. I need to know what he knew. What Sarah might see next. And more importantly, what I have to do to stop it.

***

Once I have finished, I know I need to listen to that audio file. Holding my breath I click it. The sound is scratchy. Poor quality. Old recording tech. Two voices, distorted, metallic. Altered. One is slightly deeper, more clipped. The other, urgent but hushed.

"She's not compliant."

"Mitchell?"

"Too clean. Too careful. We can't seed her directly."

"Then we duplicate her profile. Thread it through OPEX. Have it routed by Monroe's old chain."

"She's already connected to Lewis. Too close."

"Keep her distracted, promise of a promotion?"

"In progress."

The file cuts out.

My stomach turns to ice. I know this conversation. Not word for word, but I know it. The tone. The rhythm. The strategic shorthand. The manipulation disguised as procedure. I was in that room. Or on that call. I *was* one of those voices. And the other, Julia.

My breath catches. My hands go cold. It's us. But the distortion works. It blurs the edges. Masks the identities just enough. The voices could be anyone. Electronic ghosts.

But I *know*. I *remember*.

Sarah could hear this. *Has* heard it, maybe. And if she connects the dots, if she *recognises* the cadence, the phrasing, the clipped way I pronounce certain words...

I push my chair back from the table, heart racing.

She can't know. Not yet. Not like this. The audio is vague, abstract enough not to be damning unless she starts lining it up with everything else. With the files. The logs. The patterns.

I scrub my hands over my face and stare at the waveform on my screen. My name isn't said. But my voice. *My voice*, is there.

I should delete it. But I don't. Instead, I bury it deeper. Encrypt the clone again. Hide it behind another firewall.

I tell myself it's just in case. Just in case Sarah *does* recognise it and I need to know what she knows.

But the truth is simpler.

I'm scared.

Scared of her hearing what I hear. Scared of losing what little time I have left. Scared, most of all, of what happens if she stops trusting me. Because once she does... There's no coming back.

~ 46 ~

I barely sleep. The audio file plays on a loop in my head, distorted voices, mine among them, saying things I can't take back. It haunts me through the restless hours of the night and into the grey quiet of morning. By the time I'm at my desk, caffeine pumping through my bloodstream like a poor substitute for courage, I'm still shaking.

I keep seeing Sarah's face from the café, soft in the light, trusting. The image now feels so fragile. Like something I could shatter just by breathing wrong.

My stomach knots as I step out of the lift and into the office corridor. The hum of the fluorescents is too loud. My shoes sound like sirens on the polished floor. And then I see her through the windows of the Project Room.

Sat at her desk. Her posture is relaxed, one hand curled around a pen, tapping it rhythmically against a notepad. No laptop open yet. Just the quiet ritual of settling in. But it feels like the floor drops out from under me. She's here.

Has she listened? Maybe not. Maybe she hasn't played the file yet. Maybe she doesn't know.

I move toward the break room on autopilot. My hand trembles slightly as I reach for the cup. I pour her coffee, the good one, she always says, from the little French press I keep hidden behind the sink. Then I grab a blueberry muffin from the stash I keep in the top cupboard. She always reaches for blueberry.

With each step back to her desk, my pulse quickens. I have rehearsed this. Keep it normal. Keep it casual. Do not let her see the cracks.

"I brought you the good one," I say, holding out the coffee and muffin like offerings to a god I have betrayed, and who might know it.

Sarah looks up, startled for half a second, then smiles. "Thanks. I needed it."

Her eyes are tired, a little dull. But there's no sharpness. No suspicion. No recognition.

Not yet.

I set the cup and muffin on her desk gently, and ask, "You okay?"

She lets out a quiet huff of breath, more amused than anything. "Define okay."

We share a look, and I let my hand brush hers, solidarity, comfort, familiarity. A practiced gesture, but one that hits me harder than I expect.

"Glad you're back," I say. Then I lower my voice, watching for a sign, any sign, she suspects me. I need her attention elsewhere. Anywhere but on me. "Mark's been twitchy since you vanished."

That makes her blink. "Twitchy?"

I nod. "After you called out sick, he started asking questions. About project files. Audit trails. Way more than usual. It felt like he was... looking for something."

Sarah frowns, thoughtful now. Exactly what I need.

"He's acting weird," I continue, keeping my voice low but urgent. "I don't trust it. But ignore me, I'm looking at everyone differently since we met."

I drop my hand from hers, step back slowly. My heart is hammering again. Every word I just spoke was calculated. Each one a seed. Each one leading her somewhere that isn't me. She watches me go with a puzzled look. But not an accusing one.

I make it back to my desk without collapsing. The door hisses shut behind me, and I exhale. I take my seat and I push into the secure test environment server logs, building more misdirection. I want her to find this part eventually, on her own. But she needs a trail.

When I am done I grab my tablet and head back to the Project Room, I'm surprised to see Mark standing next to Sarah's desk. I feel myself tense. What is he saying to her? It could be nothing... But what if it's not?.

I take a breath and walk into the room, Mark flashes me a look I can't quite put my finger on, setting my pulse racing. Guilt or attraction, I'm not sure.

"Sarah, did you see the test server errors that came in when you were off? There's a weird IP pinging internal logs."

Sarah makes her way over to me and I angle the tablet so she can see the data I have spent the last hour fabricating.

Mark heads towards the door, he smiles at me as he leaves, it feels genuine and I feel a flutter in my stomach, despite myself.

She checks the audit logs I planted, she sees that same IP interacting with the deprecated Horizon Alpha file structure, she finds Mark's secondary credentials buried in the approval logs from last year, she's starting to build the picture I want her to see.

***

As I return to the rhythm of my workday, keyboard clacking, spreadsheets ticking, meetings filled with too many acronyms and too few answers, the echo of that audio file still haunts me.

"Keep her distracted..."

It could be anyone's voice. But I *know* it's mine. I can feel the shape of it in my throat, like a bruise.

If Sarah ever listens to it again, *really* listens, if she slows it down, filters it, cleans it, uses one of the NexTech audio tools we both know how to access...

She'll know.

Or she might suspect.

And that's enough to end me.

So I have to stay ahead. I have to make sure that what she hears next is louder than anything I've said before. Distraction. Doubt. Distance.

I check the cloned files again at lunch. James's folders are clean, organised. There's a new unease building in my gut, not because of what's there, but because of what *isn't*.

What else did he know? What else did he give her?

***

I take a walk around the block after work. Not to clear my head, nothing could do that right now, but to test if I'm being followed. A woman with a navy umbrella crosses the street just before I do. Not unusual. But when I pause at a bookshop window, so does she. When I speed up, she doesn't. She just disappears.

Alex is out there. Somewhere. Watching.

She hasn't approached me. But I feel her in the negative space. The empty chair in the café. The silent corner of the lift. The reflection in the glass when I'm not expecting it.

There are too many players now. Too many threads.

***

When I get home, I load the waveform again. The audio file. I lower the volume, just to hear the cadence. It's still there. That terrible, damning rhythm. I turn it off.

I need to plant more seeds, make their guilt undeniable.

Hours have passed by the time I shut down my laptop, lock my front door, and climb into bed.

The room is quiet. But in my head, I'm still in that café. Watching Sarah watch the screen. Watching myself betray her with every calm word. And knowing I'll do it again tomorrow. Because I have to. Because she can't know. Not ever.

~ 47 ~

The following day, I leave the note on Sarah's monitor like I've done a dozen times before. Neat handwriting. A tone that says "routine" without inviting questions.

Meeting in the sub-basement server room. IT audit. E x

It's believable. Dull. Perfect. She'll probably roll her eyes and heat up her lunch in the microwave that burns the edges of everything. I can almost hear her now: "*You always get the glamorous assignments.*" It hurts how easy it is to imagine that. It hurts more knowing it might be the last time she looks at me without suspicion.

I walk past our favorite vending machine on my way out of the third-floor hallway, the one with the ancient honey-roasted peanuts she buys when she's too stressed to eat real food. The sight of it makes my throat tighten. It's strange what details you cling to when you feel the ground shifting beneath you.

Today, I'm not walking towards routine. The building I enter is one of NexTech's overlooked outposts, a gray-glass husk buried in the shadows of its glossier siblings. No reception. No cameras in the foyer. Just badge access and silence. The kind of place you only learn about when someone asks you for a new mouse or monitor, or you need an extra HTML cable for one of the meeting rooms.

Inside, the corridor is uncarpeted. Every step echoes like a reminder that I'm alone in this. That this meeting, unofficial and unlogged, doesn't just bend protocol. It eviscerates it.

Room 3 looks like it should be filled with forgotten chairs and busted AV cables. Instead, Dr. Julia Voss waits inside, seated with her back to the vent, the same pale-coffee blazer I've seen her wear a hundred times, and an expression as blank as a whiteboard. She doesn't rise. She doesn't gesture. She simply watches me enter with that same unsettling calm.

She nods, once. "Emily."

"Julia." My voice feels like it doesn't quite belong to me. I sit across from her. No handshake. No smile. The silence stretches.

"I assume this is about Sarah," she says. "She's too close." I let the words hang, unadorned. "She's asking questions about other budgets and financial reports. She's flagged two offshore routing chains. She hasn't named ZettaCore yet, but she's seen the Liechtenstein link. It's a matter of time."

Julia raises an eyebrow, her face unreadable. "And you've tried to misdirect her?"

"Extensively. I've planted fabricated anomalies, noise around Mark, noise around Daniel. I've twisted the logs inside out. But she's not letting go."

Voss leans back, steepling her fingers beneath her chin. "Because she trusts you."

"She did," I say. "I don't know if that's still true."

"Then this is the moment," Julia says. "Before she finds her footing." A pause. "She hasn't gone to anyone yet," I add. "She's just... looking."

"For now," Julia replies. She slides a folder across the table. Thin. Clinical. Efficient. I don't reach for it.

The label reads:

Provisional Exit Strategy: Horizon Division – Staff Level D

Inside, I already know what I'll find. A resignation template, post-dated. Severance terms. HR flags. Scripts for the termination call. Offboarding instructions for IT. The digital equivalent of slipping out a side door and never being heard from again.

"Same protocol as Monrow," Julia says calmly. "She's made herself a liability. We respond quietly, effectively. She gets a story that makes sense. We keep control."

I stare at the folder like it might burn me. "She's not Monrow."

"She's a risk."

"She's my friend."

"I know she is, which is precisely why she's dangerous. She knows enough to keep digging, and you won't stop her." I shake my head, slow. "Let me try again. I can divert her attention. Give her something else to chase." Voss raises a brow. "Mark?"

"He's already suspicious in her mind. I can solidify that. Give her a pattern to track that ends nowhere."

"And when that doesn't work?"

"Then we reevaluate," I say, hearing the shake in my own voice.

"She has access, Emily. Raw logs. Archive snapshots." I go cold. I curse silently. Sloppy. Too fast. Too much pressure lately.

"If she finds the full context..." I don't finish the sentence. I don't need to.

"She'll unravel the entire architecture. ZettaCore. Horizon. The wellness funnel. You. Me. Daniel. And she'll do it believing she's saving people."

"And you're proposing we make her disappear."

"Discreetly," Voss corrects. "Like we did with Alex. No threat. No accusations. Just a quiet exit and a generous severance."

"Alex didn't deserve that."

"She was going to talk, she knew too much." Julia says sternly. "And now Sarah is treading the same path. and they all lead to us. Do you want us to be found out Emily? because that's what you are risking."

I go silent.

Julia's gaze is sharp. "You want Sarah to keep her job? Then stop her. Or she won't have one."

I reach for the folder slowly. But my hand doesn't land. "I don't want to be the one who does this."

Julia tilts her head, almost sympathetically. "No one ever does."

"I need more time."

"Time for what?"

"To spin the web tighter. Give her just enough evidence to think she's winning. Let her go after Mark. Let her bury herself in the wrong narrative."

Julia considers. "How long?"

"the end of the week"

She's quiet. Then... "That's all you'll get."

The folder stays on the table between us. I don't take it. I don't touch it. But its weight settles in my chest like a stone.

Outside, the sky is cruelly blue. I stand on the pavement and press my phone to my chest. It buzzes with a new message from Sarah:

"Lunch was boring without you. Hope the servers didn't explode."

I want to scream. I want to tell her everything. I want to drag her out of this company and into the light before I become the next shadow over her shoulder.

Instead, I type, "Still stuck in the basement. You didn't miss much."

She sends back a laughing emoji.

I almost drop the phone.

Back at my desk, I sit in silence. The folder may be gone, but the ultimatum has teeth. Seventy-two hours.

I open the terminal window again. Start scanning last year's Q2 logs. Mark's entries. Daniel's credentials. I begin to bend the shapes of their data.

I keep telling myself it's a net. Something to slow Sarah down. But maybe it's a veil. Maybe I'm not trying to protect her at all.

Maybe I'm just trying to give her a reason to stop looking, before Voss gives her no choice at all.

~ 48 ~

The office is quiet now, it has a kind of hush that wraps itself around you like static. The kind of silence that doesn't feel peaceful, it feels loaded. Full of things unspoken, unfinished. I've been running on fumes since the meeting with Julia. The sticky note I left on Sarah's monitor like it was nothing. Like I hadn't just spent an hour discussing her potential erasure from the company she's sacrificed everything for.

***

By the time I make it home, the sun is long gone, and the sky is the color of static on a broken screen. I drop my keys on the counter. Kick off my boots.

The glow of my laptop screen feels like a beacon in the darkness, something alive and waiting.

I sit.

I work.

My fingers move almost automatically now. The rhythm of fabrication is familiar, nauseating in its predictability. I start with the logs, nothing flashy, nothing too bold. It's about layering. Subtle misdirection.

A login from Daniel's terminal at 03:11 a.m. last year, well outside his usual hours. I backdate it through one of the admin override tunnels I used during the ZettaCore reroutes. I layer in a request for expense clearance on a dummy training invoice.

Amount £17,280. Large enough to matter. Small enough to pass under the quarterly radar.

I pull up Mark's digital signature history. Reconstruct a chain from his approvals in the Horizon subgroup from six months ago. Duplicate the pattern but alter the timestamps. Just enough overlap to suggest awareness, collusion. One approving the route, the other pushing the funds. The implication is clear if you know how to look, they worked together.

They didn't. Not really. But that doesn't matter anymore. The trick is always in the metadata. That's where truth dies, or is born. I seed overlaps in system access logs, reroute packets through the asset tags that were decommissioned six months ago. Sarah's own login appears once or twice, just briefly. A blink. Enough to muddy the water.

Nothing will point to me.

Not this time.

I check the system time: 02:42 a.m.

I should sleep. My muscles are starting to ache from the way I've been hunched over the keyboard. My eyes burn. But adrenaline is a cruel god, it never gives back what it takes.

I scroll through the fabricated logs again, checking alignment. The records now show that Mark accessed the backup server for Horizon Alpha in April, just before Daniel submitted the quarter review. There's even a local copy saved to a folder that never really existed. I seed a system error log to reference it.

Then I build in a trace of a reimbursement request from Daniel's profile, approved under Mark's VPN route, for travel to "client engagement, Luxembourg." Tied to a vendor that doesn't exist. Wrapped in wellness funding.

My code compiles cleanly. No errors.

By now, my hands are shaking slightly from fatigue and too much caffeine. I've drained two mugs and half a thermos. I reach for the remainder of the coffee and sip, its cold. The taste is bitter and wrong, but it's something to do with my hands.

The deeper I go, the more tangled it becomes. The narrative I'm building is nearly airtight. Mark and Daniel, financial collusion, hidden vendor routing, unauthorized system access. With the breadcrumbs I planted earlier this week, Sarah won't need much more convincing.

I'm making them the villains.

And maybe, in their own way, they are. Daniel's been exploiting the promotion pipeline for years. Mark's been quiet and clever about what he touches, what he questions. I don't know why yet, but they're not innocent.

I tell myself I'm not doing this because I want to. I'm doing this to survive.

03:09 a.m.

I blink hard. The screen swims for a second. I minimise the logs and just... stare at the desktop.

My reflection catches in the black void of a dormant secondary monitor. Pale. Hollowed out. My eyes looking increasingly sunken, like I've been sick for a week, not spinning digital thread into lies that will shape the downfall of two careers. Possibly three. Maybe more. I wonder if Mark would see the patterns I've built, or if he'd see me inside them.

It wasn't supposed to be like this.

I slam the laptop shut before I can spiral.

What kind of person have I become?

I asked Julia that once. During the James fallout. I'd sat across from her in that sterile office, eyes bloodshot, hands still shaking from wiping a system that should've never existed.

And she'd looked at me, calm, always calm, and said, "You did what was necessary."

It was meant to comfort. But it didn't. Because what if "necessary" is just a prettier word for monstrous?

What I've done tonight... it's not just manipulation. It's character assassination. I am rewriting reality, I know that they don't deserve it, no matter how many times I try to justify it to myself. But I need to make sure the blast radius doesn't reach me.

I close my eyes and think about Sarah. Her smile when she laughed over ramen two weeks ago. The way she touched my hand in the café, grateful, trusting.

I can still feel the shape of her hand holding the thumb drive, cold plastic. Solid. Like truth in miniature, which she passed to me with the ultimate trust. Trust I will never deserve. I still see the files, the raw data. She's close. She doesn't know how close. But she will get there soon.

And when she does, I don't know what I'll do.

Because I care about her. I care so much it hurts. And that's the cruelest irony of it all. She's the only one I never meant to lie to. But now, she's the only one I can't afford to tell the truth.

I push out of the chair and walk to the kitchen, the motion sluggish. I fill a glass of water and drink it slowly. My hands are trembling. My pulse is still racing.

I return to the desk. Reopen the laptop. Everything is saved. Archived. Synced to an encrypted sandbox that will self-wipe if tampered with. I've done my due diligence. Laid the landmine. All I have to do is wait.

The last thing I do before shutting everything down is scroll through my notes on Sarah's behavior, keywords she's searched, files she's accessed, phrases from Julia's session logs.

She's not letting this go. Even if I buy myself another week... she'll keep digging. And eventually, she'll dig me up. I can't decide if I want her to or not.

It's 03:27 when I finally shut the system down and crawl into bed, fully clothed again. The sheets are cold. I lie there staring into nothingness, counting seconds between thoughts, waiting for sleep. The last thing I hear before I drift into a fitful half-dream is the echo of my own voice from the audio file, warped and distant: "Keep her distracted..."

But how long can I?

And what happens when I can't?

~ 49 ~

The audit entries I'd manipulated the previous night were intricate, cross-linked, timestamped, and masked in layers of believable logic.

I should feel triumphant.

Instead, I feel... Empty.

By the time I get to the office, the lights feel too sharp, the voices too loud. I step into the bathroom and splash my face with cold water, I need to look believable.

My hands grip the travel mug like a lifeline as I walk toward the Project Room, every step weighted with what I am about to do.

Sarah is already there, hair pinned up, sleeves rolled back, brows drawn together over some report. She looks tired but focused. Resilient.

When she sees me, she smiles. "Morning," I say brightly, then lowering my voice. "I've been busy."

I set my tablet on the table beside her, hoping that she doesn't notice my trembling fingers. Or if she does, she takes it as excitement and not nerves. I try not to think about what I've done. I try not to look at her face.

"What is it?" she asks, leaning closer.

I pull up the document recovery log first. The one I'd spent hours crafting down to the last metadata signature.

"I found this last night," I said. "Old log. It shouldn't exist anymore, which is why it stood out."

Sarah leans in, her eyes scanning the screen. The document header looks benign. Just code, server logs, time stamps. But I watch her expression shift as she hits the part I'd planted. Unauthorized access attempts, audit trail inconsistencies, and buried deep in a document recovery log, two names.

Daniel Reed.

Mark Bishop.

Her voice is quiet. "Where did this come from?"

"The audit cache," I say. "Old server backups. Things no one ever checks unless they're bored or suspicious."

She doesn't say anything for a moment.

"Are you saying they tampered with the files?"

"I'm saying, there's a log entry showing Mark accessed the project financials folder after the board signed it off. And Daniel approved an internal transfer that doesn't exist on our end."

Sarah leans back, lips pursed. "So they're both involved."

"I think so."

But I also know that *I* had built this implication. I have written the guilt across their names like a surgeon crafting evidence out of tissue and blood. Daniel has his sins, yes. Mark has his secrets. But what I've constructed was something else. A trap. One with Sarah's trust at the center of it.

"Why didn't you tell me this yesterday?" she asks, and my heart skips a beat, knowing that the reason I didn't tell her earlier, is because earlier this didn't exist.

"I needed time to confirm it wasn't just noise.." She is too focused to notice the tremor in my voice or the exhaustion in my bones.

She found what I wanted her to find. The right names. The right timestamps. The right ghosts.

I go back to my desk and stare at the wall for ten straight minutes.

I should feel better. But all I feel is... the weight of her trust. Of the lie. Of the next step I was already planning.

That evening, Mark texts, "Dinner? My turn to pick. Something quieter."

I hesitate for exactly three seconds before replying. "Sure. Send me the time."

I don't want to go, I just want to sleep. But I have to. I need to know what he knows. Or doesn't.

***

The restaurant he's chosen is tucked into a quiet street, a converted townhouse with soft lighting and exposed brick. Small tables. Cloth napkins. Muted jazz.

Intimate.

Mark is already there when I arrive, seated at a corner table with a glass of wine already in front of him. He stands when he sees me, ever the gentleman, and pulls out my chair.

"You clean up well," he says with a smile. "You've said that before." I laugh. "Still true." I let the smile touch my face.

The server brings wine. Then water. For a while we talk about unimportant things, film recommendations, office politics, a ridiculous story about someone stealing the third floor's milk frother.

Then, slowly, I pivot.

"Do you remember the old training logs?" I ask. "The ones from Horizon's alpha cycle?"

Mark tilts his head. "Why?"

"I came across something weird yesterday. Made me think of those legacy approvals. I didn't realise you ever worked with that team."

"I didn't, not directly," he says. "I inherited some of the database scaffolding. Why?" His voice is easy. "Just curious," I say. "Have you ever worked with Dr Voss?"

"Only during compliance reviews. She's intimidating. And a little... opaque." He isn't lying. Not exactly. But he's editing.

"And Daniel?" Mark pauses. "Daniel likes to be the smartest person in the room. Doesn't matter what the meeting is about." he says shrugging. I look down at my glass. "You know," I say casually, "you deflect better than most people I know."

He laughs, but then he looks at me more closely. "And you ask better questions than most of our auditors." There it is again. The *almost* compliment. The challenge buried in velvet.

I smile. "That's because I never liked auditors."

Mark watches me for a second longer than feels comfortable. I can't tell if he is trying to read me, or just trying to anticipate what I will ask next. Either way, I'm not sure I like what he sees.

After dinner, we walk in the cool night air, our shoulders occasionally brushing. I don't speak. I don't want to break the silence. I am listening too closely to the sound of my own heartbeat.

When we reach the edge of the park, he stops. "I like you," he says.

"I know."

He smiles. "I mean it."

"I know that, too." I laugh.

He looks at me, searching. "But I feel like there's a part of you always standing five steps behind your own shadow."

I blink. "That's a poetic way to say I'm distant."

"It's not distance," he says. "It's something else. Like you're always watching yourself. Like you're afraid of what happens if you stop."

I don't answer. Because he is right. Because he isn't just looking at me. He is *seeing* me. And I hate it. Not because it is wrong. But because it isn't.

I kiss him before we part. Just enough. A promise. A diversion. I need him close, but not too close.

I watch him walk away. And for the first time, I'm not sure who is playing who.

***

Back at home, I stare at my laptop, then close it without opening the cloned folder. I can't face it. Not tonight.

Because if I look too closely, I might start asking questions I don't want answers to.

Like: *What if Mark isn't guilty? What if I just made him look that way?*

Or worse: *I lose not only my friend, but a real chance of happiness. Or at least the scraps of happiness I could cling onto.*

~ 50 ~

The following day I sit in the IT room, when Sarah finds me, eyes still a little red from whatever Julia has said during their session. She's holding her coffee like it's the only thing anchoring her to reality.

"I need you to see something," she says, breathless. She holds out some strips of paper, her hand trembling as she does.

I glance at them and my heart instantly starts to hammer against my chest. "She had his notes?" I breathe, knowing exactly where they came from. "She shredded them?"

I feel my expression harden. I had warned Julia, explicitly told her to dispose of them and she hadn't listened.

"When I was in Dr Voss's office today," she begins slowly, "I dropped my notebook while I was leaving. Bent down to pick it up and... I saw something under the shredder bin."

My mouth is dry. I don't speak.

"I couldn't get all of it, I didn't have much time. But it looked like pages. Torn. Partially shredded. Some of the corner bits had handwriting."

"James?" I ask, keeping my voice low, careful.

Sarah nods. "There were words I recognised, internal routing, project codes. It looked like part of his notebook. I couldn't read much, but I'm sure of it. She's in this."

I let my shock register just slowly enough. Not too much. Just enough for her to believe it. "Are you sure?" I ask. "That it wasn't something else?"

"I know his handwriting," she says firmly.

I nod, slow, measured. "Did you tell Dr Voss?"

She snorts. "No. All that would do is alert her to the fact that I am looking. Right now she is in the dark and I need it to stay that way."

I give her a look of concerned solidarity. But all I can think about is the god damn shredder. The one in Julia's office. The one I used.

The moment Sarah heads off to grab her second coffee, I leave. No hesitation.

The walk across the building to the lower floors feels longer than usual. I flash my access card. No one asks questions. No one stops me. Juila's door is closed, but not locked. When I enter, she doesn't even look surprised.

"Emily," she says without turning from her screen. "To what do I owe the pleasure?"

"You left evidence," I hiss, closing the door behind me.

That gets her attention.

"Evidence?" She repeats calmly. "You're going to have to be more specific."

"Shredded pages. The ones I told you to get rid of." I snap. "From the notebook. Sarah found scraps under your bin."

"I know."

The admission cuts through me. "You, what?"

"She knocked the bin," Voss says smoothly. "It tipped slightly. Some shreds escaped. She didn't even realise she had done it. I've gathered the rest of them. She's hunting Emily. She might've seen something, but there is no real evidence."

"I don't care that there is no evidence. You said you'd get rid of it."

"I forgot," she says evenly. "I had a busy schedule and I didn't expect her to come in and start snooping around."

I step closer, fury rising in my chest. "I told you to destroy everything. Properly. You said you'd double-check."

"You insisted on using the shredder. You should have got rid of it, or you should have burned it."

"You wanted a fire in your office?" I snap.

"I wanted certainty," she replies, folding her hands calmly on the desk. "But you made the decision. This is the consequence."

"You're playing semantics."

"No," she says with terrifying calm. "I'm playing survival chess. Same as you."

For a moment, I just breathe. In. Out. Trying not to explode. My hands are shaking.

"This was sloppy," I finally say, voice low.

Julia raises a brow. "And whose hands were on those pages, Emily? Mine? Or yours?"

I want to scream. Instead, I turn and pace to the window, watching people walk across the carpark, unknowing, innocent, irrelevant. I feel like a balloon stretched to the point of tearing.

"If she puts the pieces together... I've spent hours manipulating the truth"

"She won't," Voss interrupts. "Not fully. Not unless someone confirms what she suspects."

That cuts too close to the truth. I whirl back toward her. "She's smart. She's methodical. And she cares. That makes her dangerous."

Voss watches me for a beat. Then she nods, just once. "I agree."

I don't sit. I can't. My limbs are tight coils of tension. The walls of this office feel too close, too clinical. This was supposed to be under control.

"You told me you were monitoring her. Watching what she accessed. Did you see her take anything else?" I say, my thoughts spiralling.

"No," Julia replies. "Her behavior is focused, not erratic. She's following a trail, but she hasn't deviated from it. Not yet."

"She found the shreds."

"And told you, didn't she?"

I stop. She has a point. She is still coming to me. But it doesn't matter. Every time I misdirect Sarah, it only buys a little more time. She always circles back. She always re-checks.

"What happens when she finds something we can't explain away?" I whisper.

Julia folds her arms, but says nothing. I turn to the door. "Emily," she says quietly. "Don't let guilt make you reckless." I freeze. Too late.

She continues, "You care about her. That's obvious. But care doesn't undo what's already in motion."

I leave without another word. My silence feels heavier than any threat I could make.

***

Back at my desk, I sit numbly for a while. Just... existing. I imagine Sarah in the Project Room scribbling something into a notebook, jaw set with concentration. I wonder if those scraps are still on her mind. If she's turning them over in her memory like puzzle pieces that almost fit.

I open a new terminal window, start running basic queries on archive data again. Not because I need to, but because doing something feels better than sitting still.

The reality is sinking in, I've lost control of the cleanup. It was never meant to spiral like this. I remember the first time I rerouted a training fund. The thrill of it. The elegance. Not just stealing, solving. Like finding music inside code.

It's not music anymore. It's noise. Panic. Mistakes. I keep hearing Sarah's voice from earlier, soft and low: "I know his handwriting."

Of course she does. She's seen enough of it by now..

If she hadn't believed in me, this wouldn't hurt as much. But she did. She still does. At least for now. And I'm going to keep lying to her.

I pull up the internal risk audit logs. Begin masking my old accesses again. Deeper this time. I route one through an obfuscated sandbox environment. Strip another of its user tags completely. I'm covering my tracks. I'm erasing myself.

I close the terminal window. My fingers linger over the keyboard. I think of Sarah's face when she spoke to me that morning. She wasn't angry. She wasn't accusing. She was worried. She still thinks I'm on her side. And for as long as I can keep it that way, maybe I still have a chance to survive this. But part of me isn't sure I deserve to.

~ 51 ~

That evening I'm staring down a choice I don't want to make.

I've been sitting in front of a muted TV, laptop on the arm of the sofa with a blank document open for twenty-five minutes. Not to fabricate anything, not this time. Not yet. It's just the blinking cursor and me, and this thought I can't shake. Maybe I need to try something else. Something honest.

I've tried misdirection. Planting evidence. Scrubbing logs. Weaponizing Sarah's trust. But she's not stopping. If anything, she's accelerating. She's pulled enough threads that I can feel the pressure on the web I've spun. It won't hold forever, no matter how carefully I crafted it. One more clue, one more mistake, hell, one more memory she manages to stitch together, and it could all fall apart.

She's smart. Too smart.

And the worst part? She still thinks I'm on her side.

There's a version of this where I just... tell her to stop. Not because I need to throw her off the trail, but because I'm genuinely afraid for her. Julia's already talking about cutting her out, watching everything through more layers than I can map. And I, well, I'm tired. So tired that my bones ache when I climb the stairs in the morning. So tired I forget if I've eaten. Or what day it is.

I've spent weeks becoming someone I barely recognise. Maybe what Sarah needs isn't misdirection. Maybe she just needs a friend to look her in the eye and tell her it's time to stop.

I don't expect her to listen. But I have to try.

I arrive earlier than usual, the building still caught in the lull before the buzz kicks in. The corridor lights flicker like they always do near the elevator, another thing on the never-ending maintenance backlog. I don't head to the IT Room. I take the internal route, cutting through Finance, then past HR, until I reach the Project Room.

Sarah's already there.

She's hunched slightly, head down, her laptop is closed beside her, but I can see the way her body tenses in rhythm. She's not relaxing. She's calculating. And I know that rhythm too well, it's what I do when I'm building a lie so carefully I forget to breathe.

She doesn't notice me at first, so I knock gently on the open door. "Got a minute?"

She glances up. Her smile flickers across her face like a breeze over still water, barely there, but visible.

"Of course," she says. "Come in."

I walk in slowly, cradling two coffees. "I brought reinforcements."

She chuckles and takes the cup I hand her, eyeing it like it might carry answers in the foam. "You always bring the good stuff when you're about to ask me something difficult."

"I'm not," I lie.

She raises an eyebrow.

I settle into the chair beside her and let the silence hang for a moment. The air between us is different now, charged, wary, like glass under pressure.

"I've been thinking about that scrap you found," I say finally, keeping my voice low.

She doesn't pretend not to know what I mean. Her eyes sharpen slightly. "From Dr. Voss's office."

I nod.

We sit in stillness, the clink of her spoon stirring the coffee the only sound.

"I'm worried, Sarah," I say. My voice is quiet. Measured. Honest, but not too honest. "That piece you showed me, 'Merge,' 'Monrow not responding,' your initials... That's not just stray notes. It's part of something. If Voss had it, and shredded it..."

"She knew," Sarah finishes. "She was either complicit or trying to cover her tracks."

Exactly. But hearing her say it out loud makes it feel heavier.

"You're in this deeper than we thought," I say.

Sarah studies me for a long second. Her eyes aren't angry, but they are searching. Measuring.

"I can't walk away from this," she says. "James didn't just write this stuff down for fun. He died trying to reveal it."

Her words land like stones in my stomach. I look down at the table, let the silence answer for me for a beat too long.

"I get that," I say finally. "I really do. But you have to think about your safety too."

She stills.

I can see it then, the shadow of everything she's holding up. The weight of truth. The uncertainty. The way she's inching closer to the edge without realising how far the fall is. And I'm standing behind her, heart pounding, wondering if I'll be the one to push.

I sip my coffee, stalling. Then I lean forward.

"Maybe it's time to let the James stuff go," I say carefully. "Or at least slow down. Focus on what's happening now. Your project. That promotion that's probably already being discussed. You've already uncovered so much. Maybe someone else can pick up the trail."

She stiffens slightly, and I brace for resistance.

"Letting go of James's legacy isn't an option," she says. "Not yet."

Of course not.

She's better than me. More principled. More stubborn. It's why I picked her at the start, why I used her. Because she was so clean, so consistent. But now I'm watching that very integrity become the blade that might split us both in half.

I set my cup down and exhale. Slowly.

"Then promise me you'll be careful," I say, quieter. "I'll keep looking through logs and vendor approvals. Quietly. I'll keep an eye on the compliance team too. But Sarah... don't get reckless."

Her eyes soften. "Thanks. I'm not trying to be a martyr. I just want the truth."

I give her a tight smile. "You and me both."

Except we're hunting different versions of it.

She shifts in her seat, glancing back down at her notepad. She's still holding the pen, still tapping it. Slower now. More methodical. I watch her scan a series of numbers. Old grant approvals. She's chasing the threads again.

I return to my desk, but I don't settle.

Instead, I sit there staring at the half-loaded server dashboard, the reflection of myself ghosting back in the monitor glass. I look tired. Too many nights creating false leads and planting digital footprints. And still, Sarah keeps finding the cracks.

She's so close.

Too close.

I lean forward, elbows on the desk, and rub at my eyes with the heels of my palms.

This was supposed to be simple. And now? Now I'm looking at a girl who still offers me coffee, still trusts my help, and knowing that my next move might be to destroy her.

Julia had said it in that windowless room, the hum of the backup server vibrating through the concrete walls.

"If she won't stop," she'd said, her voice even, "we'll have to do what we did with Alex. Sever the access. Control the narrative. You know how this works, Emily."

And I do.

I lean back in my chair, the silence of the office pressing in like guilt made real. I don't want to hurt Sarah. But I also don't want to burn for what I've done. But if she keeps digging, I won't have a choice.

I open the secure sandbox again. Run a trace script through the Horizon folder Sarah keeps revisiting. The fabricated markers are still in place. Daniel. Mark. A few ghost edits pointing at legacy systems and overseas accounts. Misdirection dressed as truth.

But it won't hold forever.

I close the terminal window and press my fingers to my temple. My skull aches. Everything feels loud. The whirr of the server. The tick of the old analog clock. The faint buzzing light above my head.

This has to end soon.

One way or another.

~ 52 ~

I'm not dreaming. I know because in a dream, my body doesn't jolt upright like this. My phone buzzes on the nightstand with the urgency only real life carries. The screen glares too bright in the dark room. The screen says Sarah calling and 1:26 a.m.

I answer immediately, heart hammering even before I speak. "Hey"

"Sorry for calling late. I just... needed to hear a familiar voice." she replies. Then without wasting time, "We found something," her voice stripped raw from adrenaline. "There's a fake HR profile. ZettaCore Consulting. Routing funds internationally through Liechtenstein."

For a second, I say nothing. My heart isn't beating, it's grinding. Not because I'm caught. Because it worked.

The thing I planted. The backdoor breadcrumb. It led her exactly where I wanted. And she took the bait. And soon she will find Daniel's approval credentials are all over it.

But I have to sound shocked. "Wait—what? ZettaCore? Liechtenstein?" I fumble with my voice like I've just been yanked from sleep. "Jesus. Are you sure?"

"It's hidden under a wellness funding memo," she says. "But the routing instructions are wrong. The bank doesn't line up. And the HR contact, 'Maria H.' there's no one by that name in the system. Not even a hire record."

I let a beat pass. "Be careful" I say "If you're right, you're dealing with professionals. People who know how to disappear."

There's a pause, and I can hear her breathing, shaky, caught between exhaustion and exhilaration. "I think we've found how they're laundering the money," she says quietly. "We're getting close."

We.

It sticks in my throat.

"You're not alone, Sarah" I say finally. "Just remember that."

The call ends. I stare at the screen, the time burning into my eyes. 1:34 a.m. I drop the phone onto the duvet beside me, then let my head fall back onto the pillow.

ZettaCore Consulting. I created it almost two weeks ago. A shell initiative hidden in NexTech's older onboarding archives, fake onboarding memos, ghost email threads, buried expense justifications all signed off using Daniel's old credential override. All those nights building the digital scaffolding, imagining what a compromised director might design if they were lazy and greedy and thought no one would ever check.

And now Sarah had found it.

This was the shift I needed. The realignment. A way to get her off my scent. I'd been so careful. And it had worked. She was chasing Daniel now. But I don't let myself feel relief. Not yet.

Instead, I crawl out of bed and walk barefoot to my desk, the house silent except for the distant buzz of refrigeration and the creak of old floorboards under my steps. I open the encrypted sandbox terminal on my laptop.

It only takes a moment to pull up the logs. Maria H. is still active in the system until the purge I scheduled at the end of this week. A perfect cover. The image I attached to her profile, stock photo, smiling middle-aged professional, glasses, sleek bob, was pulled from a public university website before I uploaded it. Except, as a final twist, I reattached a version of the original filename and tagged it with "public/training-assets."

Subtle fingerprints. Just enough to scream "sloppy embezzler," not mastermind.

I scroll down and look at the paper trail I left Daniel. The admin override ID#7712B used to authenticate the fund transfer request. The timestamp placing the access at 2:17 a.m., the same hour he was known to work late and handle fiscal adjustments. The IP trail cloned from one of his Saturday VPN sessions.

It was perfect.

Sarah had finally stumbled onto it, and now every ounce of her focus would be laser-locked on Daniel and the false horizon I'd carefully constructed.

I close the log window and sit back in the chair. This should feel like a win. But all I feel is exhausted. I look over at the clock again. Almost 2 a.m.

I think back to the phone call, Sarah sounded shaken. But energized. She believes she's close. And she's not wrong.

That's what unsettles me most. She *is* close. Closer than she knows. And not just to Daniel. I've made too many mistakes. If she doubles back, if she finds the fingerprint I left somewhere I forgot to clean. Too many what-ifs.

I return to bed exhausted, but sleep doesn't come easily. I just lie there, in the dark. I think about what it means to manufacture truth. To shift someone's reality by design. It's power. But it's also a burden. And I've been carrying it so long, I don't know who I am anymore.

Each breath feels like an hour. Every shift of fabric on skin feels loud in the quiet. I keep thinking of Sarah's voice on the phone. That edge of urgency. The conviction in her words. *We found something.*

She thinks she's on the verge of truth. But what she's finding is a lie I wrote. And even that might not save me.

I sit up. I don't make the decision all at once. It comes to me like fog forming on a window. Thin, slow, inevitable, as I make my way back down stairs.

I open my laptop. A blank email form stares back. I keep the headers clean. No routing from my usual alias or sandboxed relay.

Just this:

To: NexTech Internal Compliance
Subject: Concerned Staff Tip

There may be irregularities in billing and vendor approvals related to the Horizon Initiative. One of the team members, female, director-level, is involved.

Check Q2 disbursements. Start with ZettaCore.

No name. No signature. Just a push.

I hover over "Send" for a full minute. My hands are shaking. I tell myself this isn't betrayal. Its a risk, but its also prevention. If I can stall her, if I can shake her confidence or restrict her access, it'll give me time. It'll protect both of us.

I hit send.

The quiet whir of my laptop fan is the only sound in the room. I stare at the sent folder until the message disappears from the queue.

It's done.

I close the screen and wrap myself in a blanket, sitting in the silence until the sun rises through the blinds. Then I get up, get ready and make my way into the office.

***

By 8:17 a.m., the email has been read.

I watch it happen in real time from my terminal, sipping coffee that tastes like regret. My secure listener picks up the auto-routing of flagged terms: “irregularities,” “Q2,” “ZettaCore.”

By 8:15, it’s been upgraded to “Priority Two” and escalated to Legal.

By 8:30, a permissions sweep begins. Someone in IT is pulling access logs from the Horizon team directory.

By 9:21, Sarah receives an invitation to a meeting she never saw coming.

I’m sitting at my desk with my headphones on when I see her walk in, a confused knot between her brows. She doesn’t look scared. Just... off-balance. A little disoriented. That’s good. Confusion is a buffer. Panic comes later.

"You okay?" I ask. "Yeah. Just got flagged for a meeting. Something about Q2 finances." she replies

"Weird. You’re probably fine, though. These things pop up every so often." I say trying to keep my tone neutral.

***

When I find her afterward, she’s sitting at her desk with her laptop locked, staring at the floor like she’s doing math in her head.

I approach slowly. My stomach turns with every step. “Hey,” I say softly. She looks up, eyes wide and blinking like she’s still catching up. “Emily,” she breathes looking lost. My heart cracks in two.

I sit beside her, trying to look surprised, concerned, but not too eager. “They locked your system?” I ask, looking at the blank screen.

“Yeah,” she sighs, “Compliance got an anonymous tip.”

I give her a sympathetic frown, like I'm working it out with her. "Look, I'm sure it's temporary. I'll talk to someone in IT. Maybe it's just standard during investigations."

Sarah nods slowly, eyes rimmed in exhaustion. "They're saying it's just a standard review. That it'll clear up. But they looked at me like I'd hidden something."

She looks small, like all the adrenaline from last night is gone and now she's just left with fatigue and disbelief.

She reaches out and I take her hand and squeeze it. "We'll get through this."

***

The second she disappears down the hallway to find her bag, I stumble into the nearest stairwell and collapse onto the bottom step.

My body seizes up like it's finally registering what I've done. I cover my mouth with both hands. For a second, I think I might vomit.

I sent that message. I triggered that audit. I watched her walk into that room and pretended I didn't know.

I told myself this would buy time. But watching her face... it broke me. I did this, to my friend. It feels like I have passed the point of no return.

Later that afternoon, I sit in the IT Room, alone. I don't do anything. Just stare into space. I should be watching the compliance queue, tracking their progress, seeing what they uncover, or don't.

But I don't open anything. I can't.

Instead, I scroll through old photos of us. Her birthday last year. Takeout on my floor. Team building in London, when we stayed up too late talking about what we'd build if we ran the company.

I always imagined I'd be standing beside her when we got there.

Now I'm the one cutting her off at the knees.

~ 53 ~

I shut my phone off, and unlock my laptop. I should feel safer, but I don't. My stomach twists tighter every minute I sit here. The guilt sits on my chest like lead.

Then, a message. one that I did not expect. Alex. "Can you get me into Voss's system?" No greeting. No small talk. Just that one line. I don't hesitate. I can't afford to. "Read-only access. Decision logs. Session activity and behavioral folders."

I send it through the sandboxed gateway. Seconds later, her system pings back. She's in. I lean back in the chair and exhale slowly. My fingers are trembling.

When I created the breadcrumb trail for Sarah to find, fabricated invoices, fake HR identities, and deep-rooted corruption, I'd hoped she'd chase just far enough to stop asking questions about me. About what I did.

But I also embedded real things. Real crimes. Not just to sell the lie. Because some of them deserved to burn. Voss is one of them. And Daniel... he lit the match.

It's almost poetic, in a horrific kind of way. I spent months laundering money through fake vendors and ghost accounts. But what Julias system holds is proof that her and Daniel are laundering something else. Truth. Compacted, redacted, filtered through intent.

And for once, I'm not faking it. They really did this. They really deserve what's coming.

I didn't want this. But I've run out of places to hide. And if it means letting them take the fall? Then so be it.

They used people like data points.

They profiled people for deletion.

James. Clara. Ian. Maybe even Sarah, if she hadn't been clever enough to catch the ripple.

So I won't mourn what happens to Voss or Daniel. Even if the evidence I've provided is selectively filtered. Even if I tailored it to fit a story I need others to believe.

Because the bones are real. The motives are true. And some part of me, some small, rotting part, still believes this is justice, even if I'm doing it for the wrong reasons. Even if I'm not sure where the line is anymore between stopping a monster and becoming one.

By the time I shut down the console, it's after 18:00. The building is quiet. I hear heels on tile, quiet conversation through glass.

Alex will make her report. Legal will start asking questions. And Voss and Daniel? They won't see it coming. Neither of them ever thought someone like me was dangerous.

But then again...

Neither did I.

***

A message from Sarah comes through just after 22:00. Short. Direct.

"Emily, Need help decrypting backup sets. Think they're tied to Voss. Are you up?"

I stare at the screen. My fingers hovering above the keyboard. My first instinct is panic. The second is relief. She's still coming to me for help. She doesn't suspect, not yet.

"Yeah. Send the details of what you need and I will load it on a thumb drive for you."

I set down my cup of tea beside me and wipe my hands across my face. I haven't slept properly in days.

Sarah sends the details through and I get to work. The real files are there. Julia's notes on profiling assessments, flags tied to Daniel's override codes. But I redact key timestamps, and route the trace lines away from anything with my name. I substitute session info tags to Voss's assistant. Harmless. Disposable.

It's 23:48 when I finish the scrub and insert the modified index into a blank thumb drive. I encrypt it again, with Sarah's preferred toolset, so it looks like she found it, not that I shaped it.

I stare at the little drive in my palm for a long moment before sealing it in a generic envelope.

Sarah wants the truth. I'm giving her the part of it that's safe to know.

***

At 08:10 the next morning, I slip through the maintenance stairwell and down into the storage alcove behind the server room. It smells like old wiring and floor polish. The space is quiet, the overhead fluorescents half-lit. We've used this alcove before, during audits, for project triage, or just to avoid being seen. Today, it's our safe zone.

Sarah arrives at 08:15 sharp, coat unbuttoned, face flushed from the walk across the carpark, the Autumn air is bitter this morning. Her hair is a little wind-blown, a pen is tucked behind her ear. She looks like she hasn't slept either.

"You got it?" she asks, her voice low. I nod and pass her the envelope. "Encrypted backups. I ran a blind crawl through Voss's system. Found a set of flagged archives that don't match her standard file structure." She pulls the thumb drive halfway from the envelope, eyes scanning the label. "Is this everything?" I nod.

"Thank you."

There's something in her tone. Gratitude, but also distance. Like she's beginning to walk into a place I can't follow. "You're doing the right thing," I tell her, softly. "Just... be careful. Voss plays the long game."

Sarah nods, then tucks the drive into her pocket. "She picked the wrong game this time."

I don't say anything else. I just watch her go, footsteps echoing as she disappears around the corner. I remain behind, pulse thudding. That drive could be a weapon. But not against me. Not anymore.

***

I'm not surprised when Sarah calls me. I've been half-expecting it ever since I gave her the thumb drive earlier this morning. She's been scraping through Julia's data like it's scripture.

I swipe to answer on the second ring, keeping my voice steady. "You found it?" There's a pause, and then her voice, tight, clipped, already raw. "It's worse than I thought."

I press the phone harder against my ear and close my laptop slowly. "It's not just a cover-up," she continues. "She's weaponising her position. And Daniel is behind it, he's been receiving her reports for months."

I don't breathe. I don't move.

So she found the Voss–Daniel pipeline. The psych profiling logs. The buried tags. "Does it mention you?" I ask, already knowing the answer.

There's a silence that stretches across the line. Then she says it.

"Mitchell, Sarah — Monitored since Q2 FY. Flag: Over-compensatory Behavior, High-Stakes Project Risk, Elevated Suspicion Threshold. Recommendation: Soft Exit Strategy if Threat Profile Escalates."

I feel it like a punch to the chest, even though I already knew what Julia had written. But hearing her read it aloud like that, in her voice, is worse than anything I could've prepared for.

I stay silent.

"She's building the same case against me," Sarah whispers.

"Sarah..." I say, softer than I intend to. Because it's real.

"She's not just diagnosing," she says. "She's scripting. Giving Daniel a clean excuse to erase people. If we hadn't found that prescription, if we hadn't followed the trail..."

"You'd be next," I finish. My voice barely makes it out.

And it's not just a theory. I know it's true. Because that's exactly what we did to Alex Monroe. What Julia proposed for Sarah only days ago. What I sat silently through in a locked office while pretending it wasn't a death sentence for my best friend.

"She knew James was close," Sarah says. "So she prescribed him something to accelerate the outcome. She did it quietly, through channels no one watches. And she's doing the same thing now, only this time she's using policy."

There it is. The full shape of what we've built, wrapped in Sarah's voice, parsed through her heart. And it lands like a stone in my throat.

I should say nothing. I should steer. Re-direct. Distract. But instead, all I say is, "You have to go to the board." She doesn't hesitate. "I will. Soon."

Another pause. And then, even though I have no right to say it, no place to let it pass my lips. I say. "I'm sorry."

It's real. For a second, it's real. Not for the data I forged or the lies I built, but for not stopping any of it sooner. For letting it get this far. For not protecting her when I still had a clean chance to do it.

"For not seeing this earlier." There's a beat. A silence between us that's gentler than anything I've felt in weeks. Then Sarah's voice, softer, "You helped today. That's what matters."

I close my eyes, and I want to believe her. I want to believe there's still a way out where both of us survive this.

I don't say anything else. My throat's too tight. Eventually, I manage, "Just... be careful. Okay?"

~ 54 ~

I lie awake with the tracker app open on my phone, its signal pulsing softly in the darkness of my bedroom. Sarah hasn't told me where Alex lives, she'd only ever referred to it as the "cottage." I never intended to have to use it, but if Sarah is planning to confront the board soon, I need to know everything. That first thumb drive, the origin of all this, is still out of my reach. If Sarah presents unverified evidence, it risks unraveling everything I've built. I refuse to let that happen.

There's no choice but to go after it. To take control, one last time.

I sit up, breath tight in my chest, and slip on a dark hoodie, the one that falls low around my face. I grab the slim utility kit I keep hidden under my bed, a tension wrench, spare driver bits, a flashlight with a silent flick switch. I leave my phone on vibrate, silent, tracking Sarah's coat ID like a silent tail. I step into the dark of the early hours.

My car weaves through streets lit only by distant street lamps, I follow the blue dot. The tick of adrenaline pushing through my veins matches the beat of the song playing quietly on the radio. At each intersection, I double-check the signal, the tracker pings again, a heartbeat guiding me down street after street until I arrive at a country lane, surrounded by trees. Their forms are looming dark silhouettes. The app shows the tag icon through an opening that I would have missed if I hadn't been looking. Alex's cottage.

I kill the engine, letting the car coast the final few metres in idle. No headlights. No music. No trace. I park beneath the skeletal shadow of a tree, far enough that no one will hear the engine tick or see the faint glow of dashboard light. The silence stretches wide around me.

I don't slam the door. I don't even close it fully until I've shouldered my bag and scanned the deserted lane twice. Then, with a quiet, deliberate nudge, I seal the car shut. The click sounds loud in the cold air, but nothing stirs.

I pull my hood low and melt into the hedgerow shadows, sticking to fences and overgrown garden walls. Alex's cottage sits hunched at the end of the lane like a sleeping thing, old brick, gabled windows, a sloping roof. No streetlamps. Only darkness, deep and absolute.

The tracker pings again, Sarah's coat, right inside. I feel it like a jolt. She's here. They're both here.

I move to the side gate. It's wooden, weather-worn, barely latched. I press it open with a single finger. The hinges groan, soft but accusatory. I flinch and wait. One second. Two. Nothing.

I step through into the garden, overgrown and quiet. Leaves crunch underfoot. I wince. My boots press softer now, careful. Around the back, I spot a large window, its panes fogged slightly from within. A weak amber glow leaks through the drawn curtains. A lamp maybe. Not a screen.

I creep closer and peer through the corner where the curtain doesn't quite meet the frame. No movement. No sound. But I feel the static tension in the air.

I crouch low beneath the window frame, pull my pick set from the inside of my sleeve, and slide the tension wrench into the lock. It's old, stubborn. I feel each pin shift beneath the pick, my breath held tight behind my teeth. The final tumbler clicks into place with a sound that feels louder than it is, amplified by the knowledge of what I'm doing.

I freeze.

Wait.

No footsteps.

No door creaks.

I push the door open inch by inch, slipping inside like smoke.

The smell hits me first. Not dust, cleaner than I expected. The warm, lived-in scent of fire, wood polish, electronics, and cocoa. There's something unsettling about the quiet intimacy of it. A home, not a hideout. I'm intruding in a way I never have before.

The kitchen tiles are smooth under my shoes. I move like I've rehearsed it, low to the ground, limbs measured, breath shallow. To my left, a narrow hallway disappears into deeper darkness. To the right, the main room.

Sparse furniture. Storage boxes against the wall. A low hum of electricity.

I scan for signs of life. No glow beneath the door frames. No shuffle of blankets. But I pass a pair of shoes by the mat, Sarahs. Worn, practical. The kind of footwear that means she's here. Sleeping a wall away.

I stop moving. I listen harder. Still nothing.

A laptop rests on a side desk near the far wall, angled slightly toward the window like it's been used recently. Cables snake around it. I feel a rush of cold through my chest. This is it.

I check the shelves first. The drawers. Underneath the desk. A box in front of the fire. No thumb drives, none of the ones I saw Sarah use. No encrypted sticks, no stashed backups. Just notebooks. Charging bricks. Logs. The usual signs of paranoia.

My hand hovers over the laptop.

Do it.

No. Wait.

I glance toward the hallway again.

Still nothing.

I kneel, check the laptop, hoping its the one Sarah used with the first thumb drive. It's got to be. Session caches, mount logs, handshake data, probably buried in there somewhere. But I can't risk turning it on here.

My pulse is fast now. Too fast.

I don't plug in. Don't search. I pull my gloves tighter, check the time, past 2 a.m. The risk window is closing. They could wake up at any sound.

I slide the laptop into the messenger bag I brought, padding it with a folded sweatshirt so it doesn't knock. One wrong sound and everything collapses.

I rise slowly, holding my breath. My knee brushes a chair. It squeaks. I stop breathing. I wait. Nothing.

Maybe a creak upstairs, but it's faint. Could be the house settling. Could be Alex shifting in bed.

I don't wait to find out.

I retreat backward across the kitchen tiles, each step measured like I'm dancing across a minefield. Past the hallway. Past the entry. Through the same door.

Outside, the air hits my face like ice.

I move fast now, heart hammering against my ribs. Back through the gate. No lights flip on behind me.

I don't breathe fully until I'm back inside my car, engine cold, hands trembling as I place the bag beside me.

***

Back in my flat, lights off, windows shut tight. I plug the laptop into my locked backup terminal, an isolated network with no connection to NexTech's systems. It hums quietly.

I sift through caches again. Session fragments, old passwords now useless, IP chains, deleted logs, all the breadcrumbs. I don't risk checking live credentials; too dangerous.

I'm relieved. Nothing ties me directly to the laundering or shell company. Nothing screams "Emily hid this." This laptop, this flash drive, becomes my insurance.

Still, a tension coils deep in my gut. I unplug the laptop, place it in a nondescript canvas bag. It's evidence that I need to get rid of quietly.

Breathing low I slowly make my limbs feel real again. I've done what I went to do. I've taken the risk, broken in, and taken back control.

But the guilt is a weight, heavier than any midnight operation. Because I've crossed a line, too many lines now, not just tonight, the hoodie, the pick, the betrayal. All of it.

Resigned, I set the laptop under the bed. I plug my phone in and lie down on the bed, falling into exhaustion. I fall asleep in the dark with the sound of my heartbeat flooding my ears, haunted by the soft promise of evidence that could save me, or doom me, when Sarah finally stands before the board.

~ 55 ~

I wake to a kind of stillness that feels strange after the last few nights, the weight of the cottage gone quiet, the tension eased, as though the world has let me catch just one breath. I slept through until 7:45 a.m., the first decent sleep in weeks. It takes me a moment to remember what I did, drove back at 3 a.m. with Alex's laptop, verified the session logs, found nothing incriminating. Just fragments and cached data. Enough to breathe easier, but only just.

Now I'm in the IT room, the pale glow of the screen illuminating my face. I'm running a few low-impact diagnostics, nothing too obvious, just enough to check network health and log integrity. I pause on a line of code, something I planted yesterday to flag unauthorised Horizon folder access. The entries show access by that fake "Maria H." profile, I smile at how neatly it fits into place.

My fingers hover over the keyboard when the door opens.

Sarah steps in, once again. I flick my eyes up and offer a small, real smile for the briefest second, tied and genuine, the best I can do without giving away everything inside. Then I drop my gaze again and resume typing. Pretend routine.

She pauses before my desk, holding her coffee like a shield. I can feel her watch me, the way she always seems to. Maybe she's testing for cracks. Maybe looking for the same reassurance I desperately need.

She clears her throat softly. "I'm going to the roof for some air. Do you want to come?"

For a moment, I hesitate, even though I knew this moment was coming, I know her too well. Maybe I want to stay here where I can see the logs, check the trails again. But I push away the code and shut down the diagnostics window. "Sure," I say, rising from the chair a touch too fast.

We exit the room together. I linger at the door a second, scanning the hallway. It's quiet. Only hums and faint clicks behind closed office doors. We pass through and ride the elevator up, metal box stillness holding us both.

On the rooftop, the door swings closed behind us. The city stretches out across the horizon in low morning light, soft and forgiving. A breeze stirs.

Sarah walks to the edge, leaning on the barrier slightly, one sleeve pushed back. I linger near the back, hands in pockets, pretending to watch but really measuring her silhouette, strong but quiet, burdened but not broken. She stands there in silence, staring at the distant skyline. I stand a few feet away and sit on the low concrete ledge.

The air smells fresh.

The world is quiet around us, as we both process the aftermath. She breathes deep. I close my eyes, try to imagine what she sees. Opportunity? Danger? Maybe both. My mind races, turning toward the logs, the breadcrumbs, the falsified approvals.

Inside, I'm calculating, if anything leaks now, if the board or investigators trace something to me... The fake Maria H., the backdated approval chains, Mark's linked credentials, it's all toxic if discovered. But more than that, it would unravel everything I've worked so hard to control.

My heart pounds. I can almost hear a clock ticking inside my skull. I sit beside her, pretending calm, while everything I've built sits on a knife's edge.

Her posture stiffens. She shifts slightly. I recognise the moment, she's processing, she's thinking, but not expressing. Maybe because she knows me well enough to trust that I already know.

I swallow. "Nice up here," I say. She offers a small nod. "Yeah." I don't push. Sometimes silence is safer.

Minutes pass. I look down at my watch. Light slants across the deck. We're technically on NexTech property, surveillance aside, this is neutral ground.

I want to say, "Sarah, drop it. Just leave it alone." But I can't. Because no matter how much I've built to protect myself, part of me still believes in exposing Julia and Daniel. That the truth, even half-truths, could break the rot. And I've given enough false flags to steer her down that path. But today, right now, part of me wants to stop the charade. To confess what's genuine, my care for her, my fear of losing her, my hope, yes, still hope, that there's a version of justice that doesn't destroy us both.

Yet the logs remain. The entry about Maria H. sits in the database. The fake credentials are timestamped. Daniel's approval chains, Mark's pin as "accessor" of the project spreadsheet, they're all there, feeding the trap I set.

I'm not ready to lose her. And the logs whisper a promise, stay calm. Keep code clean. And she just might never look.

She exhales. just as her phone starts to ring.

"I'll head back in." I say, my voice quieter than usual.

She glances at me and smiles nodding.

I hold onto her smile through the whole walk back, storing it somewhere safe.

~ 56 ~

The night before Sarah's Project presentation to the board, I can't sleep. I lie in bed, mind racing through worst-case scenarios. What if something glitches in the logs while I'm not there to watch? What if Voss sees through the fabrication or accuses me outright? I can't quiet the voice that asks, *What if Sarah finds me out?*

In a moment of panic-born clarity, I make a decision. I slide out of bed and log into my personal laptop. I book a flight under a new name, departing in two days to a quiet destination I'd scouted months before. I transfer the last of my savings into an offshore account tied to that identity, the one that contains millions in laundered funds.

I already hold the documents to my new identity, they have been on standby since the incident with James, I knew one day I might need to escape, I just didn't know when.

I hold the passport in my hand and read my new name, Alice Torre. It looks strange written next to a photograph of my face. A driver's license sits on the table next to a thumb drive containing work credentials and references, it's all arranged. Not because I ever planned to run, but because I couldn't risk having no way out if everything collapsed.

I close the laptop and stare at my reflection in the dark windowpane. "You'll be there tomorrow," I murmur to myself. For Sarah. For appearances.

Then I let myself rest, even if sleep remained elusive.

***

The boardroom lights feel colder today. The glow of the large wall mounted monitor casts a blue corporate light on the table, making me shiver even more. Outside the window, rain presses against the glass in slow, heavy drops. The storm is coming, Voss called it.

I watch from the side of the room as Sarah stands at the head of the polished table, her voice steady. I expect this to be a project presentation. Instead, the presentation that leaps out from the monitor is her whistle-blower exposé. My palms rest on the polished conference table, they grow clammy as my anxiety spikes.

Sarah begins presenting. The hush is immediate, total. One by one, she lays out the evidence. I quietly observe. Nothing prepared me for the clarity in her eyes. And for one shining moment, I felt real pride.

Daniel's fingers curl around his chair arms. Mark leans in.

"We've uncovered falsified wellness evaluations, unauthorised financial flows tied to shell entities. The evidence is time-stamped, cross-verified."

She clicks through each slide, her calm presence a blade in the silence. I feel the clock in my chest: *Tick. Tick.* My hands curl into fists in my lap.

I sit frozen, each word she speaks scraping at my heart. Above the low hum of air conditioning, I hear Daniel's ragged breathing. The board's expressions shift, curiosity becomes concern.

At no point do I imagine Sarah will flinch. She's calm. Commanding. In control. And I, I'm frozen with guilt, am complicit in every shadowed corner of what she reveals.

***

Once Sarah has finished, two representatives make a quiet call from the corner, speaking in hushed voices. After a moment, one of them steps toward the hallway and gestures for security.

The door opens. A moment passes. Julia walks in. The boardroom feels suspended. Drums beat in my head. She stops at the door, appraising. She doesn't smile, doesn't blink. She looks at me first, a slow deliberate moment, before taking a seat beside Legal, a single drop of sweat glints on her temple.

I nearly stand, ready to confess, *It was me. I made the logs.* But she remains quite, poised. The room shifts on its axis, more charged.

Security arrives. I watched Daniel and Julia's hands tremble, looking towards the security officers standing, clear and official. Not loud. But final. The soft clack of their badges echo in my ear.

My eyes glance towards Daniel, I can feel Voss's eyes slide past me, silently accusing. I know she saw it, my refusal to look back, as they are escorted out. My breath comes in rattled gasps, shoulders hunched.

When the door closes a final time, an oppressive weight lifts for a moment, but the board has seen enough. They shift papers, murmur, the legal team hovers.

Mark remains seated, immaculate. He catches my eye but says nothing.

***

Outside, the rain has slowed to a drizzle. Sarah and I step out, shoulders brushing, the city breathing under neon glows. She pulls her suit jacket tight around her, I watch, in admiration of how composed he remained under the weight of this day.

She doesn't look at me at first. She just stares at her shoes, slow as though she is waking from a difficult dream. Then quietly she says "We did it."

Her words are fragile, hope, guilt, relief mixing in the tremor of her voice. "Yeah," I reply softly. "We did." and those words, knowing all that I have done, press heavily on my shoulders.

We find ourselves in our favorite coffee shop nearby, one cup each, steam weaving between us. She watches the amber swirl against the white ceramic.

Sarah reaches across the table, touches my hand. "Thank you. For everything." My breath catches. It was both accolade and burden, praise and sentence.

"You should get some rest, you haven't stopped in days." I say to Sarah as much as I am saying it to myself.

"I don't think I can. Not yet." she sighs, "Then don't," I reply, knowing that this means I need to follow through and disappear, I know deep down, she won't stop until every thread has been severed. I know what I must do to save myself, knowing it will break both our hearts.

"I'm still not sure what Mark was doing," Sarah says. I feel tension rising at the sound of his name. "He didn't stop you. That counts for something. Maybe he was waiting to see which way things would break." Sarah looks at me before adding. "Or maybe he was working an angle we haven't seen yet." I nod slowly. "We'll find out. Eventually."

***

After work, I return to a house that feels impossibly changed. The floorboards groan with guilt. The windows stand open, raindrops tracing patterns on the sill.

I sit at the kitchen table, the glow of my laptop illuminating the lines of code I'd planted. I open a terminal session in root. One by one, I revert admin overrides, wipe alt credentials, blank my footprints from the audit queue. Every entry linked to Maria H.

Removed. Deleted. Every backdated approval chain tied to me vanishes into the void.

The cursor blinks, waiting for the final command.

I pause. I think of Sarah's eyes under that presentation light. I think of Julia, escorted, broken. I think of Daniel, pale, defeated.

I enter the last line of code. The script runs. It empties folders, hashed timestamps, proxy configs. Gone.

The screen goes blank. My reflection stares back, a silhouette on a slate of black. Outside, the storm clouds break, but in me... clouds still churn.

~ 57 ~

I wake to the soft hum of early morning. For a moment, everything feels surreal, like I'm watching someone else's life unfold in someone else's body. Today's the day. It's my last day at NexTech. I should feel relieved. Instead, there's a thickness in my chest, a quiet ache.

I shower, dress in clothes that look like "me" but feel like costumes. At the airport, a ticket awaits. I've transferred funds, erased traces from corporate accounts, and turned off my phone's tracking. But all that is for later. Now, I have a job to finish.

I arrive at the office just before nine. Sarah's already there. Her face is calm, bright, like the sunrise after a storm. She meets my eyes with a quiet smile, the slightest upturn, and I hold it too. We're connected by truths I can't confess, by betrayals I'll take with me. For a heartbeat, I try to forget everything I'm about to walk away from.

During the day, I transfer my responsibilities, create handover notes, and complete some final IT checks. Each click feels hollow, echoes a part of me being left behind.

Part way through the morning, I leave my desk and make my way towards the Project Room. The door to the Board Room opens behind me as I pass. I pause. Inside, that now-familiar polished table, dark leather chairs. In the center, Sarah sits opposite the Executive Team. Her posture still, composed, arms uncrossed, face resolute. I slip back into the IT hallway, heart pounding.

***

Two hours later, I am sitting waiting for her in the hallway when she emerges. Her expression is calm, yet unmistakable, she's changed.

Well?" I ask. "I'm the acting CEO." She says, her smile is immediate. Wide. Genuine. "Are you serious?" *It's happening.* My throat tightens. I wrap my arms around her. "You deserve it." She squeezes me back. "It doesn't feel real."

Sarah invites me out for a celebratory coffee. We choose a corner café with big windows and green plants, bright and hopeful. I order two lattes, extra foam, and we sit across from each other, the weight of everything hanging just beneath the surface.

***

I go back to Sarah's house after work. Mushu greets us at the door. His ears twitch, his tail arches in that strange, cautious dance cats do.

Inside, the confidence I carried all day cracks. The house smells familiar, cedar, chamomile, pages from old books, and it's almost unbearable knowing this is the last time I will be inside these walls.

Heading to the kitchen, Mushu prowls around me, He pauses outside the room I broke into, eyes fixed on me with uncanny stillness. I swallow.

"He's obviously annoyed at me" Sarah says, with a gentle laugh.

I smile at her, but the room floods with memories, the trackers planted, the laptop taken. In that moment, I realise the consequences of my choices are alive in this space. I swallow hard and turn away.

Sitting on the sofa I swallow hard before I tell her I'm heading to Sicily to visit my parents. The words hang between us.

"Sicily?" she repeats, excitement dancing in her eyes. "You deserve it."

"Yeah," I add in a whisper. "I should've gone years ago."

She leans in for a hug. Strong. Warm. Long enough for me to memorise the tilt of her shoulder, the scent of her hair, the pulse at the base of her neck. "Bring me back something Italian," she says, finally releasing me from her grasp.

***

Back at my apartment, I start a box. Clothes, cables, burned drives. Each item is a piece of identity I'm laying to rest. I pause over a framed photo, me and Sarah, shoulder to shoulder in the rooftop garden. I close my eyes, press the picture to my heart, then gently slip it into the box.

My breath comes ragged. I sink onto the couch, the weight of what I've done, what I'm leaving behind, crashes down. I rest my head in my hands and sob uncaged and hard.

***

I wake early and pack the few remaining items I am taking with me. I open my front door, pulling my cases behind me and take a few deep breaths. I watch Sarah as she approaches. "Taxi for Emily?" she calls through her car window. She's wearing a soft scarf and that calm look, the kind she has when she knows she's ready for what comes next.

"You'll be great," I tell her when the topic of her new position comes up, voice steady when inside I've shattered. She hugs me tight. "Don't worry about me. Go have fun."

"Promise me you'll 'holiday' enough for the both of us." she says, teasing. "I will." I flick on a smile, but my eyes sting.

I do everything in my power to make the short journey to the airport as fun and full of laughter as I have in me. I want to remember this part for the friendship, not the betrayal.

When we arrive, she helps with my bags. I linger at her car for a moment, taking her all in for the last time, trying to burn every last detail of her in my mind.

Inside the terminal, a crowd hums under airport lights. I stand in the foyer, pressing my forehead to the cool glass while she disappears out of sight.

I find a seat near Gate 23, in a chaise facing the windows. Boarding is in forty-five minutes. I open a crisp, brand-new laptop still wrapped in plastic. My fingers tremble as I connect it to Wi-Fi. The device hums with possibility.

I navigate to my new email account and type:

Subject: Interview Acceptance - Technical Director (Finance Dept)

Hello, Francesca,

Attached is my itinerary. I will arrive in Montreal tomorrow morning. Let's pick up where we left off.

Alice Torre

I smile, a genuine curve of uncertainty and hope. My new identity forms on the screen. I look one last time at Gate 23. Sarah's gone. Emily is gone. But maybe... maybe *Alice* can begin again.

~ 58 ~

SARAH

The email comes through just after midnight.

I'm not even at my desk. I'm sitting cross-legged on the floor of my bedroom, a mug of hot chocolate in my hand and Mushu curled up by the door. The house is dark and still, except for the soft hum of my laptop, left open on the nightstand. The board fallout is still rippling through the company. Voss is gone. Daniel's name is scrubbed from the internal directory. Mark is silent.

For the first time in weeks, I let myself think the worst is over.

Then the notification pings.

From: noreply@ghostmail.net
Subject: For you, from Emily

My heart skips.

I open it, not breathing.

Sarah

This is the last message I'll send you. I need you to know the truth, because you deserve better than the half-stories I let you believe. You deserve better than what I was brave enough to give you while I was still standing in front of you.

You didn't find ZettaCore.

I gave it to you. I built it.

The vendor trail, the Maria H. profile, the timestamps pointing to Daniel. I created all of it. I planted the clues so you'd follow them. Because you were getting too close. To the real trail. To me.

My hands start shaking. My eyes blur the words. I scroll slowly, afraid of what else I'll read and needing it all anyway.

I thought I could protect you by giving you something real enough to chase. And I justified it to myself by saying it led to people who were guilty. Daniel was laundering. Voss was profiling. But you were never supposed to know what I did to get you there.

You trusted me. And I weaponised that trust. I kept feeding you just enough to steer you away from the truth. From me.

I told myself I was helping. I told myself it was survival. But the truth is, I was afraid of losing you. Even as I lied to your face, I didn't want to watch you walk away.

That rooftop coffee? I was already erasing logs that morning. The day I told you not to be reckless? I'd just rerouted audit trails to keep my name clear.

I watched you fight so hard for justice, while I built the frame that made it look like someone else's crime. I sat beside you while you cried for James.

And I said nothing.

I feel the breath leave my body like a punch. My vision goes hot and sharp. I scroll again. The final paragraph lands like ash in my throat.

I'm leaving. By the time you read this, I'll be on a flight. New name. New city. I won't contact you again.

I didn't write this to be forgiven. I know I don't deserve that. I wrote it because somewhere in all the lies, you were the only real thing.

You once said we were the kind of friends who'd survive anything. I broke that. And I will carry that weight for the rest of my life.

I have left you a file. It's in the network. It's called Mushu.

Emily

I read it again.

Then again.

I sit frozen, blinking at the screen. Not moving. Not breathing. Like if I stay still long enough, the truth won't collapse everything inside me.

But it already has.

She's gone.

Emily, my best friend. The person I built my trust on, the one I ran toward when the world was falling apart, lied to me. Every night we sat side by side in the IT room. Every shared coffee. Every joke. Every moment I thought I had someone beside me in the fight, she was shaping the battlefield.

I feel the heartbreak as something physical. Not a metaphor. It's a sharp, seizing pain that hits somewhere between my chest and my throat and makes me gasp like I've been punched.

Mushu shifts near the door, sensing the change.

I press a hand to my mouth, like that can stop the sob building in my chest.

She made herself a ghost. She erased herself. And now she's gone, *really* gone. No more rooftop talks. No emergency text. No late-night knock on my door with takeout and a bottle of cheap wine. The woman who told me *"I've got you"* with tears in her eyes also signed the lie that made me doubt everything.

How do I reconcile that?

How do I mourn someone who *chose* to disappear?

How do I grieve a friendship that never really existed the way I thought it did?

The sob escapes despite me. I cover my face with my hands and cry into the darkness. Not just for the betrayal. Not just for the truth.

But because she was my *person*. My anchor.

And now all I have left of her is a ghost in my inbox.

Eventually, the crying stops. My chest still aches, but the tears are gone. I sit on the floor and stare at the email. I don't delete it. I couldn't if I tried.

Instead, I open a new draft. Just one line. I type it, then leave it there, cursor blinking beside it.

I would have forgiven you

But I don't send it.

Because she's not there to read it.

And she never will be again.

~ 59 ~

I step out of the elevator onto the top-floor corridor and pause, breath catching in my throat. The office feels impossibly quiet, The quiet echoes of a lost friendship, her missing presence. In my hand, I clutch the printed email, folded carefully like a fragile confession and a wound I can't heal.

It doesn't feel real.

I raise my head and stare at the door to the boardroom ahead of me. I can already envision the polished table inside gleaming under the overhead lights, and in that moment, I feel the weight of who I am and what I have pressing down around me. I thought I was walking in to deliver evidence, to finish a job I began weeks ago. But now it feels like I'm walking into a funeral. A goodbye. To the Emily I believed in, my best friend, my confidante, my anchor.

The email folded in my hand is heavier than any file I've ever carried. The crisp lines of the page, subject line, sender block, timestamp, stare back at me like a judge. I want to rip it to pieces. I want to hide it. I want to curl into a corner and pretend I never received it. But I need to finish this. Because I still believe, in some strange corner of my soul, that truth matters. Even if it breaks me.

I push open the heavy door. Inside, Legal are already seated. Two board members flank them at the head of the table. Their expressions are formal, polite, but I see the flicker of curiosity behind their eyes. They know something is coming. I straighten my shoulders and walk confidently to the polished mahogany, even though I am anything but. I sit, kneading the envelope between my hands.

"Sarah," one of the Legal counsels says softly, "thank you for coming. Please, go ahead."

I exhale, steady. I place the envelope gently on the table. It's as if I'm laying down a truce. Or a confession. "Emily was part of it," I say, unexpectedly calm. "She was involved in ZettaCore's laundering. She falsified documents, rewrote logs, and created backdoor credentials. She... she built an entire false vendor ecosystem."

My words echo. A blank hush falls over the room. The board shifts. The first board member, a pale woman in severe tailoring, tilts her head. "And how do you know this?"

I unfold the email, exposing the typed lines to the glow of the overhead lights. My voice trembles, just slightly. "She told me. It's right here." I pause, clearing my throat. Emotion pools behind my eyes. "She signed off the note." I breathe.

"Subject: For you, from Emily.

'You didn't find ZettaCore. I gave it to you. I built it.

The vendor trail, the Maria H. profile, the timestamps pointing to Daniel. I created all of it.'"

I say, pointing to the words as I pass them. The words hang in the room. I push a thumb drive toward the center. "She also left this on the network. It holds the folder she mentioned. She called it Mushu." Saying Mushus name stings more than I expect, It's as though by using it she has tainted him as well.

Legal plugs it into their laptop. The dull whirl of the disk activation fills the silence. One by one, documents appear on the screen. Transaction logs, IP traces, credential chains, dates three layers deep in audit backups. All real. All damning. All meticulously engineered.

A third board member glances at me. "And what are we looking at here?"

I swallow. I explain, "Forged vendors. Shell companies. Documented IP use. Maria H. a ghost HR profile manufactured to facilitate fund transfers. It's all here."

They scroll. Close-ups on signatures. Redacted but still clear enough. Another window, chat logs from secure nodes. Another, timestamp metadata with scope and volume. Another, X-ray views into masked code that auto-generated the layers. All built by someone who knew every corner of the system, who bent it, shaped it, made it vanish.

Then they call Mark's name. He enters the room. My throat clenches. He doesn't approach me directly. He nods to the board, eyes flicking toward mine just long enough to let me know he's aware I'm here. Then, composed, he steps forward.

The board show Mark the email from Emily, then pass him the laptop to enable him to view the files from the thumb drive. When he has finished he clears his throat and closes the laptop lid before sliding it back across the table.

"Mark," says Legal. "You're now permitted to explain your involvement to Sarah."

He straightens, hands folded, and looks at me for a long moment. I see the eyes of a stranger. Or at least someone I never truly knew.

Finally he speaks. "Sarah," he says, voice low, "I'm with the Financial Fraud Office. I've been embedded inside NexTech for eighteen months under Directive 311-B." I suck in air so fast it hurts.

He continues. "Emily's actions were under surveillance, early on, we didn't have the evidence to confidently move on her. But since your tip pointing to Daniel Reed and Julia Voss, legal has escalated. You've uncovered far more than we expected. We're grateful for your work."

I barely register the words. He's the one who asked me last week if I was okay. He's the one whose concern was actually genuine. It was real, yet I had suspected him, despised him for a long time. But now that I understand him, I feel ashamed for those thoughts.

He continues: "The financial fraud involved shell entities, ZettaCore being a primary conduit. Emily initially worked alone. But the partnership with Voss... we're still investigating her motives and intent. But as you've provided the blueprint, we now have a clear trajectory to prove full infiltration."

My heart drifts up, floats, then sinks. I feel the oxygen emptying from the room. Every truth I told myself about loyalty, about trust, I feel it crack.

Then the board murmurs. Among them is a small nod. "Internal legal escalation will follow." The board members exchange names, Julia. Daniel. Emily. Sarah. I close my eyes for a moment, fighting to keep them open.

When I look back, Mark glances at me with something approaching sorrow. "I'm... so sorry, Sarah." His voice barely a whisper.

I nod. No words can come. Everything breaks.

I leave the room, legs heavy, chest as though a fist is squeezing my heart. Outside, drizzle paints grey streaks across the windows. They cling to me. I press into the wall, leaning on its cool tile. Rain and recrimination run in tandem through me.

Moments later, Mark finds me beneath the overhang, damp and shaking. I don't look at him. My reflection is someone else entirely: bloodless, abandoned, lost.

"She left a clean slate," he says softly. "Everything will be investigated. Recovered. You can rebuild from this."

But I don't want a slate. "I don't want to rebuild," I whisper. "I want her." Her laughter. Her trust. The quiet moments when she said *I got you.* But those moments were buried beneath lines of code, digital ghosts, deliberate deception.

He doesn't respond. Just gently places a hand on my shoulder. A gesture I would have once taken as calculating, now it provides a little comfort. Then I walk away. And he stays.

I walk until my feet sting, rain soaking through layers. I feel numb, as if someone unstitched the seams of my chest and filled the void with grief.

***

Back home, Mushu circles my feet as I settle onto the couch. He's smaller, or quieter, maybe it's just me. The house smells like her. In every corner, coffee mugs, books laid open. Somewhere I can still smell her perfume, the late evenings we shared in laughter and conspiracy. Now those thoughts and scents feel like knives.

I slide onto the laptop, open the drive marked Mushu. I won't open it again. I know what's there now, truth, lies, shadow scripts. Nothing but pain.

Instead, I open my inbox. My heartbeat flickers as I see the "For you" email resting at the top. Its subject line still stings: *For you*. I let my pointer hover over it, and I tremble.

Not to forget, but to survive.

I right-click. Archive.

The screen clears, and I exhale. The sound of tears begins. I cry until no more pain can leave me. Until the very fabric of my core tears beneath the weight of it all.

The war is over. The villains, Julia, Daniel, they're gone. Line-by-line, they've crumbled under exposure.

But Emily, my best friend? She walked away. Not just from this building, but from me.

And I don't know if I'll ever forgive her.

~ 60 ~

MARK

The office feels different today. The kind of quiet that settles after an earthquake, not peace, just pause. No one speaks loudly. Footsteps echo sharper on the floors. Doors open and close with too much restraint. I pass desks filled with people who don't look up, all of them processing what they've just lived through. Or what they missed entirely.

I stop outside the door and look at the brass plaque with the initials CEO embossed on them. I take a breath, and knock lightly before entering.

Sarah looks up from her desk, eyes shadowed, face calm in a way that clearly costs her effort. She's here. She's doing her job. But I know that something fundamental has cracked underneath.

"Do you have a minute?" I ask.

She nods slowly. "Yeah."

I close the door gently behind me and take the seat across from her. For a moment, neither of us speaks. She waits. I gather the words carefully, like I've been doing my whole life in rooms like this.

"I owe you an apology," I begin. "For not telling you sooner. For not... being more than just another shadow in all of this."

Her gaze doesn't waver. "You were under directive. You had a cover to protect. I get it."

"I know you *understand*," I say softly. "But I still hate it."

Her jaw tenses slightly. I keep going.

"I'd been tracking Emily for months. Our data flagged anomalies, financial structures buried so deep in NexTech's backbone that they could've been part of the code. She was a ghost in plain sight. But I never got close enough. Not in any meaningful way."

Sarah exhales, almost bitterly. "She got close to me."

I nod. "That's what she was best at, building trust. She was always ten steps ahead of the people trying to catch her."

Sarah doesn't argue. Just looks down at the notepad in front of her, where a half-written to-do list is quickly becoming irrelevant in the wake of everything.

"You dated her," she says. Her voice isn't accusatory, just curious. Cautious.

"Yes," I admit. "And I hated it. Not because I didn't like her, I did. But because it was dishonest. I was dishonest."

I rub my hands together. "The first date, I took a phone call. I told Emily it was work, and that wasn't entirely dishonest, it was from my boss at the fraud office. He told me the audit data I'd already compiled was good. He said we were close, that we could make the case. But we needed something from her directly. A confirmation. A breadcrumb. Something only she could place."

"You were hoping she'd trust you," Sarah says, voice flat.

"Yes. I thought... maybe she'd slip. Maybe if she cared about me, she'd open up. But she didn't. Not once. Not even when she looked right at me over dinner, not when she held my hand, not when she kissed me."

Sarah swallows. "So what do I believe in now? Everything we did together as friends, was it even real?"

I look at her for a long moment. "I think some of it was, I believe the friendship was real. I don't think she started it with lies. I think she convinced herself she could do both, be both. Through it all she tried to protect herself and protect you. But when it came down to it... she chose survival."

A long silence stretches between us.

"I couldn't intervene," I say quietly. "It would've blown the entire operation. If I had warned you... if I'd tried to stop her, we might never have gotten the evidence."

"You were just following orders," Sarah mutters. But I can hear the strain in her voice.

"No," I say. "I was protecting a case. And it cost you something you can't replace. And I'm sorry for that."

Her eyes finally meet mine. There's something deeply tired behind them. The kind of exhaustion that doesn't go away after a night's sleep. "You're finished now?"

I nod. "Yeah. My part in this is done. I'm leaving NexTech. Quietly. I have another assignment already. Different city. Different name."

She doesn't ask where.

I reach into my bag and pull out a manila folder, placing it gently on her desk. She raises an eyebrow, but doesn't touch it.

"What is it?"

"Just in case you ever feel like a career change," I say. "It's an invitation. To the Fraud Department. Internal Investigations Unit. Field position. You'd be... exceptional at it."

She lets out a hollow laugh. "You're offering me a job as a professional lie detector?"

"I'm offering you a chance to use what you've already proven," I say. "You chased the truth. You found it. You kept your integrity when no one else did."

She's quiet for a long time. Then, finally, she reaches forward and places her hand on the folder, but doesn't open it.

"You really think I could do that?" she asks, softer now.

"I *know* you could."

She leans back, closing her eyes for a second. "I don't know what I want. Everything's still... too raw. This is my dream job, but these walls, they hold so much hurt"

"That's okay," I say. "You don't have to decide now. Just hold onto it."

We both stand. She walks me to the door. I turn back once and offer a small smile. "For what it's worth... I'm glad it was you. I'm glad you were the one who found her. If it had been someone else... I think she would've burned the whole place down first."

Sarah nods. "She nearly did anyway."

And with that, I leave. Quiet steps. No goodbyes to the others. No ceremony. Just the echo of my name erased from a door.

~ 61 ~

SARAH

NexTech doesn't crumble.

It flinches. Shudders. Stalls. But it doesn't fall.

In the days that follow, the corridors are quiet, stripped of the easy banter and frantic hallway conversations that once made the building hum. Now, people speak in lower tones. Doors stay half-closed. Everyone's waiting to see what happens next.

Damage control moves swiftly. PR prepares internal statements, legal tightens every compliance thread, and a rotating team of auditors sweeps through the finance division with the slow, relentless calm of people who've done this before. Every invoice. Every training fund. Every shadowed shell company.

But the change isn't just procedural. It's cultural.

I start making small changes first. Nothing dramatic. Just enough to signal that the era of silence and manipulation is over. Transparency becomes the new currency. I hold morning syncs with every department lead, no agendas, just check-ins. We bring in a third-party ethics team to review past oversight structures. Anonymous feedback is no longer optional.

The board responds with swift approval. They cite "remarkable resilience," "steadfast integrity," and "strong, measured leadership." They don't mention how close I came to being erased. They don't need to. Everyone in the room knows.

In private, one of the directors tells me, "You've steadied the company, Sarah. Not many could've done that."

I smile. I thank them. But inside, I carry the cracks of what it took to get here. We call it "rebuilding," but really, we're digging up roots and deciding what to replant.

Two weeks later, a news article breaks. It's a feature spread. Headline bold and clean.

"NexTech: Inside the Whistleblower Storm That Reshaped a Tech Giant."

The article is thorough. Names are named. Julia Voss. Daniel Reed. Several anonymous sources confirm misappropriations and misconduct stretching back five years. There are quotes from legal experts, a sidebar about whistleblower protections in corporate law.

My name is mentioned, briefly, respectfully:

"Sources close to the internal investigation confirm that NexTech's new CEO, Sarah Mitchell, played a critical role in surfacing and escalating the evidence that led to multiple arrests. Her leadership during the transition has drawn praise from industry figures."

There's a photo of me speaking at a company seminar, blurred faces behind me. My jaw is set. I look steadier than I feel.

But there's no mention of Emily. Not in the article. Not in any of the linked documents or statements. She's been scrubbed from the narrative entirely. She remains a ghost.

The only time I see her name now is in a file I keep buried on my home computer, under two layers of encryption. "Mushu," she called it. Her final gift. Her final betrayal.

Sometimes, late at night, I open it. Not to use it. Just to remind myself of the shape of her mind. The way she laid out truth like puzzle pieces. Sharp. Beautiful. Terrifying.

I still haven't decided if I hate her.

Alex's book was released the same week as the charges were brought on Daniel and Julia. It rockets to the top of the bestseller lists within 48 hours.

The cover is simple: a photo of a single office chair in an empty conference room, cast in dramatic light. The title:

Sanitised.

It's devastating. Raw. Honest in a way that doesn't protect anyone.

She names herself. Describes the pressure. The pills. The day she walked out of NexTech without looking back. She doesn't name Emily, but she references "a quiet architect in the walls."

The public eats it up. Bookstores sell out. Podcasts call her "the voice of modern whistleblowers." She gets invited onto panels, interviewed by everyone from tech magazines to late-night talk shows.

In private, she sends me a copy of the book with a note tucked inside:

"To Sarah,
You lit the match.
I just threw it.
—Alex"

I place it on my shelf. Right next to the framed photo of me and Emily from a rooftop two summers ago. I haven't had the heart to move it. Not yet.

NexTech breathes differently now. Lighter. But also sharper. I walk the halls and feel eyes tracking me with something new, not fear, but expectation. Accountability. Trust that isn't blind anymore.

We stop using words like "wellness funnel" and "performance flagging." We rewrite the handbook. We dissolve the approval silos. We open our hiring board to public oversight.

And still...

I catch myself sometimes, late in the day, about to turn and say something to Emily, to share a look, a smirk, a theory. But she's not there. Just empty air and a chair no one has the courage to claim.

She's out there somewhere. Under another name. Another face. And though I hate myself for it, some nights I still check airport records. Watch news feeds from Europe. Wonder if she's reading the same articles I am. If she has read the book that Alex wrote.

If she's read that, in some unspoken way, she will know we all survived. But only one of us stayed.

I end every Friday by walking up to the rooftop garden, now cleared and replanted with the help of the facilities team.

I sit on the same bench she used to lean against. The same spot where we talked about nothing and everything.

The city spreads out in every direction. Behind me, NexTech hums with new life.

We're not fixed.

But we're finally building something honest.

And maybe, that's enough.

~ 62 ~

I arrive at Susan's house just after dawn, the air still cool with morning mist. The garden gate is slightly ajar, its iron hinges whispering the same slow protest. My feet crunch on the gravel path, once again bringing me back to a woman I now consider a friend.

Susan is already tending to the flowerbed by the fence, kneeling in worn, denim jeans and a wool cardigan. Soil clings to her gloves and spreads in rich, dark clumps across the recently loosened earth. A tray of seedlings, lavender, marigold, sage, crowds the edge of the bed, ready to be planted.

"He always liked lavender," she says softly, without looking up. She presses a small plant into the ground with careful fingertips, burying roots into prepared dirt. "He said it kept the bugs away and gave the bees something honest."

The sunlight is pale, barely touching the garden.. I join Susan on my knees, letting the earth settle beneath me. The scent of fresh soil and wet grass fills my senses.

We begin planting in silence, the trowel tapping against root-bound soil, small plants pressed in one by one. I feel in that moment the simple gravity of it all, planting, growing, letting live. And I think of James.

Susan doesn't speak again for what feels like a long time. But her silence isn't heavy, it's soft, thoughtful. The kind of quiet that feels like flipping through a well-loved photo album in your mind.

Then, with a small smile tugging at her lips, she says, "You know, he used to make pancakes every Sunday. Said the only way to make them properly was with far too much vanilla and a ridiculous amount of butter."

I laugh. Susan has told me many stories about James over the last few weeks. It's been nice finding out more about the man who started all of this. The real James.

"And he was *terrible* at flipping them," she adds, her eyes crinkling. "Every week, without fail, one would end up on the floor, or half-stuck to the ceiling. We had a running bet on how many would survive."

I shake my head, smiling now, and Susan keeps going, like she's letting light in through a long-closed window.

"He had this old radio he swore sounded better than anything new. Crackly jazz, always playing in the background. And every now and then he'd grab my hand and spin me around the kitchen, usually while burning whatever he was meant to be watching on the stove."

There's a warmth between us now. I can see her younger, barefoot in the kitchen, laughing as James tried and failed to be both romantic and domestic at once.

"He once built me a bookshelf," she adds, glancing toward the house with fond amusement. "It leaned slightly to the left for ten straight years. But I never let him fix it. I said it had character."

I smile and rest my chin on my knee. "Sounds like he was always trying to make something just a little better."

Susan nods, softly. "He was the best kind of mess. Thoughtful and chaotic. Brilliant in ways that didn't always make sense. But he loved... *deeply*. That was always clear."

Her gaze drifts toward the flowers we've just planted. "He would've loved this. Being remembered like this. Quiet, gentle. Things growing instead of falling apart."

I don't speak. I just let the sun rise a little more in the sky while her stories settle in the soil between us, like seeds of something beautiful, blooming long after he's gone.

We plant the remaining seedlings in pairs, lavender beside sage, marigold beside chamomile, and water them together, letting the trickle of hose water fall calmly over our work.

When we're done, Susan pulls off her gloves and holds them in her lap. No tears fall. She doesn't need them. There's a quiet dignity in that.

"Thank you for coming," she says, voice small as an offering.

I swallow. "I couldn't not. He's the reason everything changed." My throat tightens. I don't add the part about losing so much because of it.

Susan gestures to the small mound of freshly planted seedlings. "He's still here," she says. "In the roots."

We rise, brushing soil from our knees, and lean on the fence, looking at our small garden. "And he's in you and your daughter" I say softly.

"Of course," Susan says. She takes a deep breath, then adds quietly, more for her than for me "And he's in you, too."

***

Evening comes later now, the light has softened to a deep orange. I return home and go straight to my desk, where my laptop waits. The house smells like coffee and incense sticks, the last of the ones Emily brought from a little shop we used to visit on weekends, back when we still smiled into candles and believed in bonds I now know were false.

Tonight, I sit with a single truth hovering in the air, Emily's confession, archived and unread. The screen glows in the dim room. Only one message remains. Not the admission, no, I too have tucked that away behind multiple protective walls. No... this is something else. A simple, ridiculous cat meme framed in one of Emily's lighthearted forwards. Subject line, *KittyMime.mp4.* A crooked emoji smiling at me from across the abyss of memory.

I click it open. The cat video plays; a tiny fluff ball attempting to steal cotton balls. Emily's voice echoes lightly in my mind: *"This reminds me of Mushu..."* And then laughter, warm and real. I feel her there again, for just a second.

I click the trash icon. The non-existent echo of a delete, a small flicker. Empty space swallows text. The inbox refreshes, leaving behind a pale streak of memory.

I close my laptop. All that remains now is the silence.

I wait, listening to my heartbeat, the hum of the city outside my window, the quiet ticking of the clock. I think about everything, James and his unwavering integrity, Emily and her slick deceptions, Mark's voice echoing caution, the board's masked relief, the chilling soft way Julia said the words "soft exit." I think about the Mocha's I drank and the roots I planted with Susan this morning, and I wonder what stays behind when someone deletes their Best Friend.

I go to the window and press my forehead to the cool glass. Lights flicker across the empty street outside. Shadows shift. I breathe out a slow, cold sigh and roll my shoulders. The shape of my world has changed. It will never be the same.

I walk across the room and sit. I close my eyes, lean back into the chair, and let myself rest there in the darkness. I don't know how to heal yet. I just know I have to try.

Tomorrow, I will go to the office again. There will be unanswered memos and compliance checks and the lingering ache of walking into a place where everything feels watched, recorded. Some protections were put in place. I will breathe through them. I will keep building. Quietly. Carefully.

But tonight, none of that matters. Tonight, I hold onto the space behind me, the ghost of a friendship that taught me too much, cost me too much, and changed me forever.

I lean forward, fingers sliding across the glass table. The surface feels cool, smooth, real, and imperfect. The same way life is, even when you can't delete the scars.

I close my eyes and whisper to the darkness: "I was never sure where the line was. And maybe... that's okay."

And for the first time in weeks, I let the truth there live in me, quiet, watchful, like lavender in the dusk.

www.ingramcontent.com/pod-product-compliance
Ingram Content Group UK Ltd.
Pitfield, Milton Keynes, MK11 3LW, UK
UKHW011305140126
10102UKWH00017B/180